Maui Widow Waltz

JoAnn Bassett

Maui Widow Waltz
Copyright © 2011 JoAnn Bassett
Printed in the United States of America
All rights reserved.

First published by JoAnn Bassett
Bend, Oregon, 97707
http://www.joannbassett.com
***

This book is a work of fiction. Places, events, and situations in this book are purely fictional and any resemblance to actual persons, living or dead, is coincidental.
***

ISBN-10: 1463606656
ISBN-13: 978-1463606657
***

Also by JoAnn Bassett:

"THE ISLANDS OF ALOHA MYSTERY SERIES"
Livin' Lahaina Loca
Lana'i of the Tiger
Kaua'i Me a River
O'ahu Lonesome Tonight?
I'm Kona Love You Forever

MAI TAI BUTTERFLY

For Tom Haberer: my *kane no ka oi*.

1

People marry for two reasons: love or money. So it was pretty clear what was at stake when she showed up wanting to marry a dead man. I normally run a pretty straight shop: no mai tai infused "quickies" or Elvis-on-the-beach impersonators, but my standards had slipped. In late December a line of squalls had parked over Maui dumping thirteen inches of rain in two weeks. The daily downpours continued through January, sending visitors fleeing back to the mainland like snorkelers spotting a dorsal fin. By early February business all over the island had ground to a halt. My mortgage was in arrears, my day planner was blank, and the credit card people had revoked my Visa. In other words, desperation was the new black.

On Tuesday morning I laid out my bills, solitaire-style, on my battered Balinese desk. There were supposed to be three piles: those I could pay right away; those I'd pay by the end of February; and those that would never get paid unless I won the lottery. Too bad Hawaii doesn't have a lottery. Pile number three stood an inch high. The other piles were bare, with only a Post-it note—a freebie from the real estate office across the street—marking the spot.

The door to my shop creaked open and a pale female face peeked around the jamb. In the space above her head I saw the shimmer of wind-whipped rain.

"Can I help you?" I said looking up not expecting much.

"Are you the wedding planner?" she said in a whisper I associate with people inquiring about illicit drugs.

"I am." I sprang from behind the desk and gestured for her to come in. She stepped inside and I pushed the door closed against the stiff breeze.

I figured her for early-twenties. She was a pale imitation of me at that age. Shoulder length blunt-cut blond hair, and pale topaz blue eyes. Her skin was the color of *haupia:* coconut pudding. I had about ten years on her, and since I live in Hawaii my skin's perpetually tanned. My hair's a few shades darker, and my eyes more hazel than blue. But in silhouette we shared the same five foot six height, same small build.

"Wow. What a gorgeous ring," I said zeroing in on her left hand. "I'm Pali Moon, the owner here."

"Polly? Like the parrot?"

"Well, it's pronounced the same, but the Hawaiian spelling is P-A-L-I."

If I'd been more truthful, I'd have explained that Pali isn't my legal name, but it's the one I use in everyday commerce to avoid dealing with snorts and chuckles.

Her swift glance around the small room tipped me off this probably wasn't what she'd imagined when she saw my yellow pages ad. I had no manikins dressed in wedding gowns costing as much as a small car, no displays of Swarovski crystal-encrusted headpieces, no glossy posters of demure brides and cocky grooms. Just a fifteen by thirty room, split by a plywood wall with a doorframe hung with a bead curtain. Behind the bead curtain I had a small dressing room with a carpeted step-up backed by a three-sided mirror.

"This is 'Let's Get Maui'd,' right?"

"Sure is. And please don't be put off by the simple digs. We keep overhead low so your costs aren't high. We focus on making each bride's special day totally unique, completely original. You bring the dream, we bring the team." I'd spent the past few weeks brainstorming business slogans and took the opportunity to try a few out on her.

She lifted a nostril as if detecting an obnoxious odor, but managed to twist her lips into a thin smile.

I offered her a seat in the rattan chair across from my desk and she moved toward it, the scent of tuberoses trailing in her wake. I slipped behind the desk, dumping my bills into the pencil drawer as I took my seat.

Something about the tug at the sides of her eyes and her pinched facial expression seemed out of place for a blushing bride, but I chalked it up to the lousy weather.

"Can you put together a fabulous wedding by Valentine's Day?" she said in the same low murmur as before.

"Of course," I said, my voice too loud in contrast. "Are you thinking inside or out?"

"Outside. On the beach."

"No problem. We'll rent a rain canopy if we need to. How many guests are you inviting?"

"Only a few friends and family."

"Good. The smaller the better in such a short time-frame."

"It has to be perfect."

"We specialize in perfect." I smiled, but it wasn't returned.

"No, I mean it. Everything has to be fabulous because my fiancé might not be there. He may have to watch it later on the video."

"Oh. And he won't be there because..." I let it trail off, hoping she'd fill in the blank. It's a common speech pattern with wedding coordinators.

"Because he's been missing since last Thursday."

I did tell her that for my efforts she'd pay me fifteen percent of the total cost of the wedding. When she didn't balk, I slid the file folder across the desk and asked her to fill out the contact information: address, telephone numbers and so on. As she worked on it, I checked over the marriage license and then pulled out a copy of my standard contract.

"This details the services I'll perform, and what you'll pay me. If you have any questions, now's a good time to ask."

She didn't even pretend to read the contract before scribbling a signature at the bottom.

"I need you to promise me it'll be perfect," she said, handing back the paperwork.

"With just over a week we'll be a bit rushed, but I can pull together flowers, music, photographer: everything we'll need for an unforgettable beachside ceremony."

"And video. Don't forget the video."

"Of course."

"Thank you," she said as she rubbed a phantom tear from the corner of her eye. "And don't worry. Brad'll be back in time."

She stood up and snapped open her jumbo probably-not-a-knock-off Gucci bag. After a bit of rummaging around, she pulled out a sealed business-size envelope and silently slid it across the desktop.

"I brought along a deposit," she said. "I hope you don't mind large bills. The teller at the bank was pretty snotty about giving me so much cash early in the day."

My jaw remained dropped in what I'm sure was an unflattering gape as she got up and headed for the door. I didn't recover in time to bid her *aloha* before she quietly pulled the door closed behind her.

A few minutes later, the door swung open again. I slipped the envelope into a drawer. She'd have to arm wrestle me to get it back.

It wasn't her.

It was Noni Konomanu, a former friend who'd reportedly gone over to the dark side.

"Hi Pali. I've been meaning to drop by and see you. I finally got the chance."

"Hey, Noni. What's up with you? I heard you moved to Honolulu."

"Not yet. Although I've got a new job." She surveyed my sparsely-appointed shop like a tax assessor with a quota to fill.

"Yeah, people say you're working for Tank Sherman."

"His name is Terrance."

"Yeah, well, he'll always be 'Tank' to me. Is he still buying up child care centers and old folks' homes over there?"

"He's consolidated his business interests to include a number of lifestyle verticals. We're now looking at expanding into new profit centers on the neighbor islands."

We locked stares. No way would I ask what she was dying for me to ask.

"So, how's business?" she said, dragging a finger along the window sill. She glanced at her fingertip and then blew off the dust as if blowing me a kiss.

"Business is great. In fact, when you came in I thought you were my new client who just left."

"Thought she was coming back to cancel?"

"No, I thought she'd decided to double her guest list."

"Face it, Pali. You're broke. Everyone knows it. Mr. Sherman is willing to help you out by offering five thousand dollars cash for your shop fixtures, your business name and your vender contact files. It's worth half that, but since we all go way back—"

"We don't go anywhere, forward or back. You tell Tank Sherman I'll burn this place to the ground before handing my business over to him. And while you're at it, remind him this is Maui, not Honolulu. Over here we treat each other like *ohana.* My contacts are as dear to me as aunties and uncles. Family members don't sell out to Oahu slumlords who jack up prices and squeeze out mom and pop businesses just to make a buck."

"Mr. Sherman warned me you might say something like that. Guess what? He's buying this building, and when he does, he's raising your rent. He's investigated your business and we know your lease is up next month. You'd be smart to shut your mouth and consider his offer. Five grand is a *makana:* a gift. You have until the fifteenth of this month—next Friday—to make up your mind."

She popped open an umbrella festooned with plate-sized red and yellow hibiscus flowers and turned to go back outside. She had to flip the umbrella sideways to get through the doorway.

"It's bad luck to open an umbrella inside," I said, racing around the desk to follow her out. The shrieking wind swallowed the sound of my voice. I watched as she trotted across the rain-slicked street to her black BMW sedan. She aimed a remote key at the driver door and the taillights winked a *welcome back.* Looking back at me, she smiled and shot me a *shaka:* the "hang loose" sign.

I shot her a different hand gesture altogether.

2

Although I've lived in Hawaii all my life, I'd only been a wedding coordinator for two years when the foul weather brought my business to a screeching halt. Before that, I'd worked at the usual tourist gigs: luaus, restaurants, that sort of thing. Right out of college I even did a short stint as an air marshal for the Transportation Security Administration. But after less than a year of leg-numbing flights to Tokyo and Taipei I actually found myself *hoping* a passenger would go postal so I could spring into action. Anyone who knows me will agree: I'm not the poster child for patience.

What I am is detail-oriented and punctual. I'm also a devoted student of kung fu. My workouts at the kung fu school, or *guan*, provide a welcome yin to the yang of whining, bitching, and hissy fits I deal with in the bridal business.

***

"You're kidding," said my roommate, Steve, as we dug into our thrown-together dinner of stir fry vegetables and rice. "She's engaged to that guy who disappeared off Kapalua?" His wrinkled brow underscored the disapproval in his voice. "So, in other words, your new client's doing it ass-backwards: a widow before a bride."

I shook my head. "Her guy's only been missing since last Thursday. He may not be dead, you know. It could turn out his bachelor party just got a little out of hand. And besides, if I hadn't said 'yes,' she'd just have found another planner who'd do it."

"He's toast, Pali. The Coast Guard's been searching nonstop. It's been all over the news."

I put my full attention to shoveling rice into my mouth with my chopsticks.

Steve went on. "You know, it's probably illegal to perform a proxy marriage for someone who's missing. Anyhow, I sure hope it is. Maybe she's pulling some kind of tabloid stunt, or a reality show prank. How can you be sure it isn't a joke?"

"I'm not sure about much of anything anymore. But paying the mortgage on this house is no joke, and I haven't booked a wedding in weeks. If I hadn't taken this client, pretty soon we'd both be looking for new digs."

Steve and I share the house I bought in Hali'imaile, a former plantation town on the windward slope of Mt. Haleakala, Maui's dormant volcano. As cozy as it sounds to have a male roommate, Steve and I aren't a couple. Not now, not ever. When Steve answered my ad for a roommate I learned he's a first-rate photographer, a fabulous cook, and he'd done hair and make-up in Hollywood for both movies and TV. It wasn't very PC of me to leap to conclusions about his gender preference when I first met him, but in my business, a three-in-one guy's a treasure. I couldn't care less about his social proclivities. I offered him the room at rock-bottom rent.

"What about wedding photos?" he said, clicking his chopsticks together. I was glad to hear he was already considering his role in Lisa Marie's upcoming nuptials. He went on, "There's only so much I can do with a camera, you know. The patent on bringing the dead back to life is still held by the Big Guy."

"The bride sincerely believes the groom will show up in time for the wedding."

"Right," he said, tossing his head back and splaying his fingers across his cheek in a theatrical pose. "And I *sincerely* believe I'm the next Leonardo DiCaprio. Maybe I'll get Marty Scorsese on the horn and let him know I'm ready for my close-up."

"Anyway, it's too soon to plan the photo shoot," I said, ignoring the dramatics. "So far all we've nailed down is the date—Valentine's Day—and that it's going to be a small beach wedding. She gave me a thousand dollar deposit, in cash. If it's a hoax, or he's a goner, it's still a house payment. She signed the contract so no matter what, the money's mine."

***

At seven o'clock the next morning, the phone rang. Steve picked it up in the kitchen before I'd had a chance to clear my throat and reach for my bedside extension. I heard his voice through the wall.

"No problem," he said. "Yeah, Pali told me about your situation. I'm Steve Rathburn, the photographer. I'm sure we'll be getting together soon."

There was a pause.

"No really, no problem. She usually gets in around nine."

Another pause.

"Okay, I'll tell her." There was a final pause before his 'good-bye.'

He tapped on the door before popping his head into my room.

"You didn't mention your pal Lisa Marie's got a Ph.D. in pushy."

I groaned and sat up in bed.

her dad's obsession with the original Cisco's Angels. She looks nothing like "angel" Jill Monroe, however. Whereas Jill's hair was blond, with that signature blow-dry hairstyle, Farrah's is a waist-length tumble of tea-colored frizz. Jill had blue eyes, Farrah's are espresso brown. All of the Angels had slim leggy bodies, but Farrah's figure is curvy, with a bra cup size at least five letters down the alphabet. If she'd been born a century earlier, she could have passed for *ali'i*: those plump royal Hawaiian gals who were sexy in a bountiful Mother Earth kind of way.

"Wish me luck," I said. I pulled open the stubborn front door and the annoying tinkle bell attached to the doorframe seemed to urge me to get moving. "From what I've seen so far, I'm pretty sure her DNA's sporting a few Bridezilla genes."

"Hey, don't sweat the DNA; it's her FICO score that counts. With all this wet, it's a miracle some bummed-out bride hasn't hijacked a jet to Tahiti. If we don't see sun pretty soon we'll all be flipping burgers in Honolulu."

"True," I said, recalling Noni's face as she delivered Tank Sherman's ultimatum. I glanced at the Felix the Cat clock above the cash register. It showed seven-fifty-five. "Oops, gotta run. *Mahalo* for the cream."

When I stepped outside, Lisa Marie was standing next door in front of my shop furiously text-messaging on a fancy cell phone.

"You're late," she said as I approached, key in hand.

"I am not." I glanced at my wrist for the watch that wasn't there.

"We had an eight o'clock meeting. You should have been here at least fifteen minutes early to turn on the heat and get the coffee ready."

"Coming right up," I said, hoisting the cream carton like a trophy. I didn't think it wise to mention my shop had no heat.

"I take half and half," she sniffed. "If you're going to work for me, I think you better make an effort to learn my preferences."

Luckily, the coffee maker was in the back dressing room. I took advantage of the brewing time to silently mouth a few clever comebacks, in both English and Hawaiian.

Once coffee was served and the wedding planning underway, the chip on her shoulder wobbled a bit.

"I miss Brad. I know he's all alone, washed up on some deserted beach. Like the guy in that movie, *Cast Away*. It was so sad. I got the DVD to watch it again the day after they found Brad's boat. Remember the part where Tom Hanks comes home and his fiancée, Helen Hunt, has gone and married somebody else?"

I nodded. Actually I didn't remember, because I'd never seen the movie. But it sounded sad.

"Anyway, I'm not doing that to Brad. When he's able to come back to me, I'm going to be there, waiting. Our reunion will probably be all over the news. I'll need to remember to cry, but just a little. Not enough to smudge my make-up." She dabbed the corners of her eyes as if rehearsing and then went on. "But in any case, either the wedding will be all ready to go, or it'll be over and we'll get to watch it together on the video. He's going to be so proud I went ahead and got us married on Valentine's Day just like we planned."

I took a deep breath. "Lisa Marie, there aren't too many deserted beaches on Maui. I think if Brad had washed ashore, someone would've found him by now and called the Coast Guard."

her cash in my bank account, my first deposit in almost two months.

"I hope you have the coffee ready," said Lisa Marie.

"Freshly brewed."

"Good. Maybe you're trainable after all. Oh, this is Kevin. And this is Pali." She gestured toward me, thumb extended as if hitching a ride.

"*Ho'okipa*. Welcome. It's nice to meet you," I said, shaking Kevin's hand while trying to read his eyes.

"Yeah, you too." The guy's face was as closed as a pro poker player wearing mirrored sunglasses. He was tall and powerfully built, with Calvin Klein model good looks, and dark wavy hair gelled to perfection. He appeared a bit older than Lisa Marie, maybe late twenties or early-thirties. He wore a pale blue Nike golf shirt and crisply-pressed khakis. Clamped to his left wrist was a gaudy gold Rolex.

I usually size up men relative to their martial arts potential, and this guy looked like a black belt waiting to happen. My stomach did a little bump and grind, and I had to bite back the audible swoon I'd have made if it had been me and Farrah checking out surfers at the beach. After all, Kevin was a client, sort of. As I ordered my libido back to its hole, I decided if Brad Sanders ever did show up I might allow myself the opportunity to reassess the Kevin situation.

Having reined in my lust, it dawned on me that Kevin's looks were not only hot, but puzzling. The photo of Brad Sanders they'd run on TV showed a pale, fleshy-necked guy wearing a rumpled dress shirt with a button-down collar. He sported a shopping mall haircut, a geek goatee, and funky wire-rimmed glasses. The photo was a portrait shot, so it didn't show his wristwatch or his physique, but judging from what I could see I imagined a black plastic

Casio and a belly paunch. Physically and sartorially, the contrast between Kevin and Brad was day and night.

I offered the couple a seat on the sofa in the front office while I stayed in back to pour the coffee and prepare the fitting room for Lisa Marie's try-on session. I sniffed the cream, determined it free of deadly pathogens, and placed the carton on the tray along with three brimming Hilo Hattie mugs. I slipped through the bead curtain beaming like Martha Stewart presenting a flaming dessert, but neither of them looked up. While we cranked up our caffeine quotient, we made idle chatter about the ongoing crummy weather. No one mentioned the search for Brad.

There was a lull in the conversation and Lisa Marie turned to me. "Are there any castles on Maui?"

"Castles?"

"Yeah, you know. Fairytale castles, with turnips and molts."

"Turrets and moats?"

"Yeah. And a drawstring bridge and all that."

"A drawbridge?"

"Yeah. Why do you keep repeating everything? Just answer me. Is there a castle over here or not?"

"Not that I know of. Why do you ask?"

"Well, I was looking through my celebrity wedding scrapbook and my very, very, *very* favorite wedding was Tom and Katie's. You know, at night, in that castle in Italy? Little Suri was so adorable as flower girl."

"Ah, yes. That wedding was pretty spectacular. But Bill Gates chose Hawaii. In the daytime, by the ocean, just like yours is going to be."

"Who's Bill Gates?" said Lisa Marie.

"Actually," Kevin chimed in, "Gates' wedding was on the island of Lana'i, not Maui. And it was on a golf course overlooking the ocean, not on the beach."

Score one for Mr. GQ.

"You're right. It was on Lana'i at Manele Bay. But in any case, it wasn't in a castle." I turned to Lisa Marie. "Bill Gates is the richest man in America."

"He's rich because he's an astute businessman and a software genius," Kevin said in a voice that let me know he felt I'd slighted Gates by merely focusing on his wealth.

"Brad's a software genius. Everybody says so." Lisa Marie said this in a voice so small I thought it might have come from inside my own head.

A few moments of tight silence followed.

"And I'm going to be a software genius' wife!" she said, perking up as if she'd been hit with a defibrillator. "Okay. Enough of this sitting around, I want to see some wedding dresses."

As I led them back into the fitting room, Kevin's eyes flicked across the four gowns I'd displayed for Lisa Marie's inspection. He frowned as he turned over the first price tag.

"Five thousand bucks? You must be joking."

"It's Vera Wang, Kevin." Lisa Marie shot me a sideways glance complete with arched eyebrow.

"Usually the bride brings her gown with her or she orders one from a local bridal shop at least four months in advance," I said. "But since Lisa Marie needs a dress on extremely short notice, and she said she'd prefer a designer label, I managed to pull together a few rentals."

What I didn't let them in on was the begging, pleading and bribing I'd done a few hours earlier at a bridal shop in Kahului. Lucky for me the owner's daughter had just picked up her high school senior pictures and she hated them. She claimed the photos, taken by a local school photographer, made her look fat and cross-eyed. I'd offered Steve's services for quick retakes with a money-back guarantee. In return, I'd received four sample dresses the shop owner was willing to rent. The immediate problem solved, I knew I faced more begging and pleading with Steve once I got home.

"How much does it cost to rent one of these things?" Kevin said, flipping over the tags on the remaining three gowns.

"They range from a thousand to eighteen hundred, plus alterations."

"A thousand bucks to wear a dress for a couple of hours? I'm obviously in the wrong business."

"You're Brad's business partner, right?" I said, making an effort to tone down the shrill that had crept into my voice. "At DigiSystems, a company the news reports refer to as a 'multi-million dollar tech company'."

"Yeah. Actually, I can't complain. Brad brought me in during the start up. He's the hardest working guy I've ever met." He lowered his eyes and shook his head. "Not the greatest with the business side of things, but that's my job. Now, I'm not sure what we're gonna do..." He ran a hand through his carefully coifed hair.

"Kevin," Lisa Marie said. "We're going to do what Brad would want us to do. We're going to focus on getting this wedding set up. Right here, right now."

He nodded but didn't look up.

"Hey," she continued. "Remember that time when he didn't come to his own birthday party?"

"Yeah," he said. "The guy was a maniac. We put on this huge bash for his twenty-third birthday but he stayed in the lab running QC on the beta of version three until one o'clock in the morning. I'll say this about Brad: the dude was focused, and stubborn."

"Shut up, Kevin," said Lisa Marie. She had enough steel in her voice to build an aircraft carrier. "You make it sound like he's gone forever. He's not. He'll be back soon and you'll be eating your crows for talking trash about him being dead."

"Tell you what," he said. "You girls knock yourselves out here. I'll wait for you in the front." He turned and parted the beaded curtain to leave. A few seconds later I heard the springs groan in my old sofa.

For nearly an hour I listened to Lisa Marie ponder aloud the pros and cons of the four gowns. The neckline on one was too high; there were too many bows on another; the color of the third was "icky;" and so on. It was like watching Goldilocks on crack. She tried on each dress at least three times.

At half-past noon I asked for her decision.

"I don't know," she said. "They all pretty much suck. Maybe this isn't going to work out after all." She plucked her handbag off the floor and disappeared behind the dressing room curtain. I heard her rustling around as she put on her street clothes.

"I could have a dress made for you," I said in a sprightly *buck up* tone intended to shore up my morale as much as hers. Gathering steam, I went on, even though she hadn't made a peep from behind the curtain. "We could use a local seamstress. It would be a one-of-a-kind original."

"And how much would *that* cost?" Kevin growled through the plywood wall. He'd been so quiet the past hour I thought he'd fallen asleep. I heard the sofa springs retract, and a few seconds later he poked his head back through the beaded doorway. Strings of shiny plastic beads draped across his shoulders making him look like a hunky back-up dancer on a music video.

"I'd have to check," I said. "With only a few days to buy the fabric; take Lisa Marie's measurements; cut out the pattern; and then assemble the main pieces for the first fitting it probably won't come cheap. But it would be an original gown that could be passed down to her daughter."

"Like there's ever going to *be* a daughter," Kevin muttered. I anticipated an outburst from Lisa Marie, but apparently she didn't pick up on his cynicism about Brad Sanders ever contributing to the gene pool.

"You're right. I deserve an original *couture* design," she said. "When can I start interviewing seamstresses?"

"I don't think you grasp the situation here, Lisa. In order to—"

"It's Lisa *Marie*. Only Brad gets to call me Lisa."

"Sorry, Lisa Marie," I said. "A wedding gown in a less than a week is a minor miracle. Let me call a woman in Wailuku who does alterations for all the local dress shops. She's the best on the island. If she can't do it, you'll have to fly over to Honolulu and find an off-the-rack gown."

"No. I've decided I want an original. I don't care how much it costs. And not another word out of you, buster."

Kevin stepped all the way into the dressing room and crossed his arms tightly across his chest. He looked as if he was dying to say something, but he stayed silent. Then he turned on his heel and went back out. This time I heard his footsteps cross the floor. I winced as he slammed the front door and the thin plank walls of the plantation-era building shuddered in response.

"Don't mind him," Lisa Marie said. "He's always been a nervous Nelly. Brad told me when they were first getting the company started Kevin used to freak out all the time about money, patents, industrial spies, all of it. Now I guess it's my turn to put up with him while we try to get this wedding ready. I hope Brad comes back before too long. I don't know how much of Kevin's uptight crap I can take. Especially since I'm trying to get ready for the biggest day of my entire life."

My conscience nagged. I asked Lisa Marie to have a seat on the dainty stool next to the dressing room step-up while I perched on the bottom step.

"You know, the Coast Guard's pretty sure Brad fell overboard." I didn't know how far I could push her, so I eased into it, trying to remember the high points of the hostage negotiation class I'd taken during my air marshal training.

"Yeah, so?"

"Well, it's extremely difficult to make it back to shore if a person falls into open water during the night."

"And your point is?"

"Lisa Marie, Brad may not be coming back. Do you understand that? Are you prepared to accept that?"

"You don't know Brad. I do. Brad wants to get married on Valentine's Day, and so do I. Even putting up with cranky Kevin is worth it because by next week I'll be Mrs. Bradley James Sanders, wife of DigiSystems founder and president." She narrowed her eyes. "So tell me, what's going on with you? It sounds to me like maybe you're trying to weasel out of doing this. What is it? Do you want more money? Are you afraid you won't be able to do what you promised? What?"

"No, it's nothing like that. I was just thinking—"

"Well, stop thinking. From the looks of things, thinking's not your strong shoot. Just answer me this: Are you going to do what you said you'd do and put on my perfect Valentine's Day wedding or not?"

"Of course. I just..." I decided to not point out that "strong shoot" should really be "strong suit." Obviously, the woman wasn't in the mood for grammar tips.

"No, stop. No more negative vibes, I need to stay positive. Don't talk to me unless you have something cheerful to say." She reached into her purse and brought out a hard-sided glasses case. Flicking it open, she plucked out a pair of Chanel tortoise shell sunglasses and slipped them on. She stood up and gestured for me to move out of her way. I watched as she gazed into the full-length mirror, turning her head from side to side admiring her reflection.

I fantasized shaking her by the shoulders and yelling, *snap out of it—he's dead.* But instead, I bent over and started retrieving the tangle of wardrobe bags she'd tossed across the fitting room floor. When I straightened up, she'd vanished without so much as a *tah-tah.*

I spent the next three hours phoning vendors. Concerned that my usual contacts would snub me for asking them to perform miracles on such short notice, I began each call with, "Sorry to call at the last minute, but..."

In every case, the response was, "No worries, Pali. What do you need?"

Seems I wasn't the only one feeling the pinch from the rotten weather.

A few of them asked if they could get back to me with prices, but by four o'clock I'd managed to secure most of the services I'd need. I ordered a wedding cake from Keahou's Cakes up in Kula; videotaping from Mikey O, who worked at the Lahaina Video Plus Store and used their off-the-shelf inventory on the sly; and I'd gone next door and reconfirmed with Farrah about doing the flowers and conducting the ceremony.

I'd promised to return the rental dresses by four-thirty, but before I left I needed to make one last call.

"Hi, Akiko," I said, holding the phone receiver between my chin and shoulder as I finished zipping a heavily-beaded gown into its protective bag. "This is Pali Moon. Remember me? I met you at Leilani's dress shop last summer. I mentioned I had a wedding planning business in Pa'ia called 'Let's Get Maui'd'."

"Ah yes, I remember you." She didn't sound like she did, but was too polite to say so.

"How're things with you?" I said. Any response would have been acceptable except *swamped.*

"Not bad. Kinda slow."

I pumped a fist in the air.

"Can I come over to your place and talk to you about doing some work for me?"

"You got a gown needs hemming?"

"Better'n that."

"Two gowns?" Her voice squeaked in anticipation. I cringed, knowing when she heard the job specs any delight she might be feeling at the moment would be trashed. I picked up a pen and asked for directions to her house. I didn't have a notepad handy, so I jotted the address on the back of my hand.

"I need to make one quick stop on the way, but I can be there in about half an hour."

"I'll be waiting."

Akiko's ancient clapboard house was on a steep street in a working class area of Wailuku. The scrabbly front lawn was littered with little kid's toys: a faded plastic Big-Wheel tricycle, a sodden refrigerator-size cardboard box with a hole cut in the side for a door, and a confetti of limbless action figures and naked Bratz dolls strewn about as if they'd come down with the rain.

I found a parking spot on the street across from her house. I set the brake and checked it. My ancient Geo was prone to whims of escape whenever I left it on anything approximating an incline. As I climbed out, I heard the creak of a screen door. Akiko had come out onto her porch, smiling and waving. She seemed to have shrunk a couple of inches in the six months since I'd first met her. She probably weighed less than ninety pounds.

I crossed the street and picked my way up the cracked sidewalk.

"These grandkids," she said, eyeing the clutter in the yard. "I tell them to pick up, but eh, do they listen? So, you give me some dresses to hem and I can ignore this mess for another week." She chuckled and her eyes disappeared in a fan of wrinkles.

We went inside where chaos continued to reign. Akiko was rumored to be a perfectionist with a needle and thread, but housekeeping apparently rarely made her "to do" list.

"Where are the dresses?" She said, eyeing my empty arms. "You just want a quote?"

"No, I don't need a quote. I need a dress."

A tight crease formed between her eyebrows.

"A dress? You need me to make you a dress from scratch? I not do that for years and years."

"This is kind of an emergency."

She gestured for me to follow her into the kitchen. "I'm going to make us some tea."

While we sipped green tea, she talked about the rain, the slowdown in business and the eminent delivery of her fourth grandchild. From a back bedroom I heard the hush and roar of a TV sitcom laugh track. After about a half hour, the sound of stubby bare feet on wood floors was followed by giggling and a slamming door.

"*Tutu*?" A girl of about ten or eleven popped her head in the kitchen doorway. "The boys locked the door again."

Akiko looked up at the clock and sighed.

"I gotta get these *keiki* their dinner."

"I apologize for coming over so late."

"No worry. You say you need a gown? Why not just order one from Honolulu and let me alter it?"

"There's no time for that. I need it right away. The wedding's next Thursday: Valentine's Day."

She snorted with such force I was glad she'd finished her tea or it probably would've shot out of her nose.

"You kidding, right? This some kind of joke?"

I shook my head.

"A week? No way."

"At least give me a price."

"A million dollars. I've got my three grandkids here 'cause my daughter's going to the hospital to have the next one. No way a dress in a week."

"Akiko, I wouldn't ask if I wasn't desperate. This girl is in a really sad situation."

"Pregnant?"

"No. Worse."

"What's worse? She on her death bed or something?"

"Did you hear about that guy who disappeared off the fishing boat? The *haole* from Seattle who's been on the news?"

She squinted, nodding.

"This girl is his fiancée. They planned a Valentine's Day wedding."

"So? No man, no wedding. Why she need a dress?"

I explained the stand-in groom and Lisa Marie's insistence that the wedding proceed on schedule.

"I'll need to charge a lot of money to finish a dress so fast. She needs to pay me for no sleep and buying Mickey D's every night to feed these *keiki*."

"No problem. She's willing to spend money. The most important thing to her is that she gets married on Valentine's Day."

"What if they find that boy's body?"

"No worries. I promise you'll get paid no matter what."

Akiko agreed to come to the shop the next morning after she'd put the grandkids on the school bus. I asked her to bring pictures of two or three gowns she knew she could finish in time.

"What if she doesn't like any of them?"

"It's my job to make sure she does."

***

My cell phone rang as I was getting ready for bed that night. It was Steve. He hadn't been home for dinner, but we don't keep tabs on each other.

"I've got a favor to ask."

"Not a good night for favors, I'm afraid. It's been a long day and I'm already in my pj's."

"Actually it's not so much a favor as an opportunity."

I chewed on that for a moment.

"You still there?" he said. I hummed my presence and he continued. "A friend of a friend of mine needs a place to stay. He got injured and can't work for a few weeks. He's pretty busted up and he's willing to pay good money for room and board."

"Room and board? I don't even give you board."

"Pali, work with me, okay? My friend swears he's a really great guy. He's just going to be laid up for a while. If you want, I'll do all the cooking. How about it?"

"What's his problem?"

"Busted up his leg real bad. He gets out of the hospital tomorrow."

"I suppose he'll want the downstairs bedroom." I wasn't thrilled to have to give up my first floor room and camp out in the spare room upstairs next to Steve's.

"He's willing to pay five hundred a week."

Whoa, why didn't he say so earlier? For that kind of money, I'd hand over the whole house, with gourmet room service and a chauffeur. But I hadn't yet asked Steve about doing the retake photos of the high school girl, so I played it cool. I'd trade a favor for a favor.

"Okay. I guess I could move my stuff upstairs for a while."

"*Mahalo*, Pali. I'll call and let him know."

I hung up the phone and went out to the garage for cardboard boxes. While boxing up the contents of my dresser drawers, I avoided looking at my bed. I'd jumped at the chance to make some extra money. But gazing around the familiar room I began to doubt my decision. This was my home, my private space. What if this guy turned out to be a chronic bed wetter with bone-deep B.O.?

My hippie parents had been gone from my life for decades, but my Auntie Mana often told me stories about them. And right then, their mantra of *turn on, tune in, and drop out* stood in sharp contrast to the motto I'd recently adopted: *hang on, give in, and suck up*.

4

Lisa Marie brought a long list of wedding gown must-haves to our meeting on Friday morning. She prattled on, describing multi-tiered flounces, seed-pearl beaded bodices, and seven-foot trains. She kept flipping through her celebrity wedding scrapbook, and from the looks of things, she was hankering for a glitzy get-up that would weigh in at about thirty pounds.

"Not gonna happen." I said.

Akiko said nothing; staring at the back wall in what could have passed for a catatonic trance.

"You *said* she was the best." Lisa Marie spit it out as if she'd caught me in a bald-faced lie.

"She is." I glanced over at Akiko to see if she appeared insulted at being talked about as if she weren't there. From the looks of it, she'd gone into a Zen state, imagining herself someplace else entirely. Apparently, no offense taken.

"Here's how it goes, Lisa Marie. You pick from one of these three basic dress designs and Akiko will spend every waking minute between now and Valentine's Day creating a stunning gown that will make Brad's eyes pop out when he sees you. Or, you can hold out for something else and you'll be on your own to find it."

Okay, the *Brad's eyes popping out* image was a little macabre, even for me. But Lisa Marie didn't even blink.

"It better be gorgeous."

"*You'll* be gorgeous; your gown will just accentuate the fact."

She smiled for the first time that morning.

Farrah stepped out of her store while I was stashing fabric samples into the back of Akiko's ancient seaweed-colored minivan. The dressmaker was still in the back room, measuring Lisa Marie from every possible angle

"Ad-bay oos-nay," Farrah said in a low voice, nodding toward my shop door.

"Mainlanders can figure out pig Latin," I said. "What's going on?"

"The Coast Guard's got some dish on your Brad Sanders dude. The TV said they're doing a press conference at three."

My stomach clenched. I looked up at the sun peeking through the clouds. Not quite noon.

"Listen, what are you planning for flowers?" I said in a voice that even to me sounded like a fake attempt at calm.

"Don't you want to chill on that until we hear what they say about the missing dude? No use digging ourselves any deeper."

"No. I don't care what they say. We need to move forward."

"Okay then. I'm thinking cymbidium orchids—pink—and lots of white pikake for fragrance. It's a no go on the tuberoses she wants. Wrong time of year. I'm figuring about five hundred bucks ought to cover it."

"Can you push it to eight hundred?"

"Eight hundred bucks for flowers? For a little beach wedding? If you weren't already my best *hoa aloha*, I'd be whipping out the b/f/f tiara and planting it on your head. Let's see. How's a plumeria-draped arbor sound? And I'll get flashy white and green orchid leis for the guests. By the way, how many guests we talking about?"

"She said less than a dozen. Her family, of course. And I imagine a few of Brad's co-workers will be coming over; probably more for the ghoul factor than to support Lisa Marie."

"Too weird. Well, don't sweat it, I'll get abundantly creative."

"In this case, less isn't more; *more* is more."

"Got it."

By early afternoon I finished lining up the remaining details: printers, caterers, guest favors, hair and make-up, limo service, all of it. My friends and colleagues had all gushed their gratitude for the business. The only glaring omission was a venue. I told everyone I'd be back to them that afternoon with the exact location.

I called the pricier hotels with private beaches. Since Brad Sanders' disappearance had made him something of a local celebrity, I was concerned a public beach could attract the press or curious onlookers. Maui's notorious for local gossip. If just one vendor slipped up and told his cousin who told his neighbor who told his boss's wife, a beach parking lot would fill up with looky-loos hours before Lisa Marie's "perfect" wedding.

"Not possible," sniffed the special events coordinator at the Maui Prince Hotel. "We limit our beach access to weddings coordinated by our in-house bridal staff." The sentiment was echoed by the Grand Wailea, the Four Seasons, and all the other high-end Wailea hotels. I didn't bother calling the Ritz-Carlton in Kapalua because not only did I figure the response would be the same, but it creeped me out to imagine conducting Brad's proxy wedding on the beach where his empty boat had washed ashore.

I was left pondering if I could hold it at a less swanky oceanfront hotel or one of the more obscure public beaches. I hadn't asked Lisa Marie if she had a particular beach in mind, and I wasn't even sure where she was staying. Maybe her hotel would sanction a quickie wedding on their property if I cajoled—a nicer word than *bribed*—someone at the concierge desk.

I called her cell.

"What is it *now*, Pali?" she said in an annoyed tone that made me want to pipe, *Sorry, wrong number* and hang up. "I hope this is good news. I'm just about to get a massage and I don't want any stress following me onto the table."

"Yep, I've got great news. Everything's lined up for next Thursday. Only one little detail left to decide." I took a breath to allow her time to congratulate me on being so damn good at my job. All I heard was the low murmur of New Age flute music in the background.

"Which beach?" I said.

"What do you mean *which beach*? Are you talking about my wedding?"

I started to say something smart-ass, like 'No, I'm calling to ask if you know where they're gonna shoot next year's Sports Illustrated swimsuit edition' but I held back. No doubt she was feeling a ton of anxiety over Brad. I needed to remain supportive, upbeat.

"Yes, I need to tell the people working on your big day where we're holding it."

"I can't believe you're asking me this. I already told you where I want it." She blew out an irritated breath. "Don't you write anything down? I think it's incredibly unprofessional of you to ask me to repeat myself simply because you're so ditzy."

Had she mentioned the venue? My brain raced around like someone looking for their car keys. Nope, not there. Not over there, either.

"I'm sorry, Lisa Marie. Your consultation folder says you want a 'beach wedding' but there's nothing specific about which beach."

"Well, duh. The beach right here on the property, of course. I'm sure I went over all of this on the very first day. How would Brad know where to come if we held it anywhere else? Look, I've got to go; my masseuse is waiting. And Pali, please don't bother me with stuff like this again. If I need to talk to you, I'll do the calling." She clicked off.

I've worked with difficult brides before. Not anyone I'd go so far as to label mentally ill, but women teetering darn close to the edge. I've been called 'stupid,' 'mean,' and even expletives so blue I wondered if they'd use that same mouth to kiss their groom. So, in the scheme of things, I rated Lisa Marie's snippiness at about a six-minus.

I carefully looked through her consultation folder: front, back, and all the pages inside. In the contact information area she'd provided her local address as simply, 'Maui.' She'd left no hotel name, not even a town. Like most visitors, she probably didn't know the street address of where she was staying. Most likely she'd been picked up by a taxi or a hotel shuttle at the airport and they'd whisked her off to her resort. But I was surprised she hadn't bothered to even fill in the name of the place.

A few minutes before three o'clock, I locked up and headed over to Farrah's store. Farrah kept a tiny black and white TV under the counter ostensibly to watch for storm reports, but most of the time it was tuned to the afternoon soaps. I didn't see her right away, so I peeked around the counter to see if the TV was on. On the grainy screen a tall, clean-shaven man in black tie and tails was berating a woman dressed in what appeared to be some kind of French maid's outfit. They cut to a close-up of her, and I watched as she narrowed her eyes and raised her arm into position for a dramatic slap. The camera pulled back in time to show him catching her arm mid-whack.

I was becoming somewhat engrossed in what was going on when the picture went blank and a gray channel ID screen popped up indicating breaking news. Farrah came out from the back room, humming and carrying a Sex Wax counter display. She nodded in greeting, but continued her humming.

She made her way over to the two wooden stools behind the counter, sitting on one and patting the seat of the other to indicate I should join her. At the end of her song, she held the note in a lingering finish.

"*Mahalo* for the hush," she said. "I think it's bad juju to not finish a song."

"Sure. What was that?"

"*In Dis Life*. You know: Iz."

"Right." Okay, she's my friend and all that, but the woman cannot carry a tune. She could have said it was the Star Spangled Banner and I would've agreed.

She leaned over and turned up the volume on the TV but it was still silently displaying the ID screen. When the sound came on, a booming voice blasted out of the tiny speaker.

"*We interrupt our regularly scheduled program-ming to bring you the following special report*". The screen flipped to an image of an empty podium, festooned with microphones displaying not only the call letters of television channels 2, 4, 8, and 9 in Honolulu but also the major mainland television networks, including CNN.

"Wow. Your missing dude must be some kind of celebrity over on the mainland," she said.

"Yeah, I guess. And I thought he was just some under-the-radar computer nerd who'd struck it rich."

A Honolulu police officer in a glowing white short-sleeved dress shirt stepped up to the mic. Even on Farrah's feeble TV I could see the heavily starched creases that dissected his shirt front into three equal parts. His above-the-pocket badge flashed a brilliant white when it caught the sunlight.

"Testing, testing," he said tapping the mic. His eyes were pulled into a self-conscious squint.

"I'm Lieutenant Muro, Public Information Officer for the Honolulu Police Department. I'd like to welcome my colleagues from the Governor's office, from the Counties of Maui and O'ahu, the Coast Guard, and members of the press. At this time we have an update on the disappearance of Bradley James Sanders, founder and president of DigiSystems Corporation in Seattle. Mr. Sanders was here on vacation when he disappeared off the Maui coastline sometime after nineteen hundred hours the night of January thirty-first. His rental boat was recovered, unmanned, on the beach at Kapalua at oh-six hundred hours the next morning."

He paused and looked over his right shoulder at the assembly of uniformed men standing behind him as if giving them an opportunity to step up and disagree with his facts. No one so much as twitched a cheek muscle.

"Commander Roman of the Coast Guard's Search and Rescue team will now present the latest information on the rescue and recovery effort."

He nodded toward a puppy-faced guy in dress whites who looked much too young to even be in the Coast Guard, let alone hold the rank of commander. Commander Roman stepped forward and pulled himself up to his full height in an attempt to reach the microphones. He missed the mark by a good three inches. He fiddled with the center mic, pulling it down toward his chin while the sound popped and squealed.

"Since when did the Coast Guard start recruiting munchkins?" Farrah said, peering at the screen. "That dude looks about twelve years old."

I nodded in agreement.

"Good afternoon. I'm Commander Roman of the Coast Guard's Search and Rescue Squad based here at Pearl Harbor," he said in a deep voice that added at least a decade to his appearance. "Our report today concerns the finding of debris in the waters of Au'au Channel, the strait between the islands of Maui and Molokai. At fourteen hundred hours yesterday afternoon, a Hawaiian-style shirt and rubber thong sandal were located at sea approximately one-quarter mile from where Mr. Sander's boat beached at Kapalua. An acquaintance identified the items as matching similar clothing worn by the victim at the time of his disappearance. This evidence, coupled with a weeklong land and sea operation which has failed to locate Mr. Sanders, has prompted us to halt the rescue and recovery effort until further notice." He paused. "At this time, we'll take questions from the media."

Dozens of reporters' hands shot up while some just shouted out questions. After a few minutes of mostly pointless back and forth, with the Coast Guard saying, "We have no knowledge," or "We can't discuss that at this time," Farrah turned the sound down.

"He's a goner," she said, looking up to check the round curved mirror used to spot shoplifters.

I shook my head. "An *aloha* shirt and a *rubbah slippa*? That's not evidence. I'll bet the next guy who walks through your door will be wearing those same things."

The bell on the door jingled and a bare-chested surfer wearing board shorts held up only by the grace of his protruding hipbones burst in. He was barefoot.

I glanced at the *No shirt, No shoes, No problem* sign above the door.

"Okay, well maybe not here in Pa'ia," I said. "But in Lahaina, every *haole* tourist on Front Street is decked out in either a red dirt tee-shirt or an *aloha* shirt. And everybody wears *rubbah slippas* to go on a boat."

"Pali, I know you've got a lot riding on doing this dudette's wedding. But let's face it, this thing's got only two ways to go. One, he became shark chum the night he disappeared, which means they'll never find as much as a tooth, or, two, before long totally wasted body parts will start washing up on the beach. Either way, this wedding is *pau*: over."

"I can only deal with what I know. And right now, what I know is I have just five days to pull off a big bucks wedding."

"Exactly."

"And your point is...?"

"C'mon, Pali, think about it. Why does she want this fake wedding anyway?" Farrah reached over and snapped off the TV. "Answer? And here's a big hint: everybody says this guy owns a multi-million dollar tech company. No doubt he's loaded. Your girl wants that M-R-S in front of her name before they get around to issuing the death certificate. The grieving widow is always first in line when they divvy up the goods."

"Whoa," I said. "What's happened to you? I figured you'd be firing up the incense and extolling the virtues of undying love."

"I don't extol for shameless gold diggers."

I stood up and pushed my stool back. "Okay, I get it. But I sure can't talk. She's marrying him for the money? Well, welcome to my world. You think if I wasn't dodging creditors left and right I'd have signed on to do this crazy gig?"

Farrah took my hand. "Hey, sorry. This crappy weather's making us all go a little *pupule*. Guess what? This morning I got my first collection call, from my dairy supplier in Honolulu. He wouldn't cut me slack even when I told him I had to toss out most of it. With nobody buying nothing, I had a zillion gallons of milk still sitting here after the sell/by date."

We sat in silence. I watched Felix the Cat's tail flick back and forth on the wall clock.

"We need this wedding to go off as planned," I said. "Lucky for us Lisa Marie's hell bent on spending as much as she can, as fast as she can. Who cares whose money she's using? Once we get paid, the collection calls will stop."

"I seriously need to mellow out." Farrah said. "I guess if the little gold digger's gonna toss a little moolah my way, the least I can do is hold her in my heart with *aloha*."

I couldn't agree more.

5

I'd promised my suppliers I'd be back to them that afternoon about the wedding location, but I balked at taking the time to track down where Lisa Marie was staying. It wouldn't have been that difficult since I know staff people at nearly all of Maui's oceanfront resorts, but I simply wasn't in the mood to play detective. I thought about heading down to the kung fu studio for some kicking and screaming but then realized an hour of physical release would only postpone the inevitable. I wanted to get home and learn what five hundred bucks a week was going to cost me in aggravation.

When I pulled into the driveway Steve's black Jetta was parked off to the right near the back door. Evidently, he'd wanted to avoid the steep front porch steps. I parked out front and trudged up the stairs, practicing a welcoming smile as I went. It felt bogus, like when someone's taking your picture and they fool around with the camera so long that by the time they click the shutter you're wearing a tiki god grin.

The front door was unlocked, which is the way we usually leave it. I pushed it open and saw Steve in the living room crouched down next to the sofa. The new guy was stretched out, his head propped up by pillows at the near end and his body covered by a tucked-in blanket. From the bumps in the blanket, it appeared that he took up the full six-foot length of the sofa and then some. He had wide shoulders and a well-muscled neck. His dark brown hair stuck up at odd angles. Most of the guys in Steve's inner circle would've rather been boiled in oil than be seen with their hair askew, but probably the guy's hospital stay had taken a toll on his personal hygiene routine.

"Hey, you're home," Steve said looking up. "This is Hatch Decker, our new roommate." He stood and moved out of the way so I could make eye contact with Hatch. "And, Hatch, this is your new landlady, Pali Moon."

Wow, what a face. Look-right-through-you brown eyes smoldered under thick *macho man* eyebrows. Why did all the gorgeous men prefer other men? He smiled and pulled his right arm out from under the blanket and held it straight out. It took me a couple of beats to realize he was offering to shake hands.

"Oh, sorry," I said, hustling across the worn carpet. I got a static shock when we touched, and my hand recoiled in reflex. When we reconnected, I felt a warm palm and firm grasp. I didn't want to let go. It'd been weeks since a man—any man—had laid hands on me and his touch caused my shoulders to lift in a little shudder.

"Hatch is a new firefighter with Maui County Fire and Rescue," said Steve. "He broke his leg at work."

"You fall through a burning roof?" I said. It seemed the logical way a fireman would break a leg.

"Nope. Nothing that impressive. I got sideswiped while we were working a wreck out on the Pi'ilani Highway. Guy in a pick-up blew right by the flagger. His bumper snagged my turnouts and he dragged my ass about thirty yards."

"Whoa. I hope they got the license number."

"Oh yeah. The on-scene cop was on him like Bubba at a luau."

"So, how long you going to be laid up?"

"The doc says I should be back to light duty work by the end of the month. In a couple more days the shoulder should be healed enough I can use crutches." He pointed to his left arm which was wrapped tight against his body with a giant elastic bandage.

"Well, no rush. You're more than welcome to my bedroom for as long as it takes."

"Huh. Too bad I'm a crip. That's the best offer I've had in months." His eyes crinkled as he smiled.

I nodded and smiled back at his flattery, even though I knew my bedroom—with me in it, anyway—would hardly make his top ten list of good times. I glanced over at Steve to see if he was annoyed by Hatch's phony come-on, but he just grinned as if he was thrilled to see the step-kids getting along so good.

That night, Steve knocked himself out making a complicated chicken curry with all the condiments. He served it with jasmine rice and a gorgeous Kula greens salad with tomatoes and balsamic dressing. He'd bought a chewy loaf of artisan bread at the Hale Kai Bakery, which must have drained all the cash in his wallet. If he was trying to impress his potential new boyfriend with his domestic skills, I'd say he more than succeeded.

We ate in the living room so Hatch could stay put on the sofa. It took some maneuvering to get a dinner tray to stay in his lap since his inert arm was in the way. When I cleared the dishes after dinner it seemed Hatch's smile seemed a little forced and his forehead sported a couple of deep furrows I hadn't noticed earlier.

"Thanks guys," he said. "Sorry I'm not better company, but I'm still wiped out from the pain meds. Dinner was great. We don't get much in the way of fancy food down at the firehouse. It's mostly spaghetti or chili, and we hardly ever get to finish before we're called out again, so this was pretty swank for me." He shot me a look and added, "But don't worry, Pali. I'll still be out of your hair as soon as I can get up off my sorry butt."

"No worries," I said. "Is your room all set up?" I turned to Steve, since he would have been the one who'd hauled in Hatch's things.

"Yep, his abode is ready for occupancy," he said. "You want some help getting in there, Hatch?"

"Thanks, maybe later. Is that the only TV?" Hatch nodded at the ancient twenty-four inch set in the corner.

"Yeah, sorry. We're not big TV watchers," I said.

"Well if it's okay with you guys, I'd like to watch a little basketball before turning in."

"No problem," said Steve. "I'll be down in a while to help you get to bed."

I thought it was sweet of Steve to be so gallant, but figured there was probably an ulterior motive at work. Hatch was definitely what I'd call a "man's man" and Steve appeared utterly smitten.

I went upstairs to the spare room and read for a while, but once I'd turned out the light I found it hard to sleep on the pull-out sofa bed. I tossed and turned, wondering about Lisa Marie's motives. Would she prove Farrah wrong and cancel now that the Coast Guard had abandoned their search? Or would she bull ahead, insisting that Brad was going to magically catapult from the ocean like some geek Silver Surfer? And what if he doesn't show up? I was pretty sure a proxy marriage by Power of Attorney wouldn't be legally binding in Hawaii, or in any other state, so how could she claim to be his widow?

The next morning, I got up at first light and took a quick shower before heading down to the kung fu center. I hadn't worked out in almost a week and my body resisted the idea. I pulled into the alley and parked behind a red door marked with large black Korean characters which translated into English as "Palace of Pain."

People who earn a black belt at my *guan* are not only awarded the prestigious belt, but are also a given a position of trust as special recognition for passing the rigorous test. At my black belt ceremony I'd been given my own key to the back door so I could come and go whenever I pleased. I slipped inside and entered the chilly, dark space. The floor mats were sticky and cold on my bare feet. I could barely make out my reflection in the floor-to-ceiling mirrors, but I didn't turn on the lights or the space heater. I train at Palace of Pain because the name speaks to me. I don't believe in powder puff martial arts, where the air is conditioned and the mats smell like Mountain Fresh Lysol. At PoP we pride ourselves on what Sifu Doug, our head instructor, calls "sucking it up." Take what you're dealt and use it to your advantage.

I warmed up in a matter of minutes, and after an hour of forms and work with the *mao,* the long lance, I was relaxed and centered. I took a lukewarm shower in the locker room and dressed for work, which simply meant trading my black martial arts uniform for a pair of white capris and a blue lace-trimmed tee-shirt. At the outer door, I slipped on my well-worn *rubbah slippas,* and headed out to my car.

I'd made the coffee and settled down at my desk when the phone rang. Glancing at the caller-ID I saw it wasn't an 808 area code, which meant it wasn't local. Probably a collection call from the mainland. I took a deep breath and picked up.

"Morning, Pali." It was Lisa Marie, singing my name like we were b/f/f. "I found something in a magazine I'm just dying to show you. Can you come by here this morning?"

I hesitated. I still hadn't taken the time to sleuth out where she was staying. Now I'd have to wring it out of her.

"Sure, I can come over. But I'll need the address."

"Check my client folder."

I couldn't believe she was playing that game again. "If you'll give me the address it'll save me the time of looking it up. I'll be able to get there that much sooner."

She sighed, and I heard a loud *thunk*, as if she'd banged the receiver down on a table. A half-minute of murmured voices was followed by the clatter of someone picking up the phone.

"Hello? Hello?" The voice was tentative, with a slight lilt.

"*Aloha.* This is Pali Moon. Who is this, please?"

"I am Josie. I work here."

"Oh. Is Lisa Marie still there?"

"She here, but she say to tell you where she is. She not know."

"Great. What's the name of the hotel, please?" I said.

"Is not hotel. Is house."

"Okay. She's staying in a private home?"

"Yes."

"Can you give me the address?"

"You know where is Olu'olu?"

"Yes, over on the west side."

Every Maui resident knows Olu'olu. It's a touchy subject. A supposed ancient Hawaiian burial ground, the entire area bucked development for decades. A single residence had been built there, on a spit of sand jutting into the ocean. The property flagrantly violated about half a dozen building ordinances: from Coastal Commission setbacks to the razor wire-topped fence that runs from the property line all the way down to the ocean preventing public access to the beach. But, there'd been no hearings when the building permit had been issued. Rumor had it the house was owned by a mainland mob boss who'd used creative measures to sail through the permit process. Allowances had been made; dissent had been stifled.

"It is the house on the beach. Across the street from the big banyan tree."

"I know exactly where you are. *Mahalo*."

No one I knew had ever been to the house, and even though I'd driven past the property at least a hundred times, I'd never noticed any sign of life. I wondered if the house even had an address other than simply "Olu'olu." It was so removed from the other homes on Maui's west shore, I figured it probably had its own ZIP code.

I arrived at the turn-off to Olu'olu just after eight in the morning. Making a left-hand turn off the Honoapi'ilani Highway during rush hour proved nearly impossible. After sitting with my blinker on and backing up traffic for up-wards of a quarter mile, a kind soul coming the other way slowed down and waved me across. I could see his eyes widen in disbelief as he watched my trashed-up Geo turning into the driveway of the purported mobster's mansion-by-the-sea.

I inched up to the entry gate. The driveway and gate were the only breaks in an eight-foot tall stucco wall that surrounded the house, hiding the property, and its occupants, from curious passers-by. The gate itself was substantial, made of a verdigris-colored metal, with sculpted dolphins leaping out of intricately fashioned waves. I rolled down my window in anticipation of talking into a square black box which I figured was an intercom.

"Your name and your business," a deep baritone voice boomed from the box before I had a chance to say anything. He had what we Hawaiians call a 'Southern accent,' which meant he sounded Samoan or Fijian.

"Pali Moon. Let's Get Maui'd," I said, realizing too late he probably just wanted to know the nature of my business, not the name of my shop.

"Let's not, and skip right to the honeymoon," the voice chortled back. I love my business name, but I admit it makes me an easy straight man for every joker on the island. Oh well, I figured the guy deserved a little amusement. It can't be much fun manning a rarely-used guard gate for the Sopranos.

"I'm here to talk with Lisa Marie Prescott about her wedding." I said with a certain amount of anxiety. Why was Lisa Marie staying here? Was Brad Sanders a mobster, and his high-tech gig just a cover?

The gate creaked open and I drove through. It didn't ease my tension to look in my rearview mirror and see the gate silently closing behind me.

The house was stunning. It perched on a patch of land surrounded on three sides by the crashing surf. Apparently the architect had designed the home to take full advantage of the setting by creating a floor plan that followed the curve of the peninsula. The driveway circled around so you entered on the right, drove up to a flagstone apron by the front door, and then by continuing to the far left side you'd be poised to exit back out to the roadway. I parked my ancient green Geo Metro at the outermost left edge, as far out of sight as possible.

As I walked to the front door, I felt someone watching. I glanced up, but spotted no visible cameras. I looked out toward the beach, but saw no one: just frothing surf, glistening gold sand, and an azure sky dotted with cottony clouds.

The massive double front doors were carved from slabs of koa wood. Koa forests, once plentiful in Hawaii, are now nearly depleted and the wood is rare and spendy. An eight by ten koa picture frame can set you back a hundred bucks. I approached the right-hand door and it opened before I could search for a door bell.

"*Aloha* and welcome," said a child-sized woman in a black maid's uniform. "Come in. Miss Prescott be out soon." She slightly rolled the "r" in Lisa Marie's last name, and that, plus her diminutive stature, had me pegging her as a Filipino. Not that anybody cares much about ethnicity in Hawaii. Most people pride themselves on being what we call "poi dogs"—a mixture of this and that. Racially, everyone pretty much gets along.

She showed me into a sunny room with a soaring heavily-beamed ceiling and a glass wall only yards from the crashing surf. There was a spacious flagstone lanai off to the right. I couldn't help but wonder what a tsunami would do to a place so close to the water, but it certainly was a spectacular setting. A trio of rattan-sided sofas, cushioned in a sunny yellow Hawaiian print, had been placed at a U-shape to take full advantage of the view. The pale golden walls and egg yolk-colored carpet gave the light-infused room the feeling of an architectural smiley face.

"Would you like tea?" The maid gestured toward a Chinese-style pottery tea service, as if encouraging me to say 'yes' by showing the tea was already prepared.

"Thank you. That would be lovely." I tend to slip into a snooty vernacular when in the presence of gobs of money. It was all I could do to keep my pinky finger from flipping up as I lifted the tea cup from the ebony tray.

After the obligatory five minutes of making me wait for her grand entrance, Lisa Marie walked in lugging a foot-high stack of glossy magazines. She nodded a quick greeting and dumped her load onto the coffee table. Then she plucked the most recent issue of *Hawaii Bride* from the top of the pile.

"See this?" She said as she flipped to a page marked with a dog-eared corner. She laid the magazine open on her lap and pointed to an article describing the tradition of the bride folding one-thousand origami cranes before her wedding. "I like this idea. I want oregano cranes."

"It's pronounced 'origami' and I'm afraid we don't have enough time for that, Lisa Marie. Did you read what the cranes represent?"

She gave an evasive shrug. I leaned over and read aloud the caption under a photo montage of four artfully framed origami crane collections.

"The origami crane keepsake keeps alive an ancient Japanese tradition whereby the bride presents the groom with one-thousand origami cranes demonstrating her patience and attention to detail. The groom folds one more as a promise of fidelity."

"Fine," she said, slapping the magazine closed. "I need you to get me one of those crane picture thingies for my wedding."

I closed my eyes and took in a full breath, pulling my diaphragm up tight under my ribcage. It was a pre-fight exercise I'd learned from Sifu Doug to center my mind and allow me to appear calm when faced with a daunting opponent.

"The *bride* makes the cranes, Lisa Marie," I said, slowly releasing air through my nose. "One thousand tiny perfectly folded cranes made of fragile gold-colored origami tissue. It normally takes a bride-to-be months and months to finish."

"It'd go a lot quicker if she hired some people."

"You don't *hire people*," I said, silently adding the '*you idiot*' that so naturally followed. "It's *your* job. The point of folding the cranes is to prove to your husband, and his family, that you have what it takes to be a good wife. It's not something you phone in."

"You promised me a perfect wedding. Well, it won't be perfect without a crane picture. So get with it and find me some origami folders. I'll pay them fifteen bucks an hour if they get it done by next Tuesday." She stood up and headed for the French doors before I had a chance to protest.

"Oh, and by the way," she said, turning back to face me. "I know all about the Coast Guard calling off the search for Brad. But I'm not worried. He's not in the water anyway. I had a dream last night. He was walking along a trail, high above the ocean. He wasn't even wet. In the dream he told me he has some stuff he needs to do, so he wants me to keep getting everything ready for our wedding."

I just nodded because no suitable comment came to mind.

Changing the subject I asked, "When are your parents arriving?"

"Tomorrow. Oh, and that reminds me, I'm going to need a ride to the airport. Daddy will have his car that's in storage delivered to the terminal, so you won't have to bring us back here, but I want to meet his plane when it lands."

"No problem," I said. "What time does the flight arrive?"

"I think he said around noon."

"So when would you like me to pick you up?"

"Be here at eleven-fifteen. I don't want to have to hang around the airport too long."

"How many people will be arriving with him?"

"You're sure nosy. What do you care? I already said we'll have our own ride back here."

"True, but I'll be bringing *aloha* leis. I need to know how many to get."

She blew out an exasperated breath. "Bring a dozen. There won't be that many people, but my dad's wife will probably glom on to three or four. She's kinda greedy."

Half an hour later, as I was waiting to make the turn off the highway to go toward Pa'ia, I had a flash of brilliance.

I pulled out my cell phone and punched in a number.

After fives rings, it went to voicemail. Akiko's message left no doubt she wouldn't be coming to the phone. *You leave your numba and I call you later. My daughter still not have that baby, and I busy making a bride dress. Aloha.*

I flipped the phone closed, changed lanes and made a furtive U-turn. As I neared Akiko's house, I saw two little boys out front. The girl who'd come into the kitchen last Thursday was sitting on the top porch step, her head propped on her fist. She looked like she'd been stationed there to watch over her younger siblings who were busy hurling toys at each other in the yard below.

"Hi," I said, as I passed by her on my way to the front door.

"Hi," she said in a tiny voice that split the middle between talking to strangers and prudently ignoring them.

"Is your grandmother at home?"

"My *tutu* said not to bother her."

"I know. I need to ask her something really quick. My name's Pali, and I'm the person who hired your *tutu* to make the wedding dress."

"You're getting married?" She said it with incredulity as if I didn't, by any stretch of her childhood imagination, fit her vision of a dewy-eyed bride.

"No. I'm the wedding planner. I help the bride get ready for the wedding."

"I'm Kalani," she said with a little bow of her head. "Those are my brothers." She pointed to the two boys who were now rolling on the ground grappling with each other.

"I'll watch the boys for you if you'll go in and tell your *tutu* I'm here."

"She might get mad."

"True. Well, here's the deal: actually, I need to ask you something, not her, but I don't think I should talk to you about it until I get your *tutu's* permission. Could you just tell her that Pali's here to offer you a job?"

Her small face scrunched in distress, as if she couldn't decide which was worse: risking her *tutu's* ire or not learning about a possible job offer.

"I'll be right back," she said. "You tell those boys to stop hitting."

I looked down into the yard and saw a full-blown fistfight in progress. I bounded down the steps.

"Hey, hey. What's going on here?"

The smaller boy had sunk his teeth into the larger boy's forearm. The big boy howled in protest, but didn't seem to be making much of an effort to pull his arm away.

"You hungry?" I said to the little biter. "You can choose. Keep chomping on your brother, or have some gum." I held out a half-pack of fruit-flavored Trident I'd dug out of my purse.

"No fair," the older boy screeched.

The little boy glanced toward the house, then snatched the gum and put it in his shorts pocket.

"And for you," I said, rummaging through my size-able beach bag satchel. I came up empty in the candy and gum department, so I scavenged some coins from the bottom. "Money."

The bigger boy shot out his arm and grabbed the change just as Akiko appeared on the porch.

"What you doing here?" she said. "I not done with this dress. Maybe I never get done with these *keiki* making all this *kulikuli*."

The boys hung their heads, but I saw impish grins forming as they flicked their eyes back and forth to each other.

"Akiko. I'm sorry to bother you. I just wanted to ask if your granddaughter might like to help out a little with a wedding."

Akiko looked fierce. "She's busy watching the boys."

"I can see that. But this is a job she could do while she watches them, and maybe a few of her friends could help."

At the mention of involving friends, Kalani perked up.

I told them I had a client who needed help folding her one thousand origami cranes. I avoided mentioning it was Lisa Marie, since she and Akiko hadn't seemed to hit it off too well.

"Do you know how to fold a perfect origami crane?" I bent down to look Kalani in the eye.

She sniffed as if I'd asked if she could count to ten.

"Great. Well, this client will pay a quarter for every perfect crane you and your friends make. You'll need to get the gold paper they use for the wedding cranes, and you and your friends will need to finish one thousand of them by next Tuesday. Do you want to do it?"

"Can I, *tutu*? Please, please."

"I thought you say the bride need help with the cranes. But you got the kids folding *all* of them?"

I shot her a puckish smile.

"I will ask her mother," Akiko said, throwing up her hands as she turned toward the door.

Akiko's daughter called me on my cell a half-hour later. She'd talked with a few of Kalani's friend's mothers and they'd lined up six girls from her Girl Scout troop who were eager to earn summer camp money. She told me the girls were already at work practicing their folding technique. One of the girl's fathers, a Hawaiian Airlines pilot, had agreed to pick up the special origami paper in Honolulu and would bring it home on his last flight into Kahului that evening.

I pulled into the alley behind my shop feeling like a hero. Nice moment, but short lived. Noni Konomanu's fancy black car was parked in my spot. I double parked, blocking her exit. Now she'd have to back all the way down the narrow alley to get out of there.

A few minutes later, after I'd heard what she'd come for, I reconsidered my rudeness. I shouldn't have blocked her in. I should've taken a baseball bat to her windshield.

6

I entered the Gadda-da-Vida Grocery and quickly spotted Noni and Farrah in the far reaches of the produce section. I listened, but heard nothing. I made my way back there and found them staring each other down like a couple of tomcats.

"Hey, you two. What's up?" I said.

"Nothing," said Farrah in a clipped voice. She held the small paring knife she used to trim lettuce, and she was clenching the handle so tightly her knuckles were white.

"Oh, I beg to differ," said Noni. "I'm glad you showed up, Pali, because this concerns you as well. I stopped over at your shop but you must have popped out for a latte." Her snotty attitude forced me to throw her my fiercest glare.

"I don't have time for lattes. Managing a successful bridal business requires a lot of running around handling details."

"I'm sure running a *successful* bridal business requires a lot of running around, but I think in your case any time crunch is most probably due to a lack of organizational skills." She shot me a simpering grin. "Anyway, Mr. Sherman asked me to come by and talk to Farrah about his plans to buy this building. He also said if I saw you I should let you know he's been in touch with the mortgage lender on your house up in Hali'imaile. He's going to be putting in a bid on it at the first possible opportunity."

Taunts don't rile me much. Well, anyway, that's what I'd like people to think. In my younger years I might have gasped, or talked trash back at her, but I'd trained myself to simply offer a steady stare when attacked. I hadn't quite mastered keeping my blood pressure from shooting up, though, and I wondered if my cheeks were flaming.

"Too bad," I said. "I know how much Tank hates to lose. But by the end of next week my house will no longer be available."

"Says you."

"No, says a lot of dead presidents I'll be collecting next Friday."

I glanced over at Farrah. She moved a foot closer to Noni. As if propelled by an opposing force, Noni backed away in the opposite direction.

"Anyway, girls, I've got to dash," said Noni. "I've got a million things on my smart-phone calendar. Don't you just love technology?" She waggled the small black device at us and then turned and wobbled down the cereal aisle in her four-inch stilettos. I noticed her clingy red dress was an orange-red and her shoes a definite blue-red. In the wedding business, a color gaffe like that was a career-ender.

At the back door, she hesitated as she eyed a tower of cardboard boxes waiting to be broken down and recycled.

"Oh, and Farrah, you better hang on to these boxes. You're going to be needing them. You too, Pali." She flashed us a mocking sneer; her eyes squinting into what I hoped would become permanent crow's feet.

She pushed the back door open and a blast of wind swirled her sleek dark hair across her face. "*Aloha,* see you gals later." She wiggled her fingers in a bye-bye wave.

The door slammed shut. I waited for her to bang back in and demand I move my car out of her way, but she didn't. Maybe she was smarter than she looked.

"What kind of evil shit was that?" said Farrah. "I'm going to have to hire a *kahuna* to come in and bless this place all over again. Did you know Noni had signed on as Tank Sherman's lackey?"

"Yeah. She came by my shop last Tuesday."

"Why didn't you tell me?"

"Because I completely forgot about it. I figured if I pulled off Lisa Marie's wedding I'd be able to pay his thieving rent until I could relocate my shop somewhere else. She didn't say anything about you and the Vida."

Farrah glared at the back door but kept quiet.

"So," I said, "I guess he's planning to increase your rent, too. Can you raise prices enough to manage it?"

"Are you kidding? If I jack my prices any higher they'll haul me in for extortion."

"Good point."

"And the new Wal-Mart down in Kahului has already cut into my business more than thirty percent."

"Did she say how much Tank was paying for this place?"

"She's probably blowing smoke, but she said it appraised for around two mil."

"Wow. If your folks had ever dreamed this place would be worth that kind of money, I'll bet they'd never have sold it."

"But they just wanted to run a store. The taxes and upkeep got to be more than they could handle."

Upkeep? I looked at the worn interior of the century-old building. The wood plank floor was so rutted by years of plantation workers' feet scuffling across it that Farrah had covered the high traffic areas with jute mats. The mats were frayed and dirty, making the whole place look and smell like an old army barracks.

"Two million bucks," I said, shaking my head.

Farrah's eyes darted around the store, but she didn't say anything. I'd known her long enough to recognize when she was holding something back.

"There's more, right?"

"Yeah. Noni said Tank wants to buy the store. Not just the building, but the whole business."

"She give you a number?"

"Yeah."

When Farrah made me drag stuff out of her, it usually signaled she was uncomfortable with the message. But I wasn't in the mood for twenty questions.

"Farrah, tell me the whole thing, right now. I've got too much going on to play the Barbara Walters thing with you."

"It's a boatload." She hesitated. "Okay, okay, I won't make you ask again. He's talking a couple hundred thou."

My jaw slackened.

"But, hey, that includes the inventory," she said. In a low voice she added, "I need to give him my answer by Friday."

I gripped the chrome edge of the produce case. "Why's he being so generous?"

"Noni says he's got his reasons."

"You going to do it?"

"How can I even think about it? This was my parents' store; the only thing I have left of them. Selling out to an *'okole* like Tank would be like dancing on their graves. They ran this store as a gesture of peace and love to the local people here. They didn't care about the *kala*."

"Didn't care? Twenty years ago they sold this building because of the money," I said.

She pressed her lips into a tight frown.

I went on. "And two hundred grand is some serious dough. You'd never sweat money again with that kind of stash."

"But this isn't just my work, it's my home." She glanced up, indicating her tiny apartment above the store.

"Maybe Tank will still let you live up there. Pay him rent or something."

"No, the offer is to get out. *Pau.*"

Something red caught my eye and I looked down. Farrah had pushed the blade of the paring knife into her palm. Three or four dark red drops had fallen to the floor.

"Eh, that hurts," she said. She dropped the bloody knife on a display of neatly stacked head lettuce and pressed her thumb into the cut. Blood from the knife seeped across a lettuce head making it look like it'd taken a bullet.

"He offered to buy me out of 'Let's Get Maui'd' too," I said.

"Really? How much?"

"Five grand."

"What? That's a freakin' insult."

"Yeah, but it's pretty obvious Tank's way more interested in groceries than girls. He'll probably just farm out the wedding business. Besides, like you said, you've got inventory—and a huge customer base."

"So," said Farrah, "what did Noni mean about Tank making a bid on your house? I didn't know it was for sale."

"It isn't. It's in foreclosure. I'm behind on the payments."

She opened her palm. Blood oozed from the cut. I pulled a clean white tissue from my beach bag and held it out to her. It looked like a limp surrender flag. She grabbed it and dabbed at the blood.

I went on, "I'm not going to sweat losing my house, though, because by the end of next week I'll be paying off my bills and almost caught up on my mortgage. I'm planning to tell that fatso, *tanks but no tanks*."

"Sounds good. But I'm not sure what I should do. I hate the idea of caving to that slimy *pololia* but what can I do? I need to go upstairs and consult my sources."

Farrah relied heavily on her Ouija board, tarot cards, and rune stones to manage her day-to-day life. Her apartment resembled a gypsy fortune teller's wagon with walls festooned in decades-old tie-dye, crystal prisms dangling in the windows, and every available flat surface cluttered with mystical trinkets. Although she was an ordained minister of the Church of Spirit and Light—an ultra-liberal Christian sect—her personal belief system leaned much more toward the paranormal.

I gave her a hug and went over to my shop. Before I had a chance to switch on the lights I saw the answering machine blinking a cheerful staccato. The read-out showed three messages. Was it too much to hope at least one of them was good news?

"Pali, I hate to bug you, but I'm gonna need some deposit money before I start printing these wedding announcements. Get back to me, okay?"

"Hi Pali. Keahou here. I usually get full payment before I make a cake, but since you're my good girl bringing me this business , I'll let you just give me half. When can you get that to me?"

"This is Akiko. I forgot to tell you I'm ready for the first fitting. Tell your bride we need to do it quick. Oh, and can you pay me some money? The fabric cost over two hundred dollars."

I punched in Lisa Marie's cell phone number.

"Now what?" she snapped. "I told you not to bother me."

I refused to rise to the bait. "You'll be happy to hear Akiko is ready for the first fitting of your gown."

"Why do I need a fitting? That stupid little woman already measured every inch of me. It was way embarrassing. I bet she wouldn't stick a tape measure up Paris Hilton's crotch. "

"It's up to you, Lisa Marie. It's true Akiko has all of your measurements. But the drape of the fabric and the unique design must work with the curves of your body to make a gown that fits you perfectly. If you'd like her to simply sew it up, she can. But be forewarned, without fittings it'll look more like an off-the-rack-dress than an exclusive original. You're paying for *couture* and you deserve the full package. Do you have any idea how many fittings super models have before Fashion Week in New York?" My BS meter was pegging in the red zone, but the overall gist of it was true.

"All right. But I'm not happy about this. Naomi Campbell gets paid huge bucks to have pins stuck in her. Is this the only fitting I'll need?"

"There's usually a final fitting the day before the wedding."

"The wedding's in less than a week! Does that stupid dressmaker think I'm going to pork out in five days?"

"Maybe you won't need a final fitting. I think you should discuss it with Akiko."

"Oh yeah, like she's ever said one single word to me—ever."

I let a beat go by and then ventured, "Any chance you could come by later this afternoon?" I was pushing it. She probably had her entire day planned out: napping, whining, watching a half-dozen soaps she'd recorded on the DVR.

"Today's Saturday," she said. "It's not even a work day."

It struck me odd that someone who'd most likely never worked a day in her life could differentiate between business days and weekends.

"Yes, but Akiko's been slaving non-stop on your gown. She won't be taking any time off between now and Valentine's Day."

"Bully for her."

I waited.

"Okay. I'll call Kevin and get him to drive me. We'll be there at three. Tell that little sewing lady to be on time and to make it snappy. I've got to be back home by four to catch *Entertainment Tonight, the Weekend Edition*. It comes on way early over here. My whole TV schedule's all messed up."

I offered *mahalos* for coming in on such short notice. I didn't comment on the obvious irony of a spoiled diva racing home to catch up on the antics of other spoiled divas. After all, I had a mortgage to pay.

Lisa Marie arrived a few minutes before three. Kevin excused himself immediately, saying he'd be back in half an hour. In her slim elegant gown Lisa Marie looked even more emaciated than she had on Friday. Akiko pinned and tucked, assuring both me and the bride it was way easier to take in a dress than let one out.

"I make big seams. Usually with pregnant girl, well, you know." She pinched her lips into a disapproving scowl. "Skinny girl, no problem."

After the fitting, Lisa Marie hopped off the step-up platform and dashed behind the curtain of the tiny changing room. Half a minute later, she used her bare foot to nudge the exquisite silk dress under the curtain and out onto the fitting room floor. Akiko's eyes widened in horror as she snatched up the gown. She smoothed the fabric with the tenderness of a mother comforting an injured child. Then she hung the dress on a padded hanger and slipped it into a pink satin garment bag. She turned to leave.

"Next fitting on Tuesday," she said, parting the bead curtain. I heard her bare feet pad across the reception room floor and then there was a pause as she slipped into her flip-flops. A few seconds later the front door slammed with a resolute *bam*.

"I told you I didn't want any more fittings," said Lisa Marie. She'd come out from the dressing room wearing only her bra and panties. She stood, hands on hips, glaring at me.

"Akiko had to take your gown in almost an entire size, Lisa Marie. If you keep losing weight, it'll be hanging on you like a garbage bag by Valentine's Day. You need to start eating. And you need to come back on Tuesday so she can check the alterations."

"Oh, listen to Miss Bossy Boss. Well, the queen of somewhere once said, 'There's no such thing as being too rich or too thin.' I've already got the rich part figured out, so now I'm going for super-thin. Besides, Brad will like me skinny. Kevin says bony girls are hot."

Hot wasn't the word I'd use to describe the jutting clavicles and xylophone ribcage Lisa Marie was flashing me as she stood there in her skivvies. But I managed to maintain my fake smile as she flounced back behind the dressing room curtain to get dressed.

When she came out she wore a soft leather jacket over her street clothes. I touched her elbow and asked if I could have just one more minute of her time. She rolled her eyes, but didn't make a dash for the door.

"I hate to bring this up, but your original deposit has been pretty much used up. I have a few people who've spent their own money getting things ready for your wedding and they need to get paid. So, if you could, I'd appreciate another partial payment." I held out her consultation folder which had grown plump with bills for the gown, the cake, the printing, the flowers, and at least a half dozen other services I'd ordered. "I have all the invoices right here if you'd like to look them over."

"Stop," she said, pushing the folder aside. She unclasped her boxy Louis Vuitton clutch and plucked out a white business card. "Call this number and tell the guy what you need. He'll be paying our wedding bills."

I glanced at the card. In simple block letters it read, "Todd Barker, CFO, DigiSystems Incorporated." At the bottom left corner was a post office box address in Seattle and a phone number with a 206 area code.

At that moment Kevin burst through the front door looking as guilty as a stand-in groom could look facing his ersatz bride. He'd been gone almost an hour. I braced myself for Lisa Marie's tirade, but instead she ran over and threw her arms around him.

"Oh, Kev, please get me out of here. My wedding dress is baggy and ugly, and everyone thinks they can just boss me around. I need to get home to see what's going on with my people. "

He looked confused.

"*Entertainment Tonight*, silly. It's on in a few minutes."

Kevin still looked confused. I took him aside as Lisa Marie marched out the door.

"I don't think she's feeling well," I whispered. "She keeps losing weight and it looks like she's not sleeping much either. The stress of Brad missing is probably taking a much bigger toll on her than she's letting on. Oh, and by the way, the gown is lovely. Simple, but extremely elegant."

"It better be. She told me what it's costing."

"Ke-*vin*," Lisa Marie whined through the open door. "Take me home—now!"

As soon as they left, I sat down and dialed the number on the business card. Since it was nearly seven o'clock on a weekend night in Seattle, I was expecting to just leave a message.

"Todd Barker's office," said a cheery female voice.

"Oh, hello, this is Pali Moon in Maui. I'm calling on behalf of Lisa Marie Prescott. She asked me to contact Mr. Barker regarding some invoices that need to be paid."

"Certainly," she said. "Would you like to speak directly with Todd?"

"He's in?"

"Yes. We're staffed seven days a week. We work ten hour shifts, four days on, three days off. Today is one of Todd's work days. Please hold and I'll put you through."

There was a series of clicks.

"Barker here." His voice sounded like his name.

"Mr. Barker? My name is Pali Moon. I'm the coordinator for the Brad Sanders and Lisa Marie Prescott wedding over here on Maui."

"Do you have news about Brad?"

"No, I'm afraid not. Unfortunately they found some clothing they believe may have belonged to him, but—"

"I know. It was on yesterday's Internet news links."

"Yes. Well, actually I'm calling about some invoices that need to be paid."

"For what?"

"Brad's wedding."

A long pause served as his reply.

"I know," I said. "It's kind of crazy, but Lisa Marie's convinced he's still alive and he'll return in time for the wedding so we're going forward with it. She said it's extremely important to Brad that they stick with their Valentine's Day wedding date."

He laughed: a loud, guttural laugh. I pulled the receiver away from my ear to avoid a temporary hearing loss.

When he settled down I continued. "I'm afraid I don't find this as amusing as you apparently do, Mr. Barker. After all, this self-delusion is probably all that's keeping her from going into full-blown shock. She's losing weight, she's not sleeping, and she's—"

"Ms. Moon, let me enlighten you as to what she is. She's a royal pain in the ass. We all advised Brad against doing this, but for whatever reason, he seems determined to allow her to lead him around by the nose. But isn't this rather moot? I mean, he's been missing for almost two weeks. Regardless of her fantasies, you can't have a wedding without a groom."

"Kevin McGillvary's offered to stand in as proxy," I said. "Under the General Power of Attorney he and Brad have for each other."

"That moron. What's he...oh, forget it. Let's get back to why you called. You said she's run up some bills?"

"Yeah, I'm afraid I'm looking at some pretty hefty invoices. Lisa Marie assured me you'd pay them. But perhaps that isn't the case?"

"How much are we talking about?"

I did some quick arithmetic in my head.

"She gave me a thousand dollar deposit, but there's still over three thousand currently owing and more bills coming in every day. I know that might sound excessive, but—"

"That's nothing. I've seen the way that girl blows through cash. Send me the current bills and DigiSystems will pay. But no more. With Brad gone, I figure she's no longer our problem."

I started to gush my thanks, but he talked over me. "You want some advice, Ms. Moon?"

I hesitated and he went on. "Cancel the wedding—today. Unplug yourself from this girl and her scary family at the first possible opportunity. I tried to warn Brad and now look what's happened."

"What—"

But the hum on the line told me he'd already hung up.

7

After dinner Saturday night Steve went out clubbing, leaving me to entertain Hatch on my own. I wondered how smitten Steve actually was with Hatch if he'd rather go out partying than stick around to pour on the charm. But as I always reminded myself, it was none of my business.

"You want to play cards or just watch TV?" I asked, hoping he'd opt for television, but feeling the need to act like a good hostess.

"Oh, I'm fine here with my book." He held up the new Lee Child thriller.

"Hey, I'm a big Jack Reacher fan myself. I mean, the guy's the ultimate alpha dude. I love those scenes where he's crushing the air out of the bad guy with one hand while dragging the perky blond to bed with the other."

"That's your ideal man?"

"No, that's my ideal book."

"That surprises me, you being a wedding planner and all. I'd have thought you'd go for the girly-girl stuff."

"Oh no, trust me. In the scheme of things, a wedding planner is just one tea rose away from a drill sergeant. The job's mostly kicking butt and taking names."

"Huh. I wouldn't know. Never got married. How about you?"

"Not even close."

We both nodded, as if silently agreeing not delve into that subject any further.

"So," I asked, eager to change the subject, "how long have you been with Maui Fire?"

"Only a few months. I transferred here from Honolulu. I had to get out of there. They didn't take kindly to me playing for the other team."

"Oh." I tried to look understanding, but didn't offer any comment. I'd heard Steve lament about prejudice and discrimination even though he worked in a creative field where a gay lifestyle was often the norm. I couldn't imagine how brutal the bigotry might get in a macho job like fire fighting.

"Now that I think about it," he said, "I guess I could go for a few hands of poker. You up for some five card stud?"

I nodded and pulled out a sticky deck of cards we keep in a drawer of the coffee table. I offered to deal since Hatch's left arm was still out of commission.

"What about poker chips?" he asked. "Or do you want to use quarters or something?"

Ha! I thought. *If I had a stash of quarters, they'd have gone for groceries weeks ago.* I didn't say anything, though. I wasn't ready to own up to my abject poverty to a guy I hardly knew.

"Give me a minute. I'll think of something." I considered the stuff stored in the garage and came up with a winner. Now if I could just locate the box I needed.

"I'll be right back."

The night air outside was perfect. Ebony black and balmy. If I hadn't promised Hatch a quick return, I'd have plopped down on a porch chair and star gazed a while. Instead, I went back to the garage and opened the creaking door. I grabbed the flashlight hanging by the door and surveyed the tidy shelves Steve had built for me. I came upon a box labeled *LGM-Rejects*. I rummaged through the box until I found a large plastic bag. Inside were about six dozen pale blue lapel buttons that read, *Denise & Austin, September 22*. Underneath the date was a too-cute cartoon couple with oversized lips puckered up for a kiss. I hauled out the bag and took it to the house.

"What've you got there?" said Hatch, as I plopped down the bag of buttons.

"Mementos from a stunning display of cold feet."

"That happen a lot?"

"Not often. This turned out to be a ten-thousand dollar ditch job."

"Which one blinked?"

"Truthfully, I'd say both. But the groom took the bullet."

Hatch picked up a button and fiddled with the pin on the back. "Why do you keep these things?"

"Hey, I don't throw anything away. Notice there's no year on there. What if I get some future clients named Denise and Austin who are willing to get married on September 22? I could offer them these buttons for free and they'd think I was a hero."

"No, they'd think you were blind. C'mon, these are butt ugly."

"I think you'll find the rest of the world may not share your 'queer eye for the straight guy' sophistication, my friend. The original Denise and Austin thought they were adorable. "

"Oh yeah?" He scowled. "Did you ever consider maybe these were the deal breaker?"

Having worked with the couple in question, I knew the goofy buttons were merely the proverbial tip of the iceberg. I'd never observed such wildly divergent goals, interests, and priorities in two people about to get married. But I make it a point to avoid gossiping about my clients no matter how amusing the tale.

"Are we going to play poker or argue aesthetics?" I said.

"Hey, I'm sitting here waiting for you to dole out the chips."

I counted out thirty buttons each and slid his pile across the table.

"Speaking of 'queer eye,'" he said, "how'd you and Steve get to be roommates? I'm assuming you don't run in his social circle."

"You assume correctly. Actually, I met him when he was a man on the run."

"From?"

"He didn't tell you?"

"He mentioned something about a 'sordid past' and said he'd tell me the whole story sometime. Is he wanted by the law?"

"No, nothing like that. If you promise to act surprised when he gets around to giving you his version, I'll let you in on what I know. It's nothing criminal, just pretty embarrassing."

I dealt us each two cards, one down, one face up.

"As you know," I said, "Steve's a photographer. But he always dreamed of being in front of the camera rather than behind it. So when he lived in LA he prowled open casting calls, but he never got any call-backs. Last spring he was standing in an audition line and a production assistant came by and handed him a card. It turned out to be a pass to an unmarked door at the back of a sound stage. When he got inside he discovered he'd been selected as a contestant on "Happily Ever After," a reality show where a gorgeous woman chooses her future husband from a group of hunky guys. Great gig, lots of media exposure. Problem was, it threw a klieg light on Steve's boy-girl issues while he was still way far back in the closet."

"Yow." Hatch shook his head. He hadn't even glanced at his cards.

"Well," I continued, "he told me he agonized over whether or not to do it for about five seconds. He knew a shot at a prime-time network show was a once-in-a-lifetime opportunity. And, he knew he could handle it. First, because he was an aspiring actor and he'd been perfecting the straight-guy role his entire life, and, second because there were eleven other guys. He figured he'd last a week or two."

"Uh-oh, I have an idea where this is heading." Hatch rubbed his hand against his cheek as if checking for stubble.

"Right. As you can imagine, he started to panic when week after week another guy got booted off."

"Why didn't he quit when she got down to the last few guys?"

"And come out on prime time television? His mom was sending him emails saying her bridge club ladies were praying he'd win."

"Ouch."

"Yeah. Well, on the last episode the girl pledged her undying love and he beamed. He told me when he kissed her, he closed his eyes and mentally swapped her for Russell Crowe."

"Now *that* takes some heavy-duty acting."

"Anyway, he soldiered on while the cameras were rolling, but when the studio called to schedule a televised trip to the marriage license bureau, he let it go to voice-mail. The next day he started using a different name and bought a one-way ticket to Maui. When he got here he saw my 'roommate wanted' sign on the grocery store bulletin board and he moved in that weekend."

"Whew. And I thought *my* life was complicated."

We both looked down at our cards. He was showing a king, I had a four. He threw three buttons into the pot.

I picked up my down card—a deuce—and tossed him a smile. I called his bet, and even raised him two more buttons. I pride myself on my primo bluff.

"You still in?" I asked.

"Heck yes," he said, flipping two more buttons onto the pile. "You're the one showing the lousy four."

I dealt the rest of the hand, matching his bets with every card. I ended up holding a deuce, a four, a six, a seven and a red queen. In other words, not a darn thing.

He picked up his final card and grinned.

"Seems my luck is changing." He fanned his cards and held them out so I could see. A pair of kings, a queen, a ten and a jack. I slipped my cards to the bottom of the deck without a word.

"Okay," he said. "What about you? You lived here long?"

I shuffled while I pondered my answer.

"I was born in a free love commune over on Kauai to a couple of *haole* hippies. My dad left my mom and went back to the mainland when I was still a baby, and then my mom died suddenly when I was four."

"Whoa, that's tough. So, did you end up in foster homes or get adopted?"

I wanted to point out I'd agreed to play poker, not submit to a personal interview, but I figured he was just trying to make conversation.

"Kind of a combination of both. My brother and I became *hanai* kids. You know about that?"

"Sounds Hawaiian," he said. "I didn't come to the islands until I was twenty, so I missed out on most of the cultural stuff."

"Well, *hanai* is an unofficial adoption over here. Sometimes aunties or uncles take you in; sometimes friends of the family. Since we didn't have any family members here, my mom's best friend, we call her Auntie Mana, raised us. She moved us from Kauai over here to Maui to be closer to her extended family."

"That's a pretty generous thing for her to do: to take you in like that."

"Yeah. She was a wonderful mom. I don't remember much about my real mom." I slid the deck across the table for him to cut, but he waved it away. "But I had a really weird thing happen a couple of years ago. A friend took me up to a big lavender farm up near Kula. As I crossed the parking lot, I caught a whiff of the gardens and I started bawling like a baby. I was totally stunned. I guess on some visceral level I remembered the smell. It must have been the scent my mother wore: lavender."

I cleared my throat. Hatch reached over and patted my hand. "You okay?"

"Yeah," I said, coming back to the moment and dealing out the first two cards. "It's ancient history. I really love the smell. I can't imagine why it still gets to me."

"I can."

We played for the next forty-five minutes, passing buttons back and forth.

At nine-thirty, Hatch leaned back and closed his eyes. "I hate to wuss out on you, but I'm kinda wiped out. I still haven't gotten my strength back."

"Hey, no problem. I've got to pick up some people at the airport tomorrow so I should be getting to bed."

"Before you go," he said. "I've got to ask: what's going on? You seem preoccupied, like something's eating at you."

"You're tired and it's a long story."

He scrunched down on the pillow and gently rested his good right arm on top of the bandaged-up left arm. "I'm already lying down. Fire away."

I gave him the short version of my situation: doing a proxy marriage for a cranky bride and her missing and presumed dead groom was all that stood between me and economic ruin.

"Crap," he said. "And now you've got a busted-up fireman camped out on your couch. I feel like I've come at a really bad time."

"No," I said. "It's great to have you here. I rarely see Steve, and to tell you the truth, your rent is about all that's keeping the lights on around here."

"Do you need me to give you more?"

"Oh, no," I said. "Five hundred a week is already flirting with larceny."

"No, I mean, what if I gave you a couple thousand; the whole month upfront. Would that help?"

"That'd be wonderful." I leaned in to give him a hug on his good shoulder and he reached out and gripped my hand. I jumped as if I'd been zapped with a Taser.

"Sorry," I said. "I—"

"Hey," he said, gently pulling me in.

He leaned over and lightly kissed me, the warmth of his lips firing my cheeks into what I'm sure was a vivid blush.

I pulled away. Okay, I'll admit I was attracted. But I still wasn't sure what was going on between Hatch and Steve. There was no way I'd let myself get dragged into a love triangle with my roommates.

"Uh. Well, good night," I said, standing up. "Do you need help getting to your room?" I strictly forbade myself from uttering the word *bed.*

"No, I'm good," he said thickly. "If it's okay, I think I'll just camp out here tonight." He winced and readjusted his left arm.

"You don't look so good. Can I get you a pain pill?"

"No, sorry for the waterworks. I'm fine, really." A tear hovered at the corner of his eye and then started to slide down his cheek. He swiped it away.

"There's no shame in taking a pill, you know."

"Thanks, but I swear I'm okay. I just need some sleep."

I didn't push. After all, I know a thing or two about ignoring pain.

8

On Sunday morning, my cell phone slithered across the nightstand, buzzing and vibrating with an incoming call. I rolled over and checked the time: six-thirty. The caller ID said *K McGillvary*.

"Hi Kevin. What's up?" I said, attempting an 'already had my coffee' voice. I didn't mention the early hour. I like clients to think I never sleep; as if I maintain a constant vigil until their Big Day.

"I need to talk to you. Soon."

"Is Lisa Marie all right?"

"She's fine. But I need to see you this morning."

"I don't normally work on Sundays."

"I don't need you to do anything. I want to give you a heads-up before Lisa Marie's family gets here."

"Can't you just tell me now?"

"No," his voice was tight. "Not on the phone."

We agreed to meet at my shop at nine. He offered to pick up something at the bakery, and I said I'd have a fresh pot of coffee ready.

"Will Lisa Marie be coming with you?" I said. I thought I better ask because when I'd last sniffed the cream it smelled like it was getting a little ripe.

"No," he said, practically shouting. "She's out of the loop on this."

In my line of work I'm used to functioning as mother confessor for weird personal quirks and family secrets. I've been summoned to more than a few clandestine meetings where a member of the wedding party felt compelled to dump a furtive factoid in my lap. One time I learned it wasn't the bride's first marriage—although the groom had been led to believe his bride was a blushing virgin. Or, there was the time I was warned Uncle Barney was a mean drunk so the bartender needed to have a liquor bottle watered down with colored water ready to pour. A favorite of mine was hearing the bride's older sister was really her mother. Oddly, this one had come around more than once. Family secrets rarely surprise me. Probably Kevin's big hush-hush meeting involved some petty disclosure I'd heard before and would no doubt hear again. It's all part of what I get paid to do.

Kevin arrived right on time looking downright ghastly. The gray weather hadn't lifted for more than a few sunny hours in the past week, so any tourist sporting a tan probably had had it sprayed on, but Keith's pallor reminded me of that guy in *Beetlejuice*.

"Coffee?" I said.

"Thanks." He handed over a white bakery bag. I peeked inside and saw two humongous muffins and a puffy apple turnover laced with icing. They smelled fabulous. I wanted to stick my whole face in the bag and suck up the aroma. Instead, I daintily lifted the goodies from the sack using the little piece of wax paper from the bakery. After laying them out on the bag, I offered him first pick.

With a wave of his hand he declined the scrumptious-looking carbohydrates.

"So, what's going on?" I said, laying claim to the turnover. I broke it into three pieces before biting into the cinnamon-scented filling.

"If Brad was alive, this week would have been huge for him."

"You think Brad's dead?" I said it as calmly as I could.

"How should I know? The Coast Guard says he's dead, so I guess he is."

"But if you don't think Brad's coming back, why are you standing in as proxy?"

"I've got my reasons." His eyes darted around the room. "You don't have like, uh, surveillance cameras in here, right?"

"Nope. No hidden mics or thermal imaging devices either." I smiled, but he seemed to take me for serious.

"Okay, then," he said. "I probably should keep my mouth shut, but it seems only fair I clue you in on what's going on with Lisa Marie."

"I appreciate your concern, but I think I've pretty much figured out what's going on already."

"That right?"

"Yeah. I figure she's all hot to have this wedding, with or without Brad, so she can claim to be his widow and have a shot at his estate. From what I've seen, she's gonna need some serious dough to keep up her Dom Perignon lifestyle. With Brad around, DigiSystems was footing the freight but now it looks like they're cutting her off."

"Why do you think that?"

"Because I talked to Todd Barker. Lisa Marie told me he'd pay the wedding bills, but when I called him he said he'd only pay the existing bills and no more."

"That douche bag. What's he doing? He's a clueless bean counter."

"It's fine, I'm not worried. I'll just dial everything back a tad and make it work. I've dealt with brides like her before. You know, caviar appetite on a tuna fish budget."

His lips formed a nearly imperceptible smile. "Not to dis your powers of observation or anything, but there's no way you've dealt with someone like Lisa Marie Prescott before. Let me hit the high points: You think Lisa Marie's marrying Brad for his money? That's a laugh. If anything, it's the other way around. You ever hear of Refuse Removal, Inc.? Well, RRI's the biggest garbage hauler in the country. They've got subsidiaries world-wide: Canada, Europe, Australia, you name it. The company's worth billions. That's with a 'b'."

"RRI? I think that's the name on the garbage trucks here on Maui."

"Bingo. RRI is a single proprietorship, solely owned by Lisa Marie's dad, Marv. The company was started by her great-grandfather in the nineteen twenties. Their last name used to be Prescovski—it was Russian or Polish, I'm not sure—but Marv changed it to Prescott when Lisa Marie was born. She's his only child and there's nothing he won't do for her: including giving her an American-sounding name. You following me?"

I nodded.

He went on. "The Prescotts don't give a rat's ass about money. To them, it's like the air we breathe: infinite. All that matters to them is power and respect." He paused as if he thought I might need a moment to let that sink in.

"I practice martial arts," I said. "I'm well-versed in the respect thing."

"Good. 'Cuz if you cross them, especially if you piss off Marv, you're toast. Literally. Rumor has it there's more than just garbage in Marv's landfills." He folded his arms across his chest and leaned back in his chair.

"You think that's what happened to Brad? He got out of line?" It was my turn to let a few beats go by so something could sink in.

He shrugged. "Dunno. But it's damn hard not to wonder."

"Great. Now I'll be sweating bullets about getting whacked by the Godfather of Garbage if I mess up Lisa Marie's wedding. You've got to admit what you're telling me sounds like a pitch for a really bad reality show." I couldn't keep the chuckle out of my voice.

"Look," he said leaning in, "this is serious. These aren't people you want to screw with. I had to see you this morning because I want to propose something: you watch my back, I'll watch yours. You hear anything, see anything, you let me know. I'll do the same for you. Deal?"

"It doesn't sound like I have much choice."

"You don't."

He got up to leave. As the door clicked shut, I was left alone with two cups of cold coffee, a half-eaten turnover, and the uneasy feeling maybe it was time to start locking my doors.

***

I picked up Lisa Marie at exactly eleven and we made it from Olu'olu to the Kahului Airport in thirty minutes.

"Where are you going?" said Lisa Marie as I moved into the lane for the parking lot.

"I'm parking the car. This is as close as we can get to the terminal."

"Maybe this is as close as you can get to the *public* terminal, but daddy's jet doesn't come in here. It lands over there." She pointed to a sign marked 'General Aviation.' The road led to the other side of the runway, toward a small outcropping of buildings.

I've spent hundreds of hours at the Kahului airport but I'd never been out there. The general aviation area, where private aircraft land, isn't monitored by Homeland Security. Unlike commercial flyers, general aviation passengers are exempt from the cattle chute security offered by the TSA. No 'grabbing the junk' or barefoot parades through the metal detectors for the well-heeled. And, at least while I was still pulling a paycheck from Uncle Sam, air marshals were never assigned to private aircraft flights.

As I pulled up to the chain-link fenced parking lot a uniformed guard scowled at my beat-up car. I rolled down my window while Lisa Marie dug out her ID. When she passed it to him, he looked at it and broke into a sunny smile.

"*Aloha, wahines.* You can take any open spot."

We parked and I popped the trunk. I carefully lifted out ten purple orchid leis from a flat white box and draped them over my arm. We got to the edge of the tarmac just in time to watch a sleek white Learjet make an almost soundless landing. It glided past us and taxied to a stop.

"That's daddy," said Lisa Marie.

I squared my shoulders and started walking out toward the plane. Lisa Marie grabbed my arm. "You can't go out there until they signal us."

The engines whined to a stop and a ground crew guy waved a red baton at us. We hustled across the runway, dodging the puddles from an earlier shower. A half minute later the jet's cabin door popped open and a built-in stairway slowly lowered to the ground.

When the stairway locked into place I positioned myself behind Lisa Marie, ready to hand her a lei for each passenger. Earlier, I'd demonstrated the proper *aloha* greeting: place the flowers over the head, offer a warm *aloha to Maui*, and then plant a little kiss on each cheek. An older guy I assumed was her father was first down the stairway. Lisa Marie stiffly went through the *aloha* routine with him, but then abruptly turned away and stared across the runway as if she was planning to bolt. I asked her if she was all right but she ignored me and just kept staring. I stepped up and took over. As I kissed the cheeks of the glittery blond stepmother it was hard not to notice she looked decades younger than her husband. Plastic surgeons don't come that good. She and the three bridesmaids waiting at the top of the stairs probably graduated from high school within just a few years of each other.

"Can I get a couple more?" Stepmom said, snatching four leis from my outstretched arm. "My personal assistant certainly doesn't need one, and those girls up there are just some eye candy Marv hired to play bridesmaids." She winked and leaned in. "I found out coming over here that not a one of them has ever even met Lisa Marie."

Once everyone had deplaned, the small entourage began the short trek to the passenger lounge. I hung back to walk with Lisa Marie.

"Will your real mother be coming?" I whispered as we approached the tiny building. With a pushy stepmother in attendance, I'd need to get creative with the seating chart if both "moms" showed up. It'd be a clear of dereliction of duty to seat the ex-wife mother-of-the-bride within spitting distance of the half-her-age trophy wife.

"Ha! As if I ever had a *real* mother," Lisa Marie said. "No, I doubt my bio mom will be willing to tear herself away from her latest 'Sven' or 'Julio' to make the trip. She brags about putting the 'grrr' in 'cougar.' Besides, if her twenty-three-year-old daughter's getting married, how can she explain the age on her driver's license? It says she's thirty-four."

Entering the hushed passenger lounge was surreal: as if the rigors of air travel had been given an extreme make-over. The place was a quiet oasis of leather furnishings and cool slate floors. It even had a fun tiki bar with rattan stools. A uniformed hostess, carrying a tray of tall tropical drinks, encouraged the six passengers to enjoy complimentary refreshments while the crew dealt with the baggage.

"And who is this delightful young lady?" boomed Marv Prescott as Lisa Marie and I both declined a highly-garnished mai tai. I stepped up to introduce myself, extending my hand for a shake. He grasped my fingertips and brought them to his lips. His breath smelled of scotch and peanuts. His sparse hair sported an expert dye job but his puffy face, crepe-skinned neck and watery blue eyes gave away his age. I pegged him for late sixties or early seventies.

"Daddy, lay off," said Lisa Marie in a deadpan voice.

Stepmom was giggling as if her husband's courtly antics were beyond cute: they'd veered into adorable territory. She chucked him under the chin, and with a wink, silently promised to show him her own version of adorable as soon as they were alone.

"I'm Pali Moon. I'm coordinating Lisa Marie and..." I balked at providing a groom's name. "...uh, I'm coordinating your daughter's wedding. You must be Mr. and Mrs. Prescott."

"Call me Marv. And this here's Tina." He gestured toward stepmom who dipped a slight curtsy, accompanied by another giggle. I wondered if the giggling was habitual or simply the result of a long alcohol-fueled flight over the Pacific.

"This whole thing with Brad really screws the pooch, doesn't it?" said Marv.

He didn't look like he expected an answer, so I didn't give one.

"You think he's a goner?" he continued.

Lisa Marie was clearly within earshot.

"I only know what you know, sir," I said. "The Coast Guard believes he may have fallen out of the boat."

"Hey, no 'sir' stuff with me. So, if he went in the drink he's most likely in the belly of a whale, right? You know, like Jonah." He grinned as if expecting me to high five him for his clever biblical reference.

For a moment, I considered pointing out that whales found in Hawaiian waters are herbivores and wouldn't be the least bit interested in human flesh, but decided against it. I stole a look at Lisa Marie to see if she'd overheard. Her stricken face signaled she had.

"Daddy, please don't talk like that." Her tone was pleading. "Brad's okay. I know he'll be back in time for the wedding."

"You could be right, sweetheart, but I'm somewhat of an expert on what they call 'the law of the jungle.' My money's on your boy sleeping with the fishes—or most likely *feeding* the fishes."

Lisa Marie visibly sagged, but didn't say anything. I was amazed at Marv's cavalier attitude, especially if he'd played a role in Brad's death.

Marv grabbed Tina's arm and steered her outside toward an over-loaded luggage cart waiting by door. Everyone else followed.

On eyeing the small mountain of suitcases, I leaned in to Lisa Marie and whispered, "How long are your dad and stepmom planning to stay?"

"Just until Friday morning. Daddy's got an early tee time at Pebble Beach on Saturday."

Just five days. Ever since Kevin's tip-off meeting that morning, I'd been nervous about meeting Marv Prescott. But in the flesh I found him, and Tina, oddly fascinating. And, aside from the missing groom, the wedding was proceeding without a hitch. Sucking up to Marv for a few days seemed perfectly doable.

At about noon the entourage piled into two highly polished black Mercedes and headed for Olu'olu. I followed them out of the parking lot. Driving up Baldwin toward Hali'imaile I remembered what waited for me at home: multiple loads of laundry, a sticky kitchen floor, and a lawn that had 'vacant house' written all over it. I sagged. I'm not a lazy person, but living in overdrive for nearly a week had sapped my energy. I added a quick nap to the list.

I started to turn into my driveway but two vehicles blocked my way: a late model red Ram pick-up and a dark green Jeep Grand Cherokee. The garage door was open and Steve's Jetta was parked inside. So much for getting chores done, it looked like we had company. But who? Maybe it was appraisers or potential buyers sniffing around now that word of the foreclosure was making the rounds. I did a three-point turn and parked across the street.

I'd made it about halfway up the porch steps when raucous laughter erupted from the living room. Two pair of black leather shoes were lined up to the right of the door along with Steve's flipflops. The shoes were the heavy lace-up kind working men wear. Were Steve and Hatch inside yukking it up with the vultures circling the kill? It was all I could do to force a smile as I stepped inside.

"Hey, she's home," Steve said, coming over to escort me in. Two brawny men stood by the sofa: one tall, one medium height. Hatch was stretched out in his usual prone position.

Steve made the introductions. "Pali, this is Paul and Marty. They work with Hatch at the fire department."

"Pleasure," said the two guys in unison as they each gave me an index-finger salute. I looked them up and down. I mean, who wouldn't? Even though their height and coloring was different, one dark, one reddish-blond, they were specimens of manhood that would do a Marine recruiting poster proud. Broad-shoulders, well-muscled arms, intelligent eyes—the full meal deal. Each wore navy pants and a short-sleeved blue shirt with a Maui Fire Department patch on the sleeve. After my usual check-out routine I looked at their left hands. Yep, a plain gold band on each. What kind of *karma* was throwing all this unavailable testosterone at me lately? It was as cruel as stocking a diabetic's house with candy.

Steve said, "I'll leave you all to get acquainted. I need to go down to my studio and make some prints." He leaned in and whispered to me, "Looks like our pal Lisa Marie's hired a publicist to send wedding announcements to every newspaper on the west coast. She's having me make up fifty copies of a rather mediocre snapshot of her with Brad. Maybe she's not so sure he'll show up for the wedding after all."

When Steve left I mumbled my *nice to meet you's* to the guys and turned to head upstairs.

"Hey, don't run off," the first guy—was it Paul?—said. "We want to thank you for taking in Hatch."

I turned back around.

"Oh, it's nothing. He's easy."

"That he is," said the second guy. Everybody, but me, laughed.

I felt my cheeks heat up. I couldn't believe I was feeding straight lines to a trio of spoken-for firemen.

"No, really," the second guy went on, "it was really nice of you. We're both married and, although we love this guy and feel real bad about what happened, our wives pretty much have their hands full."

"Can I get you something to drink?" I said. "Maybe a soda or a beer?" I probably didn't have either in the house, but it seemed polite to at least offer.

"*Mahalo*, but no," said the first guy. "We gotta roll. We're expecting another crazy shift tonight." He turned to Hatch. "We had six big call-outs last time. One was another major wreck at almost the same place where you went man against machine."

"Everybody okay?" Hatch said.

"Our guys are fine, but the driver was a fatal. A woman no more'n thirty. "

The mood downshifted.

"Hey," said the second guy. "But we got her baby out in pretty good shape. The guys on Ladder Two grabbed the spreaders, and bam! popped that little dude outta there in no time."

"Spreaders?" I said. I didn't like the sound of that.

"Yeah, extradition spreaders: you know, 'Jaws of Life'? We had to rip open the back door to get him out of his car seat."

All three guys nodded an unspoken 'Amen.'

They talked shop for a couple of minutes and when there was a break I said my *alohas* and started up the stairs. Just beyond the landing, out of sight, I stopped and listened.

"You're right, she's nice. Maybe's it's time to take the leap. How much does she know?" It was the first guy's voice.

Guy number two weighed in. "Yeah, what'd you tell her?"

"Look, she's my landlady, not a blind date," said Hatch.

"Still. Seems you ought to come clean. My wife says a woman can handle anything but a lie."

"I'm not lying, I'm being discreet. Besides, I'll be gone in a month and she'll forget I was ever here."

"I seriously doubt that, dude."

There was a moment of silence and then the first guy said, "We better run."

"Thanks for stopping by," said Hatch. "Tell the chief I'm raring to get back."

"Will do. And hey, you take care of yourself, man."

"Yeah," Number Two chimed in. "Get well. My wife's been bitching about all the overtime."

"Since when did your 'never met a gold bracelet she didn't need' wife decide she doesn't want you doing overtime?"

Everyone laughed and the door slammed a minute later.

I tiptoed up the stairs, trying to avoid the creak on the second-to-the-last step. I wondered if Steve knew what was going on with Hatch. Maybe I wasn't the only one he was hiding secrets from. But for the hundredth time, I reminded myself it was none of my business.

9

Monday morning I called my suppliers—one more time—to confirm everyone was still on board and things were proceeding as scheduled. My level of micromanagement borders on harassment, but everyone's come to expect it of me. Long ago I decided I'd rather be known as an anal retentive nag than a bridal consultant who doesn't deliver.

"I knew it'd be you," Keahou said as she picked up the phone in her Kula bakery. "Don't worry. I'm baking the layers tomorrow. Then I let them temper for a day; then I'll frost it early Thursday morning so the icing's nice and fresh. What time you want it delivered?"

"Two o'clock would be good. Remember, it's at Olu'olu."

"Couldn't forget that. I hope they let me in."

"When you get to the gate, tell them you're bringing the wedding cake." As soon as it was out of my mouth, I realized she probably could have figured that out on her own.

"Is that place really owned by some mafia *kahuna*?"

"I don't know. And it's not polite to gossip."

"Ooh," she said. "Touchy."

"Sorry to snap, Keahou, but this wedding's been nothing but *pilikia* from day one. You know, with the dead groom and all."

"Yeah. Seems like a pretty *hupo* thing they're doing. Oh well, we need the business."

"Yes we do."

"Will you be down there when I bring the cake?"

"I'll get there around ten that morning. And don't worry, I'll have your check all ready for you."

"Good girl. This cake is going to be *lani nui*, I promise. I have lots of time to make it extra special."

After making all the critical calls—cake, dress, videographer, limo—I was batting a thousand. Of course with tourist business at a standstill all over the island only a vendor with a family emergency, or one who'd already gone belly-up, would blow me off this week.

The weather was finally cooperating. Now we had long sun breaks interspersed with only quick showers. I couldn't be sure it'd be sunny at the time of the wedding though, so I'd ordered a canvas canopy.

At around ten I headed over to the Gadda-da-Vida. It was break time and I wanted something to go with my fourth cup of coffee. I also had Farrah on my vendor list and I needed to confirm the ceremony details and flowers. As I pushed the front door open, I heard a deep male voice off to the right by the cash register. I halted halfway in, straining to hear. I try to avoid bothering Farrah when she has paying customers, but she also has a steady stream of local folks who stop by to *talk story*, so I listened to see which this was.

"What do you think?" It was Kevin. I recognized the deep rumble of his voice.

"I think you're my knight in shining Hummer," said Farrah. Her voice had inched up a couple of octaves, just shy of kittenish.

"Well, thanks to you, I'm feeling a lot better about stuff," he said. "I'm happy to return the favor."

I stepped back onto the sidewalk and eased the door shut, hoping to avoid rousing the tinkly bell on the door. I didn't need a trail-mix bar bad enough to barge into the middle of *that*. And besides, once Kevin left, Farrah would break a leg rushing over to fill me in on the details.

Back in my shop I scrounged through my desk and found a shriveled piece of fruit leather and a sleeve of stale crackers filled with a peanut butter-like substance. The coffee had grown bitter sitting in the pot all morning. So much for my break.

I was lifting the receiver to call the final three names on my supplier checklist when the front door flew open. Kevin stood in the doorway.

"Why'd you leave?" he said, closing the door behind him. "It's not like you were interrupting anything."

"Oh, no problem, it wasn't urgent. It's good to see you. I was expecting to see you out at the airport yesterday, but ..." I let it trail off.

"No reason for me to be there. Can I ask you something?"

"Sure, shoot."

"Is there any chance I'll find myself legally married to Lisa Marie if I go through with this thing?"

"Good question. I'm no lawyer, but it doesn't seem to me you would. The marriage license was issued to Brad, and you're just signing as his Power of Attorney. To be safe, though, you may want to check with an attorney."

"You know any?"

"Lawyers? Not personally, but I can ask around and get a recommendation."

"Thanks. Oh, and by the way, Farrah's great. You know her well?"

"We've been best friends since third grade."

"She involved? I mean, does she have a boyfriend or anything?"

"Nope, the only male in her life is a very spoiled, mega-hyper dog. The last dude she dated took off about a year ago. Not a happy ending." I squinted a little stink eye his way. "Like I said, she's my best friend—ever. No offense, but I'm pretty protective."

"I get it, but don't worry. I'd just like to get to know her a little better." He winked and shot me his 'good guy' smile. "That's all, I promise."

We locked stares for a moment and he turned and grabbed the doorknob. "You won't forget to call me about the lawyer?"

"We're watching each other's backs, right? I'll get back to you as soon as I've got something."

I still had three more vendor calls to make but I was twitching with nervous energy. I cleared off my desk and locked up. A quick workout at PoP sounded good, but when I went out to my car an invisible force dragged me in another direction.

I slipped through the back door of the Gadda-da-Vida and stopped to listen for customers.

"I've been counting to see how long it'd take you to get over here," said Farrah. "I'm all the way up to two hundred and ninety."

"Well?" I said.

Her voice was all innocence. "Well, what?"

I turned back toward the door.

"Okay, okay, don't leave. I'll tell you. I know you don't believe in this stuff," she said. "But I'm absolutely sure Kevin and I were lovers in a former life." She said it the way most people would mention they'd run into someone they'd known in high school.

"I knew it as soon as I laid eyes on him," she continued. "He came over to buy a bottle of water while Lisa Marie was getting measured for her wedding gown. The store wasn't busy, so we got to talking and I got this tingly feeling. Then last Saturday when he brought her back for the fitting, he came over again. He seemed worried about something so I offered to do a quick tarot reading for him. While I was laying out his array, he came right out and said it: he said he felt like he'd met me somewhere before."

I didn't have the heart to tell her *I'm sure I've seen you somewhere before* was a rather stale *haole* pick-up line. I also kept my mouth shut about the two of them being a rather odd couple: Mu'u mu'u Mama meets Gorgeous George. After all, in my business I've worked with some pretty bizarre couples.

"I told him about Tank Sherman kicking us out and taking over our businesses." She stopped for a dramatic pause.

I nodded. My mind was leaping to conclusions, but I worked at keeping a blank face.

"And then I told him about how important the store is to the people of Pa'ia, and how Tank is a jerk who will probably turn it into a porno shop. Anyway, today Kevin came in and told me he's buying the building!"

"He's got two million bucks?"

"I guess so. He said he thinks it's a good investment."

"But what about Tank? Noni made it sound like the deal's locked up."

"Kevin's not worried about that. He says he's going to offer a little more than the asking price so the seller will take his offer instead of Tank's. Tank won't care. Noni said he's working on a bunch of projects right now."

I couldn't see Tank coolly shrugging off losing out on a business deal, but who knows? The guy had evolved from a laughing-stock fat kid in high school to Donald Trump-Goes-Hawaiian in less than ten years. Nothing would surprise me.

"Does Kevin know about Tank's Friday deadline?"

"Yeah, I told him. He said he'll get with a real estate broker tomorrow."

"Speaking of lifestyles of the rich and infamous, guess what I found out?"

"That Lisa Marie's dad is stinking rich?" said Farrah.

"Kevin must have told you."

"Yep. I sure pegged that wrong. I asked Kevin why he's doing this phony wedding for Lisa Marie and he said he owes her a favor. It's hard to imagine Miss All-About-Me doing anything for anybody. What do you think's going on?"

"Who knows? I figure the seriously rich are just as screwed up as the rest of us, maybe more. Why'd Lindsay Lohan steal that necklace? Or Charlie Sheen rant on and on about his tiger blood?"

I started for the door and then stopped. "Oh, do you have a minute to go over the ceremony and flowers?"

"Sure." She pulled a manila envelope from under the counter and opened it. Just then, a family of four burst through the front door sending the bell into a manic tinkle. The two kids took off for the beach toys section while the mom pulled out a grocery list. She sent the dad on various missions for toilet paper, cereal, and milk while she went back to referee the loud brother-sister squabble that had erupted over which boogie board to buy.

"Uh-oh, this may take a while," said Farrah. "Can I get back to you later?"

We hugged a quick good-bye. I shut the back door, pleased to hear its squeaky hinge, rather than that annoying jingly bell out front.

As I bucked the traffic on Baldwin on my way down to *guan* to work out I felt lighter than I'd felt in weeks. The Prescotts were a peculiar bunch and the proxy marriage was a joke. But with only three days to go until the wedding and Kevin buying our building, my life—like the weather— was starting to feel normal again.

10

The back door at Palace of Pain was propped open. It was too early for lessons, but Sifu Doug encourages students to come in and practice so he's often there before lunchtime.

I entered the dimly lit room and a sharp odor caught in my throat. My *sifu* was on his hands and knees, swiping a wet rag across the worn blue mats. When he sat up to wring out the rag in a plastic bucket, I bowed and we made eye contact.

"What's going on?" I waved my hand in front of my face. "What stinks?"

"It's the smell of the new plague," Doug said. "The Health Department called this morning. A high school kid's come down with MRSA and they traced the it back to a karate school in Lahaina. They've closed everyone down. Everything in here's got to be disinfected, and I need to get it checked out before I can open back up again."

"Mersa?"

"Yeah, it stands for..." He pulled out a pink 'While You Were Out' note from his pocket and handed it to me. On the message line it read, *Methicillin-resistant staphylococcus aureus (MRSA).*

"It's real contagious," he said. "If you get it, it's a bitch because they can't knock it down with normal antibiotics.

It's killed people: mostly athletes and people in their families."

"So the *guan*'s closed?"

"Technically. But if you'll help me spread this stuff around I'll let you stay and work out for a while."

The acrid fumes were making my eyes water, but I couldn't disrespect my *sifu* by not helping when asked.

"Sure, I've got some time."

Doug pulled a second rag from the bucket, twisted it out, and threw it to me.

"Start on that wall over there by the door. I'm almost done with the mats. Once we've wiped down all the walls and scrubbed out the bathrooms we're done."

"When's the inspector coming?"

"I got on the list today, but who knows? They've got more'n two dozen places to look at, so it could be tomorrow, could be a week from now. The lady at the health department clued me in that checking martial arts schools wasn't a big priority. They're gonna clear the high schools and community centers first."

"What about your classes?"

"No classes, no practice, nothin' until I get a signed release taped to the door."

Sifu Doug is a hero to me. He holds a fourth level black belt in Korean kung fu as well as advanced belts in both karate and judo. One hundred sixty pounds of lean muscle, with a face like an Army Ranger, all sharp angles and close-cropped hair. I'd come to Palace of Pain expecting him to kick my ass while asserting his superiority over the lowly brown belt I'd earned while in college on O'ahu. Instead, he welcomed me like *ohana*—like family.

Doug's a big believer in mind over matter, and he claims success is simply the result of maintaining a right attitude and acting on it. If he's ever had doubts about me he's never shown them. At times, living up to his expectations is more intimidating than any opponent I've ever faced. But without him, I doubt I ever would have earned that black sash.

We finished wiping everything down and Doug looked up at the clock.

"Gettin' late. I promised Lani I'd pick the kids up at school. Today's one of those short days for them. You okay with me leaving the windows and doors open and you close it all up when you go?"

"No problem. I really just came down here to burn off a little steam. I'll be heading out soon myself."

"Hey, I appreciate your help." He clapped me on the shoulder. I gave him a short bow in return.

"Oh, I almost forgot," I said. "Isn't one of your brothers a lawyer?"

"Yeah, James. He's got his own office now. Used to work in the prosecutor's office."

"Could you give me his number? I've got a client with a legal question."

I waited while Doug went in the back. He returned and handed me a business card. "Tell your client to use my name and ask James for a discount."

"*Mahalo*."

"No worries. Don't forget to lock up."

I stuck around for another ten minutes, but gave up when my throbbing head put me on notice that if I didn't get some fresh air I'd be popping aspirin the rest of the afternoon.

I couldn't go home, though. I still had to go over the wedding details with Farrah. When I pulled up at Gadda-da-Vida there were three open parking spaces right out front.

Farrah had a pile of coins in front of her. She'd already made up about a half-dozen rolls, but from the looks of the pile, she wasn't even halfway done.

"You able to talk?" I said.

"Yep. It's been slow since you left. That family ended up buying both boogie boards; the blue *and* the yellow. Why do parents think throwing money at their kids is a good substitute for discipline? No wonder *keiki* are so annoying." She gestured for me to join her behind the counter. "Hey, speaking of annoying, how's it going with the new room-mate?"

"It's not bad. His name's Hatch Decker and he's a fireman. Got hit by a truck and broke his leg."

"Ouch."

"Yeah. He's gonna be laid up for a month."

She squinted at me. "You're blushing."

"I'm not. I just got back from working out. I'm hot."

"Okay, maybe you're hot, but it's not from working out. C'mon, spill about the hunky fireman."

I broke eye contact.

"Not really much to say. Hatch seems like a great guy." I hesitated, and she nodded, encouraging me to get to the 'but' she knew was coming. "But, I'm pretty sure he's gay."

"Really? He came right out and said, 'Nice to meet you; I'm gay'?"

I thought about it for a moment. "Not exactly, but it sort of adds up. He said he transferred over here from Honolulu because he was being hassled by the guys at work. Seems the guys at Maui Fire are more open-minded because a couple of them came over to see him yesterday and I overheard them asking if he'd told me some big secret. Not only that, he's a friend of Steve's and almost all of Steve's friends are gay."

"I'm not gay," she said.

"No, but you're not exactly a bosom buddy of his."

She did a little shimmy which sent her generous breasts in motion. "Hey," she said. "I got the bosom. And he's my buddy."

"You know what I mean."

"So, has Steve ever talked about Hatch before?" she said.

"No."

"Well, there you go. They probably aren't bosom buddies either."

Farrah loved to have the last word. I'd already grudgingly accepted Hatch's gender preference, so I wasn't going to argue. Besides, it pained me to dwell on it.

"Before another customer comes in let's get this wedding stuff wrapped up," I said.

"Good, I'm tired of counting." She swept the coins into a coffee can and put the can under the counter.

We went over the logistics of the ceremony. It promised to be a quick one, since Lisa Marie had ordered Farrah to keep it to basic vows and skip the sermon about the sanctity of holy matrimony.

Next, we sketched out the flower placement. Farrah was still smarting over Lisa Marie going around her to get the tuberoses she wanted. I'd received a chilly call from Marv's executive assistant who'd sniffed she'd taken time from her *busy* work day to track down the flowers online. They were being flown in from South America, and 'my florist' needed to make arrangements to pick them up *promptly* when they arrived at the airport on Thursday morning.

"With the currency exchange and overnight freight charges those things are gonna cost hundreds of dollars," Farrah said.

"I know," I said. "Let it go, okay?"

"And it's going to be a huge hassle for me. I'll have to make a special trip to the cargo terminal at Kahului to get them. And then, I'll have to cram them into the bridal bouquet at the very last minute. I'm going to get everything prepared ahead of time on Wednesday. I usually make up my bouquets on the morning of the wedding, but with Thursday being Valentine's I'll be too pushed to get it all done. You know, I've got regular customers who ordered flowers *weeks* ago and it's not fair to—"

"No problem," I said. "A day early will be fine."

"If those tuberoses come in when they're supposed to, I should have everything ready to go by three o'clock. It'll be *pupule* around here, with Valentine's and all, but I'm planning to arrive an hour before the ceremony."

"And you know where Olu'olu is, right?"

"Well, duh. If the mafia dude who built that monstrosity on sacred ground was looking for privacy, he sure picked a lousy spot. It's like a ginormous zit on a bully's nose. Everybody sees it, but nobody's stupid enough to say anything."

***

I was nearly through my to-do list, but I had one last stop to make before calling it a day. I pulled into Olu'olu a few minutes after five. I hoped I wouldn't be interrupting the Prescott's dinner. Since Hawaii time is three hours earlier than even West Coast mainland time lots of visitors eat early. Stomachs don't wear watches.

"Pali Moon," I said into the gate speaker.

"And your business?" It was the same guy as before. Was he dense, or did he just enjoy coming up with cracks about 'Let's Get Maui'd'?'

"C'mon, you know me. I'm Lisa Marie's wedding planner."

No comment from Mr. Witty as the gate slowly inched open.

I parked the car and walked to the front door, once again marveling at the wraparound oceanfront setting. Who says money can't buy happiness; or at least a fabulous view?

Once again, the maid, Josie, answered the door before I had time to press the bell.

"Good evening, Miss Moon," she said, a big smile extending all the way to her eyes. I'd never seen her when she wasn't smiling. It didn't seem to me that working for a guy like Marv Prescott would be all that jolly, but then, most of the year the household help had this beautiful house all to themselves, so maybe putting up with him for a few days every now and then wasn't so bad.

"Is Lisa Marie at home?" I said. "I believe she's expect-ing me."

She looked at me with the look people give when they know you're lying but choose to ignore it.

"She here. Mr. Prescott here too."

Was that a warning?

"*Mahalo*, but I only need to speak with her. Would you please ask if I could have a few minutes of her time?" That didn't exactly jive with the notion of being expected, but she'd already given me a pass on my weak lying skills.

She escorted me to the same glorious room as before. The yellow walls and furniture seemed to hum in harmony with the approaching sunset. I gazed at the crashing surf and felt a wave of tranquility pass over me.

"What are you doing here?" Lisa Marie said, startling me. I turned around. She looked more annoyed than usual.

"I like to meet with my brides each day during their wedding week: to reassure you that everything's coming together as planned."

"You could have left a message with the maid."

"Yes, but it's part of my service to meet with you face-to-face to keep you informed and address any last-minute questions."

"I don't *have* any questions, and if I did, I know how to reach you."

"Good. Well then, I guess I'll see you tomorrow for your final dress fitting. And please remind your bridesmaids they'll need to come in as well."

"Why?"

"Because they'll need a fitting, too."

"No. Why do *I* have to remind them? Isn't that your job?"

"Oh, of course. I just assumed since they were staying here with you—."

"Well, you assumed wrong."

"No problem." I looked around, but saw no sign of the bridesmaids. "If you'll give me their contact information—"

"Talk to Josie. She has their phone numbers."

There was an awkward pause as I struggled to come up with a cheery farewell.

"Okay, then I guess I'll see you tomorrow. Oh, and on Wednesday morning I'll be down here about noon to get ready for the rehearsal, and then Thursday's your big day." I was chirping like a song bird; nowhere close to my normal 'I'm in charge' voice.

She sighed. "Where's my crane picture?"

Ah, so she had a question after all.

Lucky for me I had an answer. "The girls said they'd be finished folding the cranes by tomorrow afternoon. I'll pick them up and get them over to the framer first thing Wednesday morning, and he promised your picture will be ready by the end of the day."

"What if I don't like it?"

"I've seen this framer's work before. It's outstanding: the best on the island."

She squinted.

"The best anywhere, actually," I went on. "All my Japanese clients—and those gals are *really* picky about their origami keepsakes—swear by this guy." Okay, so I'd had only one Japanese bride who'd used this particular framer. But she'd been pleased, so why split hairs?

Lisa Marie plopped down on the sofa, and stared out of the huge window to the ocean beyond. She didn't ask me to join her, but I got the feeling she wasn't as eager to get rid of me as she let on.

"You know, I almost forgot," I said. "I've put together a three-day schedule of events for the run-up to the ceremony. Do you want to take a few minutes to go over it?" I pulled a copy from my bag.

"No, I don't. Daddy's having a patio party tonight and I need to freshen up." She didn't make a move to get up off the sofa.

The French doors burst open and Marv Prescott strode into the room. His pale, stubbly cheeks, silly comb-over and darting eyes reminded me of guys featured on America's Most Wanted. But maybe I was unfairly viewing him through the filter of his alleged reputation.

"I never forget a name. You're Patty Sunshine from the airport, correct?" he boomed, extending his hand.

I didn't know if he was joking or he'd really mistaken my name, so I went with it.

"Hello, sir. Yes, I'm the wedding coordinator. I'm just going over final preparations with your daughter."

"Please, sweetheart, no 'sir' stuff. Remember, I told you to call me Marv, or, as they say over here: *dude*."

"Okay, uh, Marv. We're pretty much finished here. I understand you're entertaining this evening and I don't want to intrude." I slipped the copy of the wedding schedule onto the coffee table and flashed Lisa Marie a big smile.

"No intrusion at all," Marv said. "And yes, we're having a little cookout. Why don't you join us?"

"Thanks, but I really should be getting home."

"Why?"

Uh-oh. Not only am I a lousy liar, but I'm especially feeble under pressure.

"Uh. Well, I have an injured fireman staying at my house and..." I hoped he'd leap to the conclusion I was sorely needed at home to nurse one of Maui's bravest back to health.

"We won't keep you out late. If your fireman gets hungry, tell him to crack open a can of chili. That's what those guys eat, right?" He turned and grinned at Lisa Marie. "Puppet, tell your little friend here I never take 'no' for an answer."

Lisa Marie's face had taken on the same vacant gaze I'd noticed at the airport. It was as if Marv sucked all the oxygen from a room, and whenever he was around she shut down to keep from suffocating.

She blinked a couple of times and in a weary voice said, "Of course, Daddy. When you came in I was just going to ask Pali if she'd be able to stay." She swiveled her gaze to me. "You can, right?"

I nodded, feeling trapped but intrigued to see the Prescott family dynamic in action.

The second Marv left the room Lisa Marie leapt off the sofa and stepped in close to me. From the look on her face I half-expected her to grab my shirt, give me a couple of shakes, and tell me to get the hell out of Dodge before her father returned.

"You promised your fireman you'd be home no later than seven, right?" Her tone mimicked me telling the lie she wished I'd been smart enough to come up with on my own.

"Seven. Right."

"Well, make sure you keep your promise."

She left the room, yanking the French doors shut with such force it rattled the glass. The setting sun washed the walls in a rosy glow and the room became perfectly still. Even Lisa Marie's surliness couldn't blot out the peace that settled over me. The low *swoosh* of waves sliding in and out along the beach reminded me of a ticking clock.

Just three more days.

11

A few minutes later, Josie came in to advise me the guests would be arriving soon and Marv wanted everyone out on the lanai. The immense space was at least the size of a basketball court. It was bordered by a knee-high rock wall on the upper and lower sides and a riprap breakwater on the *makai*, or ocean, side. The sun perched at the horizon, clouds hovering just above. Rays of sunshine shot up from behind the clouds creating what we kids used to call a 'Bible sky.'

A phalanx of butlers, bartenders and servers carrying plates of *pu'pus*—appetizers—appeared out of nowhere as soon the guests began arriving. I spotted the Blond Squad: the trio of statuesque bridesmaids who'd arrived on Marv's private jet. They were taking turns flirting with a local-boy bartender who looked like the guy in the Tommy Bahama commercials.

"Mai tai? Blue Hawaiian? What's your pleasure, pumpkin?" Marv said, sneaking up and standing so close behind me I could feel his hot breath on my neck.

"I don't usually...I mean I..." I stammered like a high school kid at a college frat party.

"She probably doesn't drink when she's on the clock, Marv" said Tina, coming to my rescue.

"Right," I said. "And I can only stay a few minutes. I promised the fireman—"

"What'd you promise him?" Marv said with a lewd chuckle. "You gonna trot on home and light his fire?"

"Marv, now don't you be naughty," said Tina, patting his cheek.

"It wouldn't kill her to have one little cocky-tail for the road," he said.

"You have other guests I'm sure you'll want to greet," I said. "Don't worry about me. I'll go over right now and get the bartender to make me something."

"Good girl. I knew I'd get you to come around. Good-looking broads can't resist me."

I asked the bartender for a virgin piña colada with extra fruit. He handed me a drink with three cherries, two large chunks of pineapple and a wedge of lime skewered on tiny plastic swords. He added a tiny pink umbrella and a long red straw. The glass was filled to the brim, but all the fruit and hardware didn't leave much room for liquid. I sipped it slowly. No doubt maintaining a full glass was essential to keeping Daddy Prescott at bay.

"How long have you and Marv been married?" I said, sidling up to Tina.

"Not long," she said. She shot me a guarded look followed by a quick smile. She didn't appear to be in the mood to discuss family history.

"Brad's disappearance was certainly a shock," I said.

"Total shock. But to tell you the truth, I was kind of surprised when Lisa Marie got engaged to him in the first place. You know what I mean?"

I nodded, hoping it would encourage her to continue.

"They were just so—I don't know—so opposite."

Again I nodded.

"Now Kevin, he's more her style. I always thought they were much more well-suited, like best friends, maybe even soul mates. *Amicos migliori*, as we say in Italian. Back home, the two of them spent *way* more time together than she ever did with Brad."

"Oh?" I said, figuring I couldn't get away with just giving her another nod.

"Yeah. With Brad it was always work, work, work. No fun at all. He'd make dates with her but then it was almost always Kevin who actually showed up. They were both real party animals: concerts, dance clubs, movie premieres—"

"Baby doll," Marv yelled from across the lanai. I prayed he meant that for Tina and not me.

"Yes, sweet pea?" Tina shot back, relieving me of the uncertainty.

Marv motioned her over like a parking lot attendant helping someone back up a car.

"I'm sorry," she said to me. "I've got to go see what he needs. He's cute but he's high maintenance. It was nice talking to you." She shot me a backward toodle-doo wave as she made her way through the crowd.

I reached into my beach bag purse and scavenged around for my cell phone. Once I had it in hand, I managed to activate the 'check ringtone' mode by touch. It started chiming and I pulled it out, doing my best to appear annoyed I'd gotten a call while I was deep into socializing.

"Sorry," I said, although no one seemed to be listening. "I've got to take this."

I put down my drink and put the dead phone up to my ear, nodding and making *uh-huh* noises as I made my way into the house.

"Oh sure. No problem," I muttered into the mouth-piece. "I'll be right there." I slipped the phone back into my bag as I closed the sunroom door. Lisa Marie was at the other end of the room huddled with her bridesmaids.

"You all need to go up there and get your dresses fitted tomorrow morning," she said, jabbing a finger at what appeared to be the wedding schedule I'd left for her.

The bridesmaids shot each other conspiratorial glances.

"Got it," they said in sing-song unison.

"Lisa Marie," I said, coming up to them. "Sorry to interrupt, but I need to leave. If you can think of anything else we should discuss—"

"There you go again, trying to rope *me* into doing *your* job." She let out a dramatic sigh, ostensibly for the benefit of the bridesmaids. "Pali, I told you from the very beginning I needed a perfect wedding. So if it's perfect, good. And if it isn't, well, Daddy's not going to be very happy with you."

As if choreographed, the bridesmaids pursed their lips and dropped their heads. They stared down at their feet as if they were the ones being scolded.

"It'll be fabulous," I said. It came out in one long string; like when you say *pleasedtomeetyou*. In other words, polite: yes; sincere: not so much.

"It better be." Lisa Marie folded her arms. "Right, girls?"

"Right," they muttered, still eyeballing the floor.

"Okay, then," I said in a squeaky voice. "I guess I'll see you all tomorrow."

When neither Lisa Marie nor the bridesmaids offered a reply, I whispered I'd just let myself out and headed for the foyer.

"*Mahalo* for coming this evening," said Josie, smiling and opening the door. She dipped her head in a quick bow. I bobbed my head in return and asked her to thank Marv and Tina for their hospitality. Then I sprinted to my car.

***

When I pulled in at home Steve's car was out front. I'd hoped to have Hatch all to myself for the evening so I could clear up a few things, but it wasn't to be.

"Hey guys, I'm home." I dumped my beach bag purse on the entry table and listened. No response. The house was eerily quiet. I crossed the hall and put an ear to the downstairs bedroom door. I wasn't really keen on hearing sounds of activity taking place on the other side of that door, but I was concerned.

I waited a few seconds but heard nothing.

I pushed through the kitchen door to see if maybe they'd left a note.

"Surprise!" Steve was arranging *pupus* on a plate. He wore a pineapple print apron over a tank top and cargo shorts. He looked adorable, his well-muscled arms deeply tanned, his hair streaked with natural highlights. "We made a special dinner to celebrate all of us getting back on our feet."

"We're not totally there yet," I said, then felt lousy when I saw their smiles dim.

"Well yeah, I've still got a few more weeks to go," said Hatch. "But at least now I'm vertical. And you and Steve will finish up that wedding this week so you've got money coming in. I'd say that's reason enough to celebrate." He was at the stove, leaning on his crutch, stirring a saucepan with a wooden spoon.

"Sorry to be a downer; you're right. I've just had a tough day. What's for dinner?"

"We have fabulous vegetarian sushi which I'll admit I picked up at Farrah's. And a fresh chopped salad. And then," Steve made a *tah-dah* gesture toward Hatch's pot on the stove, "Homemade risotto, shrimp scampi style."

"Sounds wonderful."

"Hey, it's late. Where've you been?" Steve said. "When I was down at Farrah's this afternoon, she said you'd left hours ago."

I started setting the table. "Like I said, it was a crazy day. It started out easy enough, calling my vendors. The good news is everybody's coming through. But then I went down to work out and I ended up helping Sifu Doug douse for plague—."

Steve gasped in horror.

"It's not quite as grim as it sounds. There was a MRSA infection at a karate school down in Lahaina so everybody has to disinfect. It took us a while to scrub everything down, and then I popped down to Olu'olu for a quick visit with Lisa Marie. Ends up, she wasn't in a bridal party mood, and worse, I got roped into going to a get-together Marv's hosting tonight. I managed to sneak out after an hour, but I'm beat."

"How's our pal Lisa Marie holding up?" Steve said.

I shook my head.

"Let me guess: she's not on the short list for Miss Congeniality?"

"Not even close. If I didn't need the money so much I'd have figured out a way to weasel out of this by now. It's all a charade. What it boils down to is an incredibly expensive beach party for a snotty bitch in a handmade silk dress. "

"Whew, we better get our girl here a *jumbo* glass of wine, pronto." Steve pointed to the refrigerator. Hatch hopped over and took out a bottle of Tedeschi Maui Blanc wine, already uncorked. He managed, with just one hand, to neatly fill the three wine glasses lined up on the counter.

"My favorite," I said.

"You talking to me?" said Hatch.

"Yes, you. And you, too." I leaned my head on Steve's shoulder. "Who needs sex when I get to spend my nights with great guys like you?"

"Was that a slam?" said Hatch. "Just 'cuz I'm busted-up for a while doesn't mean I'm a eunuch."

"Nothin' eunuch about you, my man. Nothin' at all," said Steve. He clinked his glass against Hatch's.

I felt like I'd crashed a honeymoon.

12

I shooed Steve and Hatch out of the kitchen as soon as we finished eating. I told them I had a rule about cooks not helping with clean-up, but really I just wanted some time to myself. I was almost finished with the dishes when the phone rang.

"Can you get that?" I yelled to Steve. "It's probably for you anyway."

Steve picked it up and after a beat I heard him laughing. Laughing was good. Laughing meant it probably wasn't a surly creditor or anyone associated with Lisa Marie's wedding. After a half-minute of conversation the swinging door to the kitchen was pushed open and Steve thrust the portable phone at me.

"It's Farrah. She's talking crazy. I told her crazy calls were best handled by the lady of the house."

I crimped the phone between my shoulder and chin. "What's up?" I said. I wiped my hands on a dish towel, expecting it might take awhile.

"You need to come down here."

"Farrah, it's almost nine o'clock and I've had a really long day."

"I wouldn't ask if it wasn't a matter of life and death."

"Farrah! If this is an emergency, you should call nine-one-one." I was getting worried.

"I don't think they'd be much help. Besides, it's not about me."

"Who's in trouble?"

"Just get down here, okay?" Her voice was tight. "I can't talk about it on the phone."

I told the guys I was headed down to Farrah's and I'd be back as soon as I could.

"You need me to come along?" Steve asked. He looked up from the TV with a face that had *please say 'no'* written all over it.

"No, it's probably some girl thing. I'll call you if it's anything serious."

Hatch said, "If it does turn out to be something serious, I'll be glad to help. Don't forget, I'm a certified EMT."

"Thanks, but knowing Farrah, her life and death emergency will probably require a hug and a big glass of wine more than medical expertise."

I parked in the unlit alley behind the Gadda-da-Vida. Farrah's living quarters were upstairs at the top of a flight of rickety wooden stairs. Her daily commute was thirteen steps down to the back door of the store. She didn't own a car, didn't even know how to drive. I climbed the pitch dark stairway and rapped on the door. Farrah whipped it open. In the backlight from a single table lamp in her living room she looked stricken but utterly healthy.

"Okay, where's the life or death emergency?" I peered into her cluttered apartment.

"It's my dog."

"Sir Lipton, the wonder dog?"

"Yeah. Well, Lipton's more of a wonder than we thought. He's been acting sick for a while, hanging out in my closet most of the time. I thought maybe he'd eaten something bad. His stomach was puffed up, like he had way-bad gas. Anyway, when I came up here after work, I found four puppies."

"What? Lipton had puppies? Like puppies came *out* of him?" I'd never checked out Lipton's equipment, and apparently Farrah hadn't either.

"I guess so, since there are four baby dogs in the closet and Lipton's nursing them. Oh, and get this: they all look an awful lot like Scooter, his b/f/f from down the alley."

"Do you need me to take them to the animal shelter at Pu'unene?"

"I called. The nightshift guy said they don't accept puppies until they're at least six weeks old. I can't keep them up here. The powers that be don't even know I've got Lipton. And I'm still getting grief about that Wilbur incident."

"It was a rat infestation, Farrah. You were harboring an entire colony of rats in a food store."

Her mouth bent into a stern frown.

"They weren't *in* the store, they were *under* the store. And I didn't harbor, I just put a few scraps out now and then. They were out of sight until that *makona* guy from the Health Department started poking around. Some people keep rats as pets, you know."

"You can't have pets where there's food. And besides, those things weren't pets. They were vermin, from the cane fields. Those rats cause tons of damage, not to mention all the diseases they carry."

She sniffed and pursed her lips in a tight line. From the looks of things, I was about to be treated to an 'all creatures great and small' speech unless I changed the subject—fast.

"I wish there was something I could do for Lipton," I said. "I know how much you love him, or her, or whatever."

"You could take him and the pups up to your place," she said. "It'd just be for a few weeks. I'll put up flyers at the store and I'm sure I'll find every one of them a good home before you know it."

"Couple of problems with that. First, Lipton's not a 'him' anymore, so you need to start saying 'she.' I think bearing offspring is proof positive of female-hood. And second, I can't have a litter of puppies in my house. Steve and I are already cramped with Hatch staying there."

"What am I supposed to do—drown them in a bucket? Just come see them. They're real cute. And besides, we're just talking about a few weeks. I bet you and Steve will end up wanting one or two for yourself."

She went into the bedroom and I followed. As she opened her closet door I got a whiff of the unmistakable ammonia smell of doggie urine.

"Lip's been inside all day," she said. "I'm afraid to let him out in case he hasn't taken well to motherhood. He might decide it's all too much and run off. You know, post-partum depression and all."

Sir Lipton whined softly from inside a cut-down Charmin toilet paper box. Farrah had put down a thick pad of newspapers on the closet floor and they were soaked through. The dog looked up to meet my gaze and I could swear she looked apologetic about the mess.

"See what I mean?" Farrah picked through the stack of furry lumps rooting around Lipton's underbelly. "Aren't they just adorable?"

She held up a brown and white pinto, with a tiny squinched-up face. There were little slits where its eyes would pop open in a week or so. Its ears stuck straight up.

"Sir Lipton's a Jack Russell, right?"

"Yeah," she said. "And if Scooter's the other dad, then these little guys are half-mini-beagle, half-Jack."

In other words, manic dog squared.

"I'll need to run this by Steve and Hatch first. They may not be all that thrilled about living in a house that stinks like a dog kennel."

She handed me the puppy she'd been holding. It was heavier than I'd expected, its little body giving off a calming heat. It shoved its back legs against my palm as if trying to nudge itself into a more comfortable position.

"Pity if I had to start looking around for a gunny sack," Farrah said. She picked up a pup the color of a coconut husk. "And filling up a bucket."

"You wouldn't."

"I sure wouldn't want to, but I'll have no choice if I can't find a place to stash them. If the suits hand me another health violation it could close me down."

It always struck me odd that Hawaiians refer to bureaucrats as 'suits,' like you hear on the mainland. I'd never seen any local government worker, even officials from the governor's office, wearing a suit. Men's business attire is an aloha shirt, untucked, and khaki pants.

"Okay, okay. I'll tell Steve and Hatch our good deed for the year is Operation Puppy Rescue. Hatch can watch them during the day, and I'll put them up in my room at night."

"*Mahalo*, Pali. You won't be sorry. This'll bring you tons of good *karma*—trust me." She put the two pups back in the box and they burrowed down, seeking milky solace. "I think the karmic energy is already balancing out. If I hadn't talked to Kevin about rescuing us from Tank Sherman we'd have lost our businesses. And if you hadn't rescued Lipton's pups, his family would have drowned."

There was probably a grain of logic in there somewhere, but I was too exhausted to hunt for it.

"Oh, and don't worry about dog food," she went on. "I'll handle that. The Lipster needs his special food, and that stuff doesn't come cheap."

"I wish you'd stop referring to Lipton as 'him.' It's definitely a *she*."

"His name is *Sir* Lipton. Always was, always will be."

"Well, then I'd suggest you get 'him' spayed."

"Neutered."

"Whatever."

We went downstairs to the store and Farrah packed up two bags of high priced canned and dry dog food; a package of pepperoni-style dog treats; and a spray bottle of carpet cleaner formulated especially for 'stubborn pet odors.' I'd seen Sir Lipton in action enough to know she definitely had her 'stubborn pet' moments.

Farrah insisted on accompanying me back home with the five dogs.

"I need to visualize them safe and happy, and it'll be easier if I'm able to be there when they get settled in," she said.

We pulled in front of the house and I didn't see Steve's car: not in the driveway, not in the garage.

I carried the puppy box up the porch steps while Farrah followed, tightly clutching Lipton to her chest. Farrah kept up a play-by-play of what was happening, whispering to her dog like an announcer at a golf tournament. "Okay, Lip-Man, we're here at Pali's. This neighborhood's called Hali'imaile, but it's only a few miles from home, so don't worry. She's being real nice to take you in for a while, so here's how it's going to go: You be a good boy and stay here for a few weeks and then you can come back to the store. Meanwhile, I'll find good homes for your kids. And, remember, the rules are the same here as at home: no barking, no whining, no chewing shit up. You got it?"

I set down the box to open the door, and I looked back to see how Lipton was handling the move. Her doggie face looked resolute: silently promising to do whatever necessary to keep her kids alive. Jack Russells are smart, but Lipton's creepy smart.

Hatch was in his usual spot on the sofa. The TV was at full volume, booming out a basketball game from the mainland. Good thing he'd paid me his rent in advance so I'd been able to pay the cable bill. A sweating beer bottle was etching an indelible ring into my coffee table.

"Hey, you're home. Everything okay?" he said.

I carted the Charmin box into the living room.

"Oh, hello," he said when he saw Farrah behind me. "I wish I could act like a gentleman and stand up, but I'm afraid I'm kind of gimped-up." He pulled the blanket from his legs to display the heavy cast.

"No, no, stay comfortable," said Farrah. "I'm just dropping off my guys." She gave Lipton a quick peck on the top of the head.

"Puppies," I said. I put the box down on the floor so Hatch could see them. "I hope you're not allergic or anything."

"No, not at all. Wow, they're real tiny—and cute."

"I'm Farrah, by the way," she said extending her right hand while trying to contain a squirming Lipton in her left.

"I'm sorry," I said. "I should have introduced you."

Farrah stared at Hatch's face as if memorizing it for a police sketch artist. I wondered if he felt as uncomfortable with the intense scrutiny as I did.

"Good to meet you. I'm Hatch Decker. I'm the first refugee Pali took in this week, but it sounds like I'm not the last." He smiled and put a hand into the box and lightly stroked one of the pups.

"They'll only be here until they're old enough to get adopted," I said. "Probably a month. Six weeks at the most."

"Great. It'll be good to have company when you and Steve aren't around."

At that point Lipton's patience wore out. She yelped and twisted out of Farrah's grasp, landing with a thump on Hatch.

"Sorry," said Farrah. "He's had a tough day. He's never had puppies before."

"This is the puppies' sire?" Hatch said, dodging his head to catch a glimpse of Lipton's underside.

"No," I said. "Lipton's a female. She's the pups' mother, but Farrah always thought Lipton was male, so it's been hard for her to make the switch."

"His name is *Sir* Lipton," said Farrah, as if that explained everything.

"Does he pee squatting down or—" Hatch said.

"I've really got to get going. Come outside with me, Pali. I need to talk to you about Sir Lipton's schedule."

Farrah and Hatch exchanged goodbyes and we went out onto the porch. Once the door closed, she dropped her jaw, put both hands on her cheeks, and wagged her head as if she'd just caught a glimpse of a naked Brad Pitt.

"Oh-my-Gawd," she mouthed. She leaned in and whispered, even though it was completely unnecessary with the door shut, "That guy is *so* gorgeous. And he is not, not, no-way-in-hell gay. Auras don't lie."

"Farrah, we all see what we want to see, but Hatch is—"

"Shut up. Really, I mean it. Shut *up*. That guy is totally smashed by you. And I should know. I read auras like most people read the newspaper, and I'm telling you, Hatch Decker is stick straight."

"Your vote is duly noted. But remember, he's Steve's friend and—"

She pushed past me and went back inside.

"Can I ask you a question?" she said to Hatch.

He picked up the remote and muted the TV. "Sure, fire away."

13

It was way past my bedtime when Farrah and I got back in the car. On the way down to her apartment she talked about Hatch's evasive response.

"He's not gay, but he's definitely hiding something. What do you think it could be?"

"I think he doesn't want to get involved with someone he lives with. Seems reasonable."

"No it isn't! You two are perfect for each other."

I snapped on the radio. She took the hint.

Baldwin Avenue was quiet and dark. Even so, as we neared the Gadda-da-Vida, it was impossible not to see the boxcar-sized Hummer parked directly in front.

"Oh no," said Farrah. "With all the jiggy over Lipton's pups, I forgot I asked Kevin if he wanted to get a drink with me down at Cisco's. You know, to toast him buying our building. You can come too, Pali." My car was dark as a cave, but her voice gave away her blush.

"Come on, we're all adults here. Besides, didn't you already admit to having carnal knowledge of the guy in a previous life?"

Kevin opened his driver door and slid a long leg down from the bulky vehicle. I tried to catch his expression, but the dim eco-friendly street lights barely gave off enough light to see a hand in front of your face. He sauntered over to Farrah's side of the car.

"Evenin' ladies," he said, leaning into the open window. "I hope you didn't start without me."

"I'm sorry, Kev," Farrah said. "I was really looking forward to seeing you tonight, but my dog had puppies, and I had to take them up to Pali's 'cuz I can't have animals at the store, and when I got there I needed to help her find out if her new roommate is gay and then—"

"Hey, no harm, no foul. Maybe another time?"

Farrah popped the passenger-side door open so fast Kevin had to hop out of the way to avoid getting hit. They huddled together, talking in low voices I couldn't hear. I was about to beep the horn and tell them I was leaving when Farrah ducked her head back in. "I'll call tomorrow to check on Sir Lipton, okay? He's never been away from me overnight."

I was about to shriek it was high time to stop referring to Lipton as male, but held off. I needed sleep way more than I needed to win an argument.

"Fine," I said. "I'll catch you then."

As I pulled away I sneaked a glance in the rearview mirror. They still hadn't climbed into the Hummer for the ride down to Cisco's. I wondered if more than a drink was on tap for the evening. None of my business, I told myself sharply. It'd been a long day and I had four bridal fittings in the morning. All I cared about was getting my weary bones back up the hill and into bed.

***

Early Tuesday morning Steve suggested we all go out to breakfast to celebrate Hatch's newfound freedom. Now that he could use his crutches his doctor had encouraged him to get out of the house and get some exercise.

"I'm looking at a pretty steep slope to get back to my fighting weight," said Hatch. "This laying around eating fancy food has turned me soft."

I wasn't sure what *soft* meant to a firefighter, but from where I was sitting, there wasn't a soft spot in sight. Steve and I exchanged a quick sideways glance. Seems the vote was two to one.

The guys coaxed me to join them—Hatch even offered to pay—but I begged off. Lisa Marie and the bridesmaids were coming in at eleven and I needed to make sure everything was ready. As much as I'd tried to deny it, Kevin's dire warnings about the consequences of messing up Lisa Marie's wedding had made an impression.

At ten I started down the hill to my shop. I pulled into the alley and went in through the back door. I had the coffee set up and was putting out fresh potpourri when it hit me: I hadn't called Kevin with the lawyer's name. I dug James Kanekoa's card out of my purse and called Kevin's cell but it went to voicemail.

At ten minutes to eleven, I opened the front door to let in a little fresh air. Kevin's black Hummer was still parked in front of Farrah's. A minute later, a bright red Porsche roared up Baldwin and pulled into the last remaining spot on my side of the road, about a half-block down from the Hummer. Lisa Marie climbed out of the passenger side and the shiny sports car backed up and took off. I didn't have a chance to ponder how the bridesmaids were going to find my shop before Akiko's smoke-belching minivan chugged into sight and pulled into the spot vacated by the Porsche.

"You better have my coffee ready," Lisa Marie shouted as she walked toward me. Then she spotted the Hummer. She slowed her gait.

"I guess Kevin showed up after all," she said pushing past me and going inside. "I called him this morning to bring me but he didn't answer."

My lips clamped shut as my brain marshaled its forces. I followed her in.

"Ke-*vin*," she called out. "I know you're in here." I watched as she parted the bead curtain and peered into the fitting area.

"Okay," she said. "Very funny, Pali. Where are you hiding him?"

I shrugged. A feeble response, I know, but it beat out faking a coughing fit.

"Wait a minute," she said. I watched clouds building behind her eyes. "He's next door, isn't he? He's with that fat hippie who's supposed to be doing my flowers. He's..." She straight-armed me and was back out the door before I could block her exit.

By this time Akiko had wrestled the bulky garment bag from the back of her van and had come up to the shop.

"Problem?" she said. We both watched as Lisa Marie banged through the door of the Gadda-da-Vida.

"She probably wants cream for her coffee," I said.

Lisa Marie was gone about five minutes. While we waited, I heard muffled shouting coming through the old plank walls. It was hard to tell who was doing the yelling or what was being said, but there were no pauses. Just a constant stream of hollering and screeching in the dulcimer tones of a cat fight. I could just imagine Kevin safely tucked in a corner watching the spectacle with a bemused look on his face.

About a half-minute after the racket died down, Lisa Marie slammed through my door, cheeks on fire.

"Akiko's here with your gown, and I'm so excited to see you in it," I said, determined to get Lisa Marie back on task. Later, Farrah would debrief me on the battle and I felt no obligation to give equal time to the opposition.

Akiko hoisted the ivory satin garment bag and nodded toward Lisa Marie. Then she silently carried it back into the fitting room.

Lisa Marie stood motionless by the door.

"Are you ready to get started?" I said.

"Fabulous," said Lisa Marie. "I'm having the very worst day of my entire life and all you and that ugly little woman care about is sticking me with pins. To hell with it; all of it!"

"I'm sorry," I said. "But is this is really the worst day of your life?" I wanted to point out the obvious: like maybe the day her fiancé disappeared might be a contender, or how about the day the Coast Guard gave up looking? But I knew saying anything would most likely bring the f-word into play.

"The *absolute* worst. First of all, last night my dad pissed off one of the bridesmaids. This morning, I found out all three of them just up and left, back to Hooters or wherever they came from. And then I find out Kevin—who's supposed to be marrying me in *two days*—has been doing God-knows-what with my florist. And then, to top it all off, I just found out she's *also* the person you forced me to use for the ceremony."

Long ago I learned silence is the better part of valor so I did my best to look shocked. I even put a hand to my mouth in a mock display of concern. I'll never be the actor Steve claims to be, but I like to give it a shot now and then.

"Now what?" Lisa Marie spit out. "Everything's ruined. And it's all your fault because you promised me a perfect wedding and instead I've got a cheating groom, no bridesmaids, and a hippie 'ho' for a minister."

Okay, I needed the money, bad. But Lisa Marie had crossed a line. I took a deep breath.

"Listen, Lisa Marie, you're not really marrying Kevin. He's just the stand-in guy for Brad. So Farrah and Kevin aren't doing anything wrong. I think you need to get a grip and calm down."

She plopped onto the sofa and crossed her arms tight across her bony chest. I waited for tears, but she just sat there: huffing and puffing as if she'd run a mile.

"Kevin owes me some respect. He *owes* me—big time."

Before I could ask, she started up again.

"And what'll I do about bridesmaids? They were supposed to hold my bouquet while I take my vows. Now where the hell am I supposed to put it?"

For once I had a really snappy comeback right on the tip of my tongue. Sadly, it was a luxury I couldn't afford.

"What about your stepmom?" I said. "It'd be a nice gesture to ask Tina to be your matron of honor."

The look on Lisa Marie's face was—as they say in the credit card commercial—priceless.

"I'd rather eat rusted glass."

"Okay then, don't worry. I'll find some replacements."

"Not ugly ones," Lisa Marie said. She seemed to be regaining her composure. "But not too gorgeous, either. Just kind of regular."

"Got it. Regular girls." I let a heartbeat or two of quiet pass before plunging into dark water. "And about Farrah. If you're uncomfortable with her doing the flowers or conducting the ceremony, just say so. I can find someone else for that too."

"Oh no, I want her there, front and center. That Ferret bitch will find out what happens to people who mess with me." She flashed me a flinty smile. "I'm not Marv Prescott's daughter for nothing."

14

I woke up on Wednesday, rehearsal day, with only one thing on my mind: in forty-eight hours it'd all be over. The fancy rehearsal dinner, the phony proxy ceremony, even sweating the evening news every night worried they'd report on body parts washing ashore. In two days my surly bride and her creepy family would be winging their way back to the mainland and I'd be trotting down to my bank. I'd coordinated some rather dubious nuptials in the past, but this dead man's sham was hands-down the worst.

By now I was on autopilot: everything had been checked and rechecked. I maintained my composure by focusing on how good it was going to feel to make that hefty deposit into my bone-dry checking account. Equally sweet was anticipating Tank Sherman's fury when he learned Kevin had outbid him for our building. I could get a smile going just imagining waving away Tank's measly five grand and showing him the door. Kevin had promised he'd renew my lease at the same rent or maybe even a bit less because we were *hoa aloha*: friends. Ol' Kev seemed to be plowing headlong into 'going native.' He'd quizzed Farrah on the local lingo and was tossing around *mahalo* and *da kine* as if he'd been born under a palm tree. I figured six months, tops, before he'd claim to be *kama'aina*: the word we use for native-born Hawaiians.

I'd managed to line up two bridal attendants for Lisa Marie. They were Maui Community College students who'd worked with Steve on a photo shoot. Each was a perfect size four, the same size as the powder blue silk dresses Lisa Marie had ordered for the previous bridesmaids. As payment for attending the ceremony I told them they could keep the expensive dresses—no charge. Since neither girl had a car I also threw in private limo transportation to and from Olu'olu for both the rehearsal and the wedding ceremony. When they inquired about a rehearsal dinner, I threw that in too. Who knew size fours even cared about dinner?

I stepped into the shower that morning feeling pretty darn pleased with myself. But two pesky things still prickled. First, since I hadn't heard anything from Kevin about the legal ramifications of the proxy marriage I wondered if he'd called the lawyer. Hopefully he had and hopefully James Kanekoa would have called me if proxy marriage was against the law. And second, I still hadn't figured out why Lisa Marie was so irate over Farrah's budding relationship with Kevin. Was Tina right? Were Lisa Marie and Kevin more of a couple than they let on? Or was Lisa Marie just pouting over another woman garnering his attention?

I warned Farrah that Lisa Marie was gunning for her, but she laughed it off.

"What's she gonna do? Cold cock me with her bouquet?"

"She can get pretty scary."

"Yeah? Well, I'm going to be in and outta there pretty fast. *Do you take this woman, yada yada. Do you take this man, blah, blah, blah. I pronounce you…*and I'm gone, baby, gone. Don't worry, Pali. She's probably just entering the anger phase of her grieving process. Once she moves on to the bargaining phase she'll mellow out."

"I don't know. She made a pretty solid point about being her father's daughter. And her father's certainly not someone I'd mess with."

"Yeah. Well, I've found bullies are mostly just little kids afraid of the dark. Watch me, I'm going to kill her with kindness. Works every time."

I'd let her have the last word on that one.

***

I got out of bed and was on a quest for coffee when I ran into Steve. He'd planned to get in a couple of hours of windsurfing at Ho'okipa Beach before going to work. After he left I considered a quick trip to Palace of Pain, but decided I'd wait until the health inspector's sign was on the door. I told myself blowing off my workout was noble, since I didn't want to get Sifu Doug in trouble, but that wasn't it. I had an entire free morning to spend with Hatch. I showered, carefully shaved my legs, and blew my hair dry to fluff it up.

I pushed through the kitchen door. Hatch had *The Maui News* spread out in front of him, but he looked up when I came in.

"You're looking chipper this morning," he said.

"Today's the wedding rehearsal," I said. "On my list of favorite days this month, it's coming in a strong number two."

"And number one was when I showed up, right?"

I eyed him warily.

"So, what's your story, Hatch?" I said. I pulled down a box of cold cereal and poured some in a bowl. I held it up as an offering and he nodded. I took out another bowl and filled it for myself. "I gave you the sad facts of my life the other day. Then you sidestepped Farrah when she tried to give you the third degree. What's up?"

"Nothing's *up*. My life's pretty boring, really. I was born in San Francisco. My folks divorced when I was eight and my mom moved us to LA a year later. When I graduated from UCLA I came to Honolulu to surf and I never left. A buddy talked me into going to the police academy—"

"You mean the *fire* academy."

"No, the police academy. I was a cop for seven years before I figured out firefighters were the heroes. Cops were 'Barneys,' 'the fuzz,' or 'bacon.' Firefighters rescue little kids and get their picture in the paper. I was pulling drunks off the road and getting my shoes barfed on."

"Bacon?"

"Yeah, you know, like pigs."

"Oh." To me the jobs were equally important, but I could see how a guy might rather be Superman than Batman.

"But when I quit the force to start my EMT training, it meant the end of some pretty tight friendships."

"Your friends dumped you for wanting a different job?"

"Big time. Cops and firefighters have a grudging respect. But it's a loyalty thing to stick with the one that's brung ya. I could have left for a million reasons and stayed friends with everybody, but leaving for the other team was not okay. I became the jerk, the traitor. My cop buddies pretty much tore up my dance card."

"Whoa, harsh."

"Yeah, it was tough. I'd known those guys since the academy. For seven years, we had each other's backs."

"How about your personal life?" I mentally patted myself on the back for the smooth transition.

"What do you mean?"

"Well, how did people other than your co-workers react to you leaving?" Not so smooth.

"Being a cop was pretty much my whole life. Made it pretty easy to move over here to Maui Fire when I got the chance."

Not exactly what I was fishing for, but it'd have to do. "Well, I better get down to my shop. Like I said, today's the rehearsal, tomorrow the big day and then it's all over. You okay watching the pups?"

"Sure. I like having them here. I'm good with kids and animals. I always figured I'd be a dad by twenty-five. Just didn't happen, you know?"

And it's never gonna happen at the rate you're going.

I brought the puppy box downstairs after cleaning up the mess in my room. Lipton had been diligent about using the doggie potty I'd made out of old towels, but still the entire second floor reeked of *eau de dog pee*.

On my way to the shop, I stopped off at the printer's and picked up Lisa Marie's wedding announcements. It was disturbing to read "Bradley James Sanders" listed as her new husband.

"I get paid this Friday," I said to the printer. "Okay if I come back next week and settle up?"

"No problem. Boy, this weather's been brutal. I've only had two wedding jobs in the past month."

"Yeah, but it's getting better. If we can just hang on until March, things are bound to pick up."

"From your lips to God's ear," he said. "Wedding stuff is generally more than half my business."

I was unlocking my shop door when my cell chimed. I dug out the phone and checked the caller ID. It was Steve.

"Pali, I'm glad I caught you. I'm afraid I've got some really harsh news." He paused. "You sitting down?"

"What is it?" I said. I wasn't in the mood for his dramatics and I didn't need to be sitting down. You know how sometimes you just know stuff?

Well, I knew. I'd been bracing for that phone call for more than a week.

15

I interrupted Steve before he could answer. "Where'd they find the body?" It was lousy of me to steal Steve's thunder but I wanted to avoid a lengthy tee-up.

"You already heard? Wow, word gets around fast. Hatch just called five minutes ago."

"I didn't hear anything. But I've been expecting it, I guess. I needed only two more days. Seems I just can't get a break."

"You want details?"

"Can you give me the short version? I just paid my cell bill and I'd rather not blow minutes on bad news."

"Okay, a couple of beach walkers spotted a man's body on Little Beach this morning. He was in shallow water, right at the water's edge."

"And they're sure it's Brad Sanders?"

"No positive ID yet, but according to Hatch, he's the only guy reported missing in the past few weeks. They flew the remains to Honolulu 'cuz I guess there's no medical examiner over here."

"It's amazing there was much left of him after all this time in the water," I said. "Ugh, I can't imagine he looked even remotely human."

"Yeah, hard to believe. I suppose this means no wedding."

"I guess. I'll go down to Olu'olu and break the news to Lisa Marie. I don't want her hearing it on TV, and I really don't want her to hear it from Marv. The guy's got a sick sense of humor."

"Sorry, Pali. It's a bummer."

"Raging bummer." I signed off and picked up my purse and keys.

The ride to Olu'olu went by in a blur of images and snatches of conversation from the past week. I wondered how Lisa Marie would take it: hearing that Brad was now, without a sliver of doubt, dead.

I planned to corner Marv and press him about paying the vendors' bills. As tacky as it felt bringing up money to man whose almost-a-son-in-law lay bloated and chilling in the Honolulu morgue, I knew I'd feel even worse if I stiffed my friends and colleagues. I wouldn't ask for my fifteen percent—after all, I hadn't completed delivery—but people like Akiko, Keahou, and the printer had all finished what I'd asked them to do so they needed to get paid.

I pulled into the driveway and was surprised to see the gate standing open. Two police cruisers were parked directly in front of the door. Looked like I'd be spared from breaking the bad news after all.

I parked far down the driveway, the best spot for a quick getaway. If history held true, Lisa Marie would blame me for Brad's body showing up at this inopportune time. I'd stick around just long enough for Marv to write a check.

Josie answered the door. This time she wasn't smiling.

"Is Lisa Marie at home?"

"She not seeing anyone. Policeman are here."

"I understand. Could I perhaps see Mr. Prescott? I need a few minutes of his time."

"He is on the phone. And then he talk to policeman."

"May I wait?"

"Of course. I will tell him you are here."

She crossed the foyer and went down a hallway to the left. I watched as she put her ear to a closed set of double doors near the end of the hall. She opened one of the doors a few inches and peeked in. Then she came back to where I was standing.

"He's not in there. Must be finished with his call. The policeman is in the sunroom. Come with me."

She led me down the hallway and gestured for me to enter the room she'd checked. It appeared to be an office or a den. The side walls were paneled halfway up in a dark wood, maybe mahogany, with the upper section papered in a deep green tropical print. The only light came from a narrow clerestory window near the top of the outside wall. A massive dark wood desk faced the double doors. It was bare except for a telephone set and a fancy leather blotter.

Behind the desk sat a swivel chair and behind that were floor-to-ceiling bookcases filled with matching leather-bound books all with gilt-embossed spines. A glass six foot tall display case was along the left wall. The glass shelves held a dozen or so odd knickknacks, including two slender white tusks carved in the image of an Asian man and woman.

Josie motioned for me to take a seat in one of two chairs facing the desk. One was modern black leather. The other was made of intricately carved wood and looked like an antique. I went with modern. The smooth leather felt cool against my bare arms.

"I tell Mr. Prescott you are waiting." She bobbed her head in a shallow bow and closed the door.

A light on the multi-line telephone blinked in the semi-dark room. I took a deep breath and shut my eyes to rehearse my 'please pay up' speech to Marv.

"I'm back," boomed Marv and I jumped. I turned, but the doors were still closed. The voice was coming from the speaker on the desk phone. "Got the damn Bluetooth thingy working after all. I'm outside now; I got cops crawling up my ass in there."

I stood up and peered over the desk at the phone set.

"So," Marv went on, "what have you got for me?"

"Not good news, Boss. I know you've got that wedding coming up quick and all, but…" It was a man's voice I didn't recognize. He had a nasal twang I'd peg as Chicago or maybe New Jersey. I'd done my air marshal training in New Jersey, but I have a tough time placing mainland accents so the guy could have been from anywhere.

"Cut to it, will ya? I told you, I got cops snooping around, every minute they're breathing more of my air and eyeing my things."

"Okay, well, 'no dice' from the judge here in town. I called a guy out in Montana who owes us for a mining deal, but he says he needs to see the paperwork."

"We're totally legit here. I'll have paperwork; you make sure he remembers he owes me. Hell, I shouldn't even have to call in a chit on this thing. What's his problem?"

"I dunno, Boss. Seems stupid to me too. Do you know when you're coming back?"

"I got a golf game at Pebble on Saturday and then I'll be back in the office on Monday. I want this guy softened up and ready to sign whatever we put in front of him. You got that?"

"Got it, Boss."

"Mr. Prescott?" It was Josie's faint voice in the background. "The policeman say they need to talk to you now."

"Fine, fine. Tell them I'll be right there," he said. Then to the caller, "Look, I gotta go. Like I said, I want this nice and clean. Shouldn't be that hard. Like anybody's gonna object, right?" He laughed. "And, don't worry. I'll get the paperwork. This place is 'moron central.' They're so busy picking the tourist's pockets they can't find their asses with both hands."

There was a chuckle on the other end of the line and then they said their good-byes. There was a click and the line hummed the disconnect sound for a couple of seconds.

I hurried back to my seat. I settled in, crossed my legs, and assumed the posture of a bored minion patiently waiting to be called before the Great One.

A half-minute later I heard a commotion outside in the hallway.

"What the hell were you thinking?" It was Marv at full volume.

"I...I...didn't," Josie's voice cowered in reply.

"Didn't what? Didn't think? I was told you slant-eye people were smart. Are you the only dumb-ass Chinaman in all of Hawaii?"

"I'm not Chinese. I'm—"

"I don't give a damn what you are. The fact is, you're an idiot. Now get that goddamn woman out of my private office." I heard footfalls stomp down the tiled hallway.

The den door opened about a foot and Josie peeked in, her eyes narrowed in anxiety as if she was expecting me to continue the barrage of insults.

"Miss Moon?" she said.

"Yes, Josie. I'm here." I stood and walked over to the door.

"I'm so sorry for making a problem," she said, her eyes welling up, her mouth a tight line. She seemed to be struggling to maintain her composure.

"No need to apologize. I'm the one who's sorry. He has no right to talk to you like that." I wanted to tell her I had the name and phone number of a guy I'd gone to high school with who now worked in the state civil rights office. But I figured it was one of those Biblical 'time to reap, time to sow' situations. I'd hold back on getting self-righteous until I had a check—with Marv Prescott's signature on it—in hand. But I wouldn't forget.

Josie silently ushered me back to the foyer. "The policeman are still in the sunroom. Is it okay for you to wait here?"

"No problem."

About ten minutes later, Josie silently escorted the police past me and out the door. She closed the door and bobbed her head toward me in a weary bow. "Sorry for the waiting. Please follow me."

In the sunroom Marv lounged on the sunny yellow sofa. He sipped his coffee and gazed out at the view.

"Hello Ms. Moon," he said after I'd stood and waited to be acknowledged for the obligatory minute. He patted the sofa. "Have a seat."

It took some deep kung fu breathing to convince my body to place itself within six feet of the guy, but I managed to perch on the edge of the cushion.

"I guess today's the big rehearsal." His voice was full of fatherly pride. "I didn't expect to see you until this later afternoon."

Okay, I said to myself. *What's going on? The police just left. They found Brad's body on the beach this morning. Had the cops failed to deliver the news?*

Marv fixed his eyes on me and I responded in kind. I'd certainly faced more intimidating opponents than this bandy-legged, racist jerk. If I'd been hooked up to a lie-detector and asked if I'd overheard anything, I'd could've pumped out a flat line, no problem.

"Well, Marv, I don't know if we're going to have a rehearsal or not. It seems something's come up."

"You talkin' about that body they picked up on the beach?" He said it as if corpses washed ashore every day. "Yeah, I heard about it. As you may have noticed, the police just left."

"That sort of puts a crimp in things, don't you think?"

"It's unfortunate that some poor soul drowned a day before my daughter's wedding, but I don't see why that should keep us from moving forward."

It was an Oscar-winning performance. He knew damn well whose body had washed ashore that morning.

Point was, he didn't care.

16

A wise person would've hit the road, but I stuck around. After all, I had promises to keep.

"Marv, sorry to bother you with this, but I've got some wedding vendors who need to get paid."

"So pay them."

"Well, I would, but I'm experiencing a bit of a cash crunch."

"Isn't it customary to hit up the father of the bride *after* the ceremony?"

"Yes, it is. But frankly, I'm pretty sure they'll identify the body they found this morning as Brad Sanders."

"And your point is…"

"My point is that if it's Brad, then I'm also sure the proxy wedding tomorrow would be invalid, not to mention in extremely poor taste."

"Sweetheart, what's in poor taste is you asking me to pay for my daughter's wedding before it's even scheduled. I don't see how waiting one more day constitutes a hardship for you or your so-called 'vendors.' Now if you'll excuse me, I've got some business calls to make and I have a long list of things I need to attend to before tonight's events. The maid will show you out."

I hated leaving empty-handed, but I pride myself on recognizing when 'no' means 'no.' Besides, my mental kryptonite protecting me against Marv Prescott's vulgarity was losing its potency. I feared if I stuck around much longer I might feel duty-bound to take him to task for the Josie incident. That could lead to my losing my temper, and that could result in me kicking his ass and kissing off any prayer of getting paid.

Josie met me in the foyer and gave me a quick, tentative smile.

"Would you mind if I used the bathroom before I leave?" I said. "It's a long ride back to Pa'ia."

"Follow me, please."

She trotted down the hallway and I kept close behind. She stopped outside the doorway to what a real estate agent would refer to as a 'powder room.' I heard banging pans and sharp voices coming from further down the hall and figured the kitchen must be down there.

"*Mahalo,*" I said. "You go ahead with your work. I'll just let myself out when I'm finished."

She hesitated. I'm sure it was tough for her to decide if Marv would place a higher value on her getting back to her chores or making sure I departed promptly.

"I have work in the kitchen." She gave me a guarded look as if silently requesting a pinky swear I wouldn't pull a stunt that might get her into even deeper doo-doo.

"Really, I'll just be a few minutes." I said. I slipped into the tiny half-bath and flicked on the light. The room glittered like an open jewelry box. Against deep carmine walls gleamed a gaudy gilt-framed mirror that would have done Marie Antoinette proud. A black pedestal sink sported oversized gold fixtures. Even the magazine rack tucked in next to the toilet looked gold plated. I considered ripping off a magazine to read later but then shuddered as I flipped through the selection: *Guns and Ammo*, *Hustler*, and *Soldier of Fortune*. Obviously, this was Marv's domain. I lost any urge to sit down on the jet black toilet.

I counted twenty seconds using the *one-thousand one, one-thousand-two* method and then flushed. I thoroughly scrubbed my hands in the sink and then poked my head out the door. Seeing the coast was clear, I retraced my steps toward the front door. As much as I wanted to get the hell out of there I felt obligated to check on Lisa Marie and see how she was holding up. I took a left at the foyer and sneaked down the hallway that extended in the opposite direction of the sunroom. The sprawling house had no second floor so I figured I'd located the bedroom wing.

I crept along the hall, listening for signs of life. The first doorway was on my left. The door was open so I stepped inside and scanned the room. It appeared to be a guest room, with a massive mahogany canopy bed elegantly draped with about a hundred yards of milky white netting. The walls were papered in natural grass cloth. A thick area rug woven in a deep green and yellow banana-leaf design covered most of the cream-colored tile floor. A ceiling fan the size of an airplane propeller slowly rotated overhead.

The next doorway was to my right. The double doors were closed. I leaned in close but heard nothing. I'd check out the remaining rooms before risking opening a closed door.

The next room was on the left. I spotted a half-inch gap between the door and the jamb.

I listened. Through the gap I made out a faint mewling sound coming from inside. It sounded a lot like Lipton's puppies back at my house.

I nudged the door open and looked in. A human form was stretched out on the bed in a tangle of sheets. I couldn't tell whether the person was male or female in the dusk of the shuttered room.

I tiptoed inside and was startled when the figure emitted a sharp animal noise: something between a grunt and a bark, and turned toward me.

It was a tiny bald man wearing a white tank top and bright print boxer shorts. His face was smooth and he had matchstick-thin arms and legs. The guy looked like drawings I'd seen of space aliens. The eyes weren't big and buggy and the ears weren't exactly pointy, but the combination of dim room, weird noises and skinny bald dude all added up to a close encounter of the kind I prefer to avoid.

"Excuse me," I said. I waved a Martian greeting and hastily backtracked to the door.

"Pali?" said the alien.

"Lisa Marie?" I whispered.

I peered harder into the gloom.

"I'm glad it's you and not Daddy," she said. "He's been bugging me about getting up and eating something."

As my eyes grew accustomed to the low light, I could make out her face. Without hair, she looked years younger—no, maybe older—I couldn't decide. In any case, she looked bizarre. Even her eyebrows were missing.

"What happened?" I said.

She propped herself up on one elbow. "Oh, this?" She rubbed a hand across her scalp. "I shaved it off."

"Why?"

"I figured it worked for Britney Spears. Remember when everything was going wrong for her and they took her little boys away?"

I didn't keep up with Hollywood gossip, and I wondered if Lisa Marie had her facts straight.

"Uh, I don't recall that. Remind me about it."

"Everyone was calling Britney crazy and a bad mother and all that. The paparazzi followed her everywhere, yelling and shooting pictures of her without her make-up. Her life was a mess. So one night she got her hair shaved off." She smiled. I couldn't recall the last time I'd seen Lisa Marie smile.

"Anyway, I know exactly how she felt. Everybody's been bossing me around and treating me like crap. When I told my dad about Kevin screwing that hippie he laughed. He said I should turn the other cheekbone. That I should be grateful to Kevin no matter who he screws."

Hard as it was, I had to side with Marv on that one.

"Look, Lisa Marie, I'm sorry you got so upset over that. I know Farrah didn't—"

"Shut up! Don't you ever mention that name around me again. That bitch owes me an apology. A huge one."

"Okay, well I think you need to rest. I'm—"

"No!" said Lisa Marie. "You don't have a single clue what I need. I needed a designer dress and you wouldn't get me one; then I needed tuberoses and that 'ho' lied and said she couldn't get them. Then I needed you to get me a stupid crane picture and so far, no picture. Working with you has been like pulling teeth uphill the whole way."

No point weighing in on that. I turned to leave.

"My wedding to Brad was supposed to be my A-list debut. Like Kate Middleton marrying that prince. But you've wrecked everything. And Kevin, don't even get me started on him. He said I was the best ever and then he heaves me over for some gypsy with hairy legs? I hate him. I hate you all!"

My abuse-o-meter was glowing orange. I crossed the room and had my hand on the doorknob when she lobbed a final volley.

"But guess what?" she said. "You're all going to look pretty damn stupid when Brad shows up tomorrow."

I mentally cursed Marv for not telling her about the body.

She went on, "Yeah, getting rid of my hair got my brain working better. I've finally figured out how to get Brad to come back."

"I need to go now, Lisa Marie."

"So go. But you better be back here tomorrow, 'cuz even with everything you've tried to do to wreck my wedding, I *will* be getting married. Mark my words, missy. Brad's coming back and when he does, we'll be all over the news. I can see it now: 'Mrs. Lisa Marie Sanders: The Bride Who Never Lost Hope.' By this time on Friday I'll be more famous than the Kardashians."

I quietly closed the door behind me. It wouldn't be long before she'd learn about Brad's fate. I'd come back later to offer my condolences, and hopefully pick up Marv's check. Right then, my goal was to hot-foot it back to the shop and cancel the rehearsal dinner. I'd still be on the hook for the food and paying the servers' their minimum wage, but at least I could avoid the bar set-up charges and mileage fees.

I'd come to Olu'olu with two goals: to break the bad news to Lisa Marie, and to pry a few bucks out of Marv. I'd struck out on both counts. Not a good start to the day, but it wasn't over yet.

17

I spent the half-hour ride back to Pa'ia hashing over a long list of 'what-ifs.' I'd pulled into the alley and turned off the engine before I remembered that once again I'd failed to pick up Lisa Marie's thousand crane picture. As I sat in my car mulling over whether I should call the frame shop and apologize or just go get the darn thing, I was startled by a knock on the window.

"Hey," said Farrah. "You comin' or goin'?"

I rolled down the window. "Good question."

"You hear about them finding that body down at Little Beach?"

"Yeah. I went down to Lisa Marie's but I couldn't bring myself to tell her."

"C'mon inside. I'll buy you a pog."

We went in the back door and I saw Beatrice, the ancient lady who sometimes filled in for Farrah, at the counter.

"Everything okay Bea?" Farrah sang out loudly. Beatrice had a hearing problem so conducting business with her was usually done at about ninety decibels.

"Fine, dear," Beatrice yelled back.

Farrah traipsed back to the dairy case and picked up two pint-size cartons of passion-orange-guava juice: pog.

"I'll be upstairs with Pali," boomed Farrah.

"You're upset with Pali? About what, dear?"

"No, we'll be *upstairs*."

"Fine, love. You two work it out. I can stay as long as you need me."

We both waved at her and headed back outside to the stairs.

"Okay, so tell me what's shakin' at Olu'olu," Farrah said as we took seats in our usual spots: she on the well-broken-in velveteen sofa and me in an orange director's chair with a permanent butt sag in the seat. "I suppose they've called off the wedding."

"Not yet. Marv's waiting for them to ID the body, and Lisa Marie's pretty much gone totally *pupule*."

"She's gone nuts? I thought you didn't tell her. Did someone else?"

"Not that I know of."

"She doesn't know? So, why's she crazy? She was in anger phase yesterday; I'd have figured she'd be moving into bargaining phase now, not depression. She's not doing the grief cycle like she's 'sposed to." Farrah chewed on a thumbnail.

I didn't know the grief cycle from a giraffe. And, as far as I could tell, Lisa Marie lived her entire life in anger phase. "I don't know whether she's angry or bargaining or any of that, but she's definitely gone around the bend. She chopped off her hair."

"What?" she said. "Nobody gets a hair cut the day before their wedding."

"It's way beyond a haircut. She's completely bald."

"Wow, did she do it herself?"

Now that she mentioned it, Lisa Marie's head was perfectly clean shaven. "It's cueball smooth. I don't think she could have gotten it so flawless on her own. But that's not the point. She's mutilating herself and she's delusional.

She's even more convinced than ever that Brad's going to show up tomorrow."

"How could you listen to her talk like that and not tell her they found his body?"

"She needs professional help."

"And you're scared of her."

"Damn straight I'm scared of her. I was all alone with her in a dark room. Who knows how she might have taken the news. She's already gunning for Kevin. Oh, and on that happy note, she's demanding an apology from you."

"An apology? For what?"

"For getting involved with Kevin."

"Why should I apologize? He's signing the wedding certificate; he's not her prom date!" By this point she was yelling so loud probably even Beatrice could hear it.

I got up and sat next to her on the sofa. "Of course you're right. But I'd appreciate it if you'd offer an apology anyway. Just to leave things on a high note."

"You mean, because if I don't you're worried her dad won't pay the wedding bills."

"Guilty as charged. I need you to do it for me." I took her hand.

There was a beat of silence.

"Okay, I'll do it. But it won't be sincere."

"Sincerity is strictly optional."

She squeezed my hand and then let it go. "Enough about that," she said. "What's going on with you and Hatch?"

"Nothing. Maybe I'm not his type. He's been kind of distant lately."

"Maybe his man parts got mashed up in the accident," she said.

If she was angling for the last word on *that* subject, she got it.

"Well, speaking of lost man parts," she went on, "how are Lipton and the babies doing?"

"They're fine. Lipton seems to be missing you. Would you like to come up and visit?"

"Sounds good. I take it you're not having the rehearsal?"

"No rehearsal," I said, "but the wedding's still on until there's a positive ID. Under my contract only Lisa Marie or Brad can cancel the wedding. You know, for the past week I was really hoping Brad would stay missing just long enough to do this wedding. But now that he's shown up, I'm sort of relieved. I think deep down I was worried this proxy thing might be against the law."

"Well, even with everything that happened, I'm glad you took the job," Farrah said. "Because if you hadn't, I wouldn't have met Kevin. And without Kevin we'd be handing over everything to Tank the day after tomorrow."

"I hope I don't have to sell out to Tank. I've still got a ton of bills, and Marv's playing hard ass about paying me. Do you think it's out of line for me to ask Kevin to spot my rent next month? I'd pay him back as soon as I could."

"Don't worry about it. And don't bother paying me for Lisa Marie's flowers. I'll sell them tomorrow. After all, it's Valentine's Day."

"*Mahalo*. By the way, how's Kevin doing with them finding Brad's body?"

"Haven't heard from him yet today. But I'll bet he's got mixed feelings. He loved Brad like a brother, but he said Brad was giving him fits about the business. I just hope that now that Brad's officially gone they won't expect Kevin to take over the company. He's really ready to move on."

"I better run," I said. "Do you know what time it is?"

We both glanced at the old-fashioned Big Ben alarm clock on Farrah's coffee table. It said eight-twenty. It had said eight-twenty since she'd first put it there.

"Hey, it's right twice a day," she said. "I think it's around half-past noon. You going home?"

"No, I'll wait at the shop until they ID Brad, then I'll start making calls. I really dread telling people I'm cancelling on them and I won't be able to pay what I owe until next week. Give me a half-hour and I'll take you up to the house."

"See you then."

My message light was blinking when I went into to my shop. I didn't need any more messages from creditors or vendors wanting to get paid. I ignored the phone and started flipping through my mail. *Urgent!* or *Immediate action required!* was splashed across the face of the envelopes, as if I needed any reminders of why I'd gotten involved with Lisa Marie in the first place. Before I'd thumbed through the entire stack, the phone rang. Without thinking, I reached across the desk and picked up the receiver.

"Hey," said Steve. "Didn't you get my message?"

"I just walked in. Everything okay?"

"You talk to Hatch yet?"

"No, should I?"

"He left you a message. Actually, he left a bunch of messages."

I felt a little flutter in my stomach, but realized he probably just wanted me to pick up some air fresheners on my way home. The doggie odor was becoming a fourth roommate.

"Do you know what he wanted?"

"Yeah. What do you want first: the good news or the bad?"

"I don't care, surprise me."

"Okay, well, the good news is the body isn't Brad Sanders."

There was a pause. I heard him suck in a breath as if he was about to jump into cold water. "The bad news it's Kevin McGillvary."

The receiver slipped from my hand and landed with a clunk on the desk. I grabbed it back up. "Sorry. Did I hear you right?"

"Yep. Looks like Kevin picked a really bad time to stand in for his buddy Brad."

"I'm stunned. Just stunned. I..." I stopped. I couldn't think of anything coherent to say, and I felt my throat closing up.

"Don't move," he said. "I'll be right there; I'm only three minutes away."

He banged through my door in two. I was still at my desk, phone in hand. *If you'd like to make a call, please hang up and try again...*

"Hey," he said. He took the receiver from my hand and hung it up.

"I can't believe this," I said. I stood and he gave me a hug.

"I know, it's beyond weird. Hatch got the news a couple of hours ago when he checked in with his fire dispatch. The Honolulu ME released the information to Maui Fire first since they found the body. Professional courtesy, I guess."

"Kevin was a nice guy," I said. "Do they know what happened?"

"No. Cause of death takes more time than a simple ID. And, get this, he was only wearing underwear. No shirt, no pants. I'm no detective, but to me 'drop trou' means either he was having a very *good* time or a very *bad* time when he died."

"How'd they ID him so fast? No pants also means no wallet or driver's license."

"Fingerprints. According to Hatch, DigiSystems does a lot of high-level government work so the people who work there have security clearances. His prints popped right up on the federal database." He nodded toward my shabby sofa. "That thing got fleas?"

"No."

"Then let's sit down. You look like you're gonna faint."

We took opposite ends. I leaned back and tucked my legs under me. The weather had warmed up considerably but I was shivering.

"I woke up in a good mood, but so far this day's been a bitch," I said. "First Marv won't pay up, then Lisa Marie goes nut-job on me, and now Kevin's dead."

"What's with Lisa Marie?"

I told him about her shaving her head and her rant about me ruining her wedding.

"Whatever you did to piss her off will pale next to this. Can you imagine? She taps two guys to be her groom and now they're both dead. What're the chances?"

I gazed out my front window and recalled Kevin's enormous black Hummer parked out there. Then I bolted upright.

"Steve," I said. "I've got to tell Farrah."

"No need. It's all over the news by now."

"Oh, no." I launched from the sofa and was out the door in five strides.

"Want me to come?"

Steve answered his own question by following me outside. There was a 'Closed' sign on the Gadda-da-Vida. I peeked inside. The lights were off and the door knob wouldn't turn.

I raced to the back stairs. Steve followed close behind. Without bothering to knock, I pushed Farrah's apartment door open. Muffled sobs were coming from somewhere in back. We crossed the cluttered living room and found her in her bedroom, face down on her sagging futon.

"Leave me alone," she sniffed.

"Sorry, sister," I said. "We're staying."

Farrah twisted around, probably to check out why I'd said *we*. When she saw Steve, she leapt off the futon and threw her arms around him, nearly knocking him over. Her stricken face cast the enormity of Kevin's shocking death in a whole new light. My stomach clenched.

Steve began patting Farrah's back as if he were burping a baby. He turned to me, shrugging his shoulders in bewilderment.

"Did you hear?" Farrah sobbed. "They found him on Little Beach." Her body twitched with a series of shuddering hiccups.

"I know," Steve said. "It really sucks."

Farrah gulped a deep breath and reached over and grabbed my hand. "Could I come stay at your place for a few days? I hate to ask, 'cuz I know how you like your privacy, but—"

"Stop. You're *ohana*. Family doesn't get any privacy." That didn't come out right, but she got the point.

Truthfully, I had no idea where I'd put her. If three was a crowd, then four people and five dogs amounted to something approximating a mob; but turning her away was unthinkable.

"I hate being away from Sir Lipton. He makes me feel safe."

"I'm sure he does." I'd given up on the he/she thing.

"What about the store?" Steve said. "Someone needs to keep the Vida open."

"The store's closed," Farrah said.

"For the rest of the day?"

"For as long as I'm in mourning."

Steve's face slackened in disbelief. The Gadda-da-Vida Grocery was a lifeline for the Pa'ia community. It stayed resolutely open every day of the year, even on Farrah's high holy days: Farrah Fawcett's birth and death days, her parents' anniversary, and Halloween.

She snuffled her nose and stared him down, eyes defiant. "If I feel like it later, I'll ask Bea if she wants to come in."

"Okay, okay," he said. "It's your store."

"Do you want to go to Hali'imaile now?" I said to Farrah. "I've got to run down to Olu'olu, but I could drop you off on the way."

"No, I need to pack some clothes and pull together some groceries. Can you give me an hour?"

"Take all the time you need." I hugged her tight and agreed to pick her up later.

Steve and I walked to my shop without saying a word.

"Okay, you want to clue me in on what's going on?" he said once we were inside. "Farrah probably met McGillvary a time or two since she was working the wedding. But I'm having a heck of a time figuring out why she's so totally freaked out about him drowning."

"You've got to keep this to yourself." I said. I waited for a nod of agreement since Steve's kind of a go-to guy for gossip. "Farrah and Kevin were a couple."

"C'mon," he said, "Birkenstocks and Gucci loafers under the same bed? No way." He grinned as if he expected me to punch his arm and admit I was joking.

"Trust me. It defies logic, but I witnessed it in action. He'd even offered to buy this building so Tank Sherman couldn't kick Farrah and me out. I think he really cared about her."

"Well, maybe it was a peanut butter and caviar thing," he said.

I gave him a confused look.

"You know, one of those weird combos that people swear is great. What did Lisa Marie think about the two of them hooking up? She okay with it?"

"Not by a long shot."

We looked at each other and held the stare.

"Now what?" Steve said.

"Now I need to head down to Olu'olu to see what they want to do and try to get some bills paid."

"Can I do anything to help?"

"Could you clear out a few shelves in the kitchen? I have a feeling Farrah's gonna haul in a load of comfort food."

"Sorry to state the obvious, but most of the shelves are already bare."

I chewed my lip. "You know, this morning my life was clipping along pretty good; just two days to go…" I shook my head. No use itemizing the dismal events of the past four hours.

"You know your life could've turned out a lot worse," said Steve.

"Oh yeah? How?"

"You could've been a guy betrothed to Lisa Marie."

18

I took my usual route toward home but instead of turning right at my street I shot right past it. I then made a right at Haleakala Highway and then a left at Highway 36 to Hansen Road and then to Waiko Road to Highway 30 over to the West Side. It certainly isn't the most direct route from Pa'ia to Olu'olu, but by snaking along back roads I avoided the Kahului traffic and the extra miles gave me time to think.

My plan was to convince Lisa Marie to scuttle the wedding out of respect for Kevin. By the time Olu'olu came into sight, I had my whole speech prepared: 'That's what Brad would want you to do; and even if he does show up tomorrow he'll be proud you respected his friend's memory,' blah, blah, blah. I cringed at shamelessly putting words in her mouth since I was pretty sure there were some serious cracks in her psyche. Cancelling the wedding could split it wide open. But regardless of whether she went along with my plan or not I was duty-bound to wrestle a check out of Marv. If I didn't get paid before he and Tina sashayed out to the airport, I had no doubt it wouldn't take long for me to become just another blocked number on his cell phone.

The gate was closed when I turned into Olu'olu. I waited at the speaker box, burning gas I couldn't afford, for what felt like five minutes but was probably more like one or two. I tapped the horn.

"Keep your shorts on," snarled a voice through the speaker.

"It's me, Pali Moon. I need to see Lisa Marie."

"She's not seeing nobody."

"How about Marv? Is he taking visitors?"

"Mr. Prescott's gone."

"Would you please open the gate? I'm here about the wedding."

"I'm not supposed to let in any cops or reporters."

"I'm none of the above."

"Prove it."

"C'mon. You know my voice by now, and I know you've got a camera on me. Look at this car. Would any self-respecting cop or reporter drive a piece of crap like this?"

"No." There was a hesitation. "Unless maybe you're undercover or something."

"I'm the wedding planner. You've let me in nearly every day for the past week. Open the damn gate—pretty please."

I parked in my favorite spot close to the end of the driveway. As I walked toward the house I was once again rocked back on my heels by the stunning ocean view. White-capped waves crashed against the jagged black rocks of the breakwater. Kevin's body had been battered by similar rocks only a few miles south.

Stepping up to the door, I pulled myself up straight and put on my combat face. I waited, but the door didn't swing open as it usually did when I approached. I knocked and waited some more. Nothing.

I knocked again—loudly this time—then followed it up with a finger on the doorbell. I heard the bell chime a few bars of *Aloha 'Oe* inside the foyer, but still no one came.

Since the guard at the gate had let me in I was sure someone must be there. I stepped away from the front entrance and headed to my left—along the *ma kai*, or shoreline, side of the house—to check if maybe someone was on the lanai.

Lisa Marie was stretched out on a lounge chair wearing only a pale pink bikini bottom. Her bare fried-egg breasts and shaved head glowed ghostly white in the mid-day sun. She sported oversized dark aviator sunglasses that covered most of her sunken cheeks. Her overall appearance brought to mind a gigantic insect larva.

I hoisted myself onto the low rock wall that circled the lanai. I was about to jump down on the other side over when a hand grabbed my upper arm in a crunching grip.

"Where you think you're going?" said a man, six feet tall and at least half that wide. I recognized his growling voice from the security gate. His *kukui* nut-brown skin and lion's mane of frizzy orange-tipped black hair stood in sharp contrast to his blazing white teeth. I pegged him as Fijian. His fierce grin reminded me that Fijians didn't abandon cannibalism until the late 1800's. I sent up a prayer he'd gotten the memo.

"Whew, you scared me." I said.

"You supposed to wait at the door," he rumbled. His jutting unibrow shaded squinting eyes. "No one allowed back here."

"Sorry. I knocked and rang the bell but nobody came. Then I noticed Lisa Marie out here. She's the person I need to talk to."

"Go back and wait at the door." He gripped my arm tighter, pulling me off balance. I had no choice except to scramble back down the way I'd come. Once I regained my footing, I looked up at him. His eyes were fixed on Lisa Marie. Though he was no doubt tempted to stay and gawk, the opportunity to shove me around must have appealed to him even more. He hauled me toward the front entry, taking such long strides I could barely keep up. I flexed my bicep, hoping to stave off a nasty upper arm bruise. He stiffened his grip in response.

Josie waited at the open front door. The security guy heaved me forward with a shove, then wordlessly stalked off.

"I so sorry," she said. "I was in the kitchen and the bell comes and I had to turn off the cooking, and ..." She prattled on, anxiety raising her voice to a squeak.

"Are you okay, Josie?" I said.

"Oh, Miss Moon. Is terrible. First Mr. Brad is lost, and now Mr. Kevin drowned...." She picked up the hem of her apron and dabbed at her eyes.

"I know. I came down here to talk to Lisa Marie about the wedding."

"There can be no wedding!" She shrieked as if I'd suggested her first-born son step in as the new proxy.

"No, of course not. We need to talk about *cancelling* the wedding."

She nodded and motioned for me to follow her to the sunroom. It was in deep shadow now, the windows tightly shuttered. I couldn't see outside, but I knew Lisa Marie was stretched out only a few feet away on the other side of the windows. Josie offered me a seat; then crossed the room and opened the exterior door.

I heard muffled conversation through the half-open door. A half-minute later Josie reappeared and gestured for me to come outside.

"She not feeling good," she whispered. "Please say only happy talk."

Like that left much to say.

"Hi, Lisa Marie." I gave her a little wave. "How're you doing?" She didn't respond. I pulled a wicker chair over next to her and sat down.

She reached down and picked up a *pareo*—a Tahitian shawl—and draped it across her shoulders, covering her bare bosom.

I waited for her to say something, and when she didn't, I did what most people do when faced with dead air: I started blathering.

"Wow, what a rough morning, huh? You look pretty darn good, considering everything that's happened. And check out that view. Like they say, another beautiful day in paradise." I looked out toward the islands of Lana'i and Kaho'olawe glistening on the horizon. "Looks like the rain has finally let up for a while...."

I yammered on, doing color commentary on island life in general and nothing in particular. When I finally took a breath, she let out a sigh with so much hurt behind it I wanted to lean over and give her a hug.

"You look like shit," she said. "Is that what you're planning to wear to my wedding rehearsal this afternoon?" She pointed to my shorts and tee-shirt.

"No." I mentally kicked myself for even considering the hug.

"It starts in two hours," she said. "Don't you think you should change?"

I stood up, fighting the urge to grab her by the shoulders and shake her until her teeth rattled. I imagined dramatically slapping her pale sunken cheek. She'd blink a couple of times and then say, *Thanks, I needed that*. Okay, not gonna happen, but it was a satisfying fantasy.

"Lisa Marie, I need to talk to your dad. Do you know where he is?"

"He left."

"Where'd he go?"

"Who cares? Tina said they'd be gone for a few hours."

"What did your dad say when he saw your hair?" *Or rather, your total lack of hair.*

"What do you think? He yelled at me."

"That's it?"

"You want details? Okay, he called me a whack-job and told me I look like hell. Then he said he was done trying to help me be normal."

"Lisa Marie, I'm afraid I have some bad news."

Her eyes flashed. "No! I'm sick, sick, *sick* of your bad news. If you say one more word I'll have security throw you out."

She jumped off the lounge and violently shook out the *pareo*, then quickly wrapped it around her, tucking and folding until she'd created a pretty impressive cover-up. Without so much as a backward glance, she went inside and slammed the door behind her.

***

At Ma'alaea Harbor I took the Kihei cutoff, turning *mauka*—inland—at the Mokulele Highway to the Haleakala Highway. I turned again at Haili'imaile Road. It was almost the reverse of the route I'd taken earlier. I floored the Geo, which amounted to getting it up to a neck snapping forty-five, through the Haili'imaile pineapple fields before taking the left at Pu'u Lane to my house.

When I pulled into the driveway, Hatch was sitting outside on the wide front porch. His head was down and his hands were busy with something in his lap. He didn't look up as my car crunched over the gravel and stopped in front of the house. If I was interrupting a private moment it didn't seem like he cared.

"Hey," I called out.

"Hey, yourself," he said still working away at his lap. "I gotta tell ya, this is the cutest pup of the bunch." He raised his cupped hands and showed me the same little brown and white patchwork pup I'd held down at Farrah's.

"Oh yeah, that little guy's my favorite too."

"I hate to start an argument, but I'm pretty sure it's female."

"Ha! No problem with me. Better to figure it out now before Farrah names it '*Paka*'."

"Which means…"

"Bob, in Hawaiian.

He placed the tiny pup back in his lap and tickled its belly. Lipton whined behind the screen door, no doubt fretting over being separated from her offspring.

"You're going to have to share the pups," I said. "Farrah's coming to stay with us for a few days. She's taking Kevin McGillvary's death pretty hard."

"Oh yeah. Steve said he'd talked to you. Why didn't you call me back?"

"I've been avoiding the phone. I figure dealing with Lisa Marie everyday gives me a pass to dodge my creditors for a while."

"Speaking of the blushing bride: how's she taking the news?"

"About Kevin? As far as I know, she hasn't heard. I was just down there, and when I tried to tell her, she threatened to have me thrown off the property. To tell the truth, I was kind of relieved. She's gotten pretty scary."

"But the wedding's called off, right?"

"I'd love to say, 'yes,' but it's not official. Seems Lisa Marie's still holding out hope Brad Sanders will magically appear tomorrow."

"So the wedding's on?"

"For now. I'm operating with very sketchy information. Marv Prescott wasn't around for me to talk to and Lisa Marie's firmly anchored in Denial Bay. It's not like I've got all the answers. I still can't figure out how Kevin managed to drown at Little Beach, in his skivvies."

"I may be able to help you fill in a few blanks."

"Great."

"You probably won't like it," he said.

"What's new? I haven't liked much of anything that's happened today."

"Well, as you know, McGillvary's death was thought to have been an accidental drowning. But now that they've done the autopsy, that's changed."

"He washed up at Little Beach, right?" I couldn't wrap my brain around how a nearly-naked body washing up on a beach didn't point to a drowning.

"They recovered him there, but the evidence points to something else."

"What evidence?"

"The autopsy showed there was no water in his lungs. But even more important, they found a severe brain injury due to blunt force trauma."

"Like he hit his head?"

"Exactly," he said. "Or, he got smashed in the head. They're bringing in Maui Sheriff's detectives."

"Do they have any idea where it happened: on land or in a boat?"

"Don't know yet."

"And he was in his underwear, right?"

"Just him and his Calvins."

I let the new information roll around my mind a little. "If they've contacted detectives it sounds like they think it might not have been an accident."

"That's what it sounds like. And guess who's on their short list for questioning?"

"Marv Prescott." I blurted it out, remembering that famous line from Casablanca: *Round up the usual suspects.*

"You're half right. It's a Prescott. But it's the grieving widow, Lisa Marie."

19

I left the house and went down to pick up Farrah at the Gadda-da-Vida. Farrah was ready and waiting—along with a Buick-sized duffle bag, five sacks of groceries and a thirty pound bag of designer dog food.

"There's still plenty of dog food from Monday." I said, fishing for clues as to how long she planned on staying. She'd packed enough kibble for a month, maybe two.

"Yeah, but since Lipton's nursing, I figured he might need more."

The ensuing silence took the place of once again pointing out to her how bizarre it sounded to say '*he*' when referring to a lactating Jack Russell.

"Any more news about Kevin's drowning?" she said once we'd made the turn off Baldwin. "I had to turn off the TV. Too depressing."

I hesitated. If I told her they were thinking he may have been murdered and I turned out to be wrong, I'd have upset her unnecessarily. If I didn't tell her, and she later learned I'd kept it from her, it could damage our friendship. I split the difference.

"At this point the cause of death seems to be a head injury, not drowning."

She shot me a puzzled look. "But he washed up on the beach."

"Right. But I guess the medical examiner also found a pretty serious head injury."

"Like he hit his head on a rock or something?"

"Could have."

"Or maybe someone hit him?"

I locked my eyes on the road ahead.

"If someone hit him in the head," she whispered, "it could have been on purpose. That would make it murder, don't you think?" She reached over and grabbed my arm.

"I don't know what to think, Farrah. But the ME has ruled out suicide or accidental drowning. At this point they're mostly just ruling things out."

"My poor Kev," she moaned. "I remember the last time he died, you know, in our former life together. I was strong then, and I'm going to be strong now."

We drove the rest of the way in silence. She broke down sobbing when Hatch opened the screen and Lipton scampered out onto the porch. Seeing Farrah, the dog flew down the stairs and into her owner's arms. It was left to me to drag her belongings up the porch stairs and then again up the stairs to my bedroom. My three bedroom, two-bath house had felt empty and even a bit lonely when I'd moved in a year ago. But loneliness was fast becoming a fond memory.

***

Later, I sat on the porch mulling over why the police might be interested in talking with Lisa Marie. Were they looking at her as a possible witness, a person of interest, or had they come up with something that would make her a suspect? Whatever it was, I was sure Marv was implicated somehow. Lisa Marie had no motive for killing Kevin: his Power of Attorney for Brad was a necessary component in the proxy wedding. And even though she'd been miffed over his budding interest in Farrah, it was hard to imagine her temper tantrum becoming anything close to murderous.

Steve pulled in the driveway, got out, and began his compulsory arrival ritual. He went to the trunk and pulled out a limp red dust wand, a bottle of Windex and a roll of paper towels. He mopped the dust wand across the car—roof, hood and sides—then sprayed the windshield with Windex. After a quick buff with a paper towel he leaned across the hood to check for streaks. Unlike my Geo, Steve's little black sedan would never know the indignity of having 'wash me' scrawled in the dirt on his back window.

Hatch came out and joined me on the porch. He plopped down in a tattered wicker chair and laid his crutch to the side. When he stretched out his leg—the one wearing the cast—he winced.

"Is it bothering you?" I said.

"Whining doesn't make it better, but between this thing aching and me not having a damn thing to do all day, I'm running a quart low on cheer."

Steve climbed the stairs and joined us. "Hey, you two."

"Hey, yourself," said Hatch. "You hear anything more on McGillvary?"

I shushed him, pointing upstairs where Farrah was settling in.

"No," Steve said in a stage whisper. "How about you?"

Hatch filled him in on the ME report.

"Whoa," said Steve. "Where'd you hear that? I didn't hear anything even close to that on the news."

"Seems we've got a mutual friend," said Hatch. "I called a detective I used to work with at Oahu PD who's now over here on Maui. When I told him I was staying here at Pali's he asked if you still lived here. I know about 'six degrees of separation' and all that, but it's driving me nuts trying to figure out how you might know Glen Wong. Over in Honolulu he wasn't exactly the most sociable guy."

He smiled at Steve, as if anticipating a long shaggy dog story about how Steve's windsurfing buddy's roommate's girlfriend's neighbor dated Wong back in high school.

"I've run into him a few times." Steve looked about as shut down as Chernobyl.

"Did you do a photo shoot for his family or something?" Hatch offered.

Steve shrugged and turned his gaze to his shiny Jetta.

I looked from Steve to Hatch and then back to Steve. "Okay, allow me connect the dots here," I said. "Glen Wong's gay, but no one's supposed to know he's gay because he's a cop. He goes to the same bars Steve goes to but nothing short of water-boarding will get anyone to out him without his permission. How am I doing so far?"

"You didn't hear it from me," said Steve.

"And I didn't ask," said Hatch.

No one established eye contact as we all stared into the middle distance for a few beats.

"Huh, so Wong's gay," Hatch finally said. He shook his head, a slight grin playing across his face.

"Just so we're clear," said Steve, "Glen's the guy who took on finding you a place to stay when you were about to get released from the hospital. He asked around, and got me to convince Pali to take you in. Without him you'd probably be recovering in a nursing home right now." He locked eyes on Hatch.

Hatch's grin faded. "Great guy. Real solid. We go way back. In fact, I was up for promotion to homicide when I left. So, they gave it to Wong instead. Kind of pissed me off at the time, but we've kept in touch; especially since we both ended up here on Maui. Word is, they're looking at him to head up homicide at Honolulu PD when the guy over there retires."

"Small world," said Steve.

"You know it," said Hatch. "Anyway, Wong's been assigned lead detective on the McGillvary investigation." He nodded toward at me. "And I'll bet since you've spent time with Lisa Marie, he'll be wanting to talk to you, too."

Steve nodded. "Yeah Pali, no way you'll avoid getting dragged into this. Not only 'cuz you're the only local who knows Lisa Marie, but also because you're best friends with the victim's latest hook-up. "

Hatch nodded in agreement.

Hatch and Steve's casual attitude toward Kevin's death was starting to wear thin with me. This wasn't some ripped from the headlines whodunit on TV or the daily crime news out of Honolulu. This was possibly a brutal murder right here on Maui: of my client; a guy who'd stuck around to help out his friend's grieving fiancée. I got up and went inside.

Hatch and Steve followed, seemingly oblivious to my foul mood.

"Pali, lighten up," said Steve. "It isn't personal."

"Are you crazy?" I said. "It's about as personal as it gets. Not only was Kevin a decent enough guy, he was a huge help to me in handling Lisa Marie and moving the wedding forward. Throw in that my best friend had a thing for him, and he'd stepped up to buy our building and save our businesses, and I'd say it's *damn* personal. If the police think Lisa Marie had something to do with it, which I highly doubt, then that piles on another layer of personal for me."

Steve leaned over to take my hand, but I pulled it away. "Okay, okay," he said. "I'm sorry. It's just that, well, this whole thing's pretty wild if you think about it. You've got the nutty diva daughter of a garbage tycoon wanting a bizarre proxy marriage to a missing millionaire geek. Now the stand-in guy's body floats up on the most notorious nude beach in all of Maui. It's like that Clue game. You know, Colonel Mustard in the conservatory with the candlestick? C'mon, Pali, you gotta admit: it's crazy."

I jumped up and went upstairs to check on Farrah. As much as I hated to concede even a single inch of my moral high ground, Steve had a point. Unlike O'ahu, where crime takes up the bulk of the nightly news, violent crime is rare on the neighbor islands. If I hadn't been so invested in this weird cast of characters, I'd have agreed the whole sorry situation was amusing as hell.

***

It was nearly two-thirty, a half-hour until the wedding rehearsal, when I made my way down to Olu'olu for the third time that day. I'd convinced myself the trip was worth it even if only to talk some sense into Lisa Marie and make one last stab at getting a check out of Marv. I'd accepted I'd be handing my business over to Tank Sherman on Friday, but I was determined to leave with my debts paid and my reputation intact.

The gate was open when I pulled in. A white Ford sedan with black rims and a heavy-duty bumper was parked at an angle, smack in the middle of the circular driveway. It blocked not only the entry to the front door, but also the exit from the driveway. I pulled in behind it and parked. As I passed by, I peeked into the car windows. I'd never seen the interior of a cop car. The upholstery on the front seat was nearly as broken down as my Geo. There was a laptop-style computer screen mounted to the dash and a sweating cup from a fast-food joint wedged in the console. But the windows were clean and the floorboards looked recently vacuumed.

I speed-walked to the door and pressed the bell. The *Aloha ʻOe* door chime brought none other than Marv himself, highball glass in hand.

"It's you again. What do you want now?" His snarl was slurred, even though cocktail hour was still two hours away.

"I came to assist Lisa Marie in getting through this horrible time."

"Now you're claiming legal expertise? You know, so far I haven't been exactly dazzled by your matrimonial skills." He twisted his mouth into a grimace he probably thought passed for a smile.

I said nothing. I'd dealt with guys like Marv before. You know, the kind who thinks saying 'just kidding' excuses a truck load of crappy behavior.

"She's talking to the cops," he said. He didn't invite me in.

I didn't move, betting Marv didn't have the balls to shut the door in my face.

"You coming in, or are you going to stand out there all day letting flies in my house?"

"*Mahalo*," I said. I toyed with the image of stomping on his foot, but it was trumped by the image of me tucking a signed check into my purse.

"They're in the family room, so let's go to my office." He started to lead the way, then stopped. "I'm going to freshen up this drink. You want something?"

"Water would be nice."

"How 'bout I nudge it with a nip of scotch?"

"No thanks, I'm driving." I didn't want to come off too high and mighty before hitting him up. "Maybe another time."

"I'd have the maid show you down to my office, but if I recall, you already know the way," he said. "And this time, sweetheart, do me a favor…" He waited for me to make eye contact. "Don't go in there until I get back. I guess your mama didn't teach you it's not polite to snoop. Maybe good manners aren't a priority out here in the middle of nowhere." He shot me an oily smile and disappeared down the far hallway.

I waited in the foyer. I couldn't care less about Marv's opinion of my manners. I had two things I needed to accomplish: cancel my contract and pick up a check. Then hopefully I'd never cross paths with the Prescotts again.

After Marv had been gone a minute or two, I picked up voices coming from the sunroom. I tiptoed to the near side of the French doors and listened.

"...back here." It sounded like Lisa Marie.

"...cooperate...take you in." A deep male voice; probably a cop.

"My God, you're a piece of work," Marv bellowed as he suddenly came up behind me. "This morning you were snooping around my office, and now you're eavesdropping on my little girl."

He thrust a crystal tumbler of water into my hand and jerked his head in the direction of his office. I followed him. The glass was heavy for its size, deeply cut in an intricate pattern that refracted sunlight from the small window high on the wall. Marv went behind his desk and took a long pull on his drink before plopping down in the leather swivel chair.

I sipped my water, waiting for him to invite me to sit. As Marv had previously pointed out, we're pretty casual in the islands, but working in the bridal industry had required me to bone up on the finer points of social protocol. I can spot a lone demitasse spoon in a pile of teaspoons from five feet away and I always wait for my host to offer me a seat before sitting.

"My daughter may be awhile, so you might as well take a load off," he finally said, gesturing to the guest chairs in front of the desk.

This time I chose the intricately carved chair. It wasn't as comfortable as the buttery leather chair I'd sat in earlier but its hard seat and stiff armrests encouraged me to sit up straight, which I thought was the best negotiating posture.

"You know how much I paid for that chair you're sitting in?" he said.

"No idea."

"Nothing, nada, zilch. It's a priceless antique, but it was given to me as a gift. I got friends all over the world, Ms. Moon. They show their appreciation in remarkable ways. Ming Dynasty, that chair. You have any idea when that was?"

"The Ming Dynasty began in the fourteenth century, in China."

"Well, good for you. Anyway, it's a very old chair. And these carvings here..." He pointed to the tusk-like statues of the Asian couple in the glass display case. "What do you think those are?"

I shook my head. No doubt he'd blasted some defense-less animal on a hunting trip and had taken its tusks as souvenirs.

"They're human femur bones. Dug up from the killing fields of Cambodia and then carved. Rather lovely, wouldn't you say?"

My breath stalled in my lungs. I'd experienced intimidation before; I'd even practiced it a few times at tournaments. I willed my expression to remain neutral. The bad feng shui brought to this house by displaying desecrated human remains didn't require comment.

"Why are the police here?" I finally said.

"Unlike yourself, Ms. Moon, I don't stick my nose in other people's business."

"They've been here a while."

He shot me a cranky look and thrummed his fingers on the desk.

"I assume they want to discuss Lisa Marie's acquaintance with Kevin McGillvary. I don't know why it's going on so long, though. It's damn obvious she's in no condition to be much help to them ." He clenched and unclenched his fists.

"I heard you were an investor in Brad Sander's company," I said. "What kind of work does DigiSystems do?" I wasn't really interested in corporate chit chat, but I thought it might calm him down and put me in a better position to make my case.

"Who said I'd invested in that company?" He fumbled in a desk drawer and brought out a soapstone coaster for his drink. He didn't offer me one.

"Lisa Marie told me. She said you were an angel investor when Brad and Kevin first started the company."

"That's somewhat correct. I underwrite start-ups every now and then, but I don't get involved. My role is to provide seed capital to companies I like; to get them off the ground, so to speak." He shot me a snake oil smile that didn't extend to his eyes. "But I'm not one to pour over business plans. I'm sure even a person of your meager resources can appreciate that a person such as myself wouldn't have the time—or the interest—in meddling in the day-to-day affairs of a little outfit like DigiSystems."

"I'm glad you brought up my financial situation, Marv. As you said, I'm not well-off. And, since we're just sitting here waiting, I'd really appreciate it if you'd take a minute to write me that check I need to pay my vendors."

"Ms. Moon, as I told you earlier, I didn't become wealthy bailing out every sad sack who came to me with a tale of poor cash management skills. This is the last time I'll say it: You'll get paid *after* my daughter's wedding. Not before."

"Marv, let's cut the crap. You and I both know there's not going to be a wedding. With both Brad and Kevin dead, even a proxy wedding is out of the question. I say we cancel everything right now and cut our losses."

"That might be what's best for you, but it's hardly what's best for my daughter. I'm willing to forego today's rehearsal. After all, what is there to practice? Five minutes of bullshit followed by choking down a hunk of stale cake. But tomorrow's wedding is on. My daughter's sanity is at stake. Until she gets jilted at the altar she'll never believe that Sanders isn't coming back."

"Seems a rather 'tough love' way to handle it."

"You got a better idea? If we cancel now, I'll never hear the end of it."

I cringed at the image: Lisa Marie in her fitted silk gown, the hired bridesmaids lined up and smiling, and the groom's side glaringly empty. "But promise me you'll have the check ready tomorrow. I've held up my side, but it's not part of the service to stick around for the tantrum."

"Fine," said Marv. "Now, if you'll excuse me, I've got to tell 'Maui's finest' they need to get the hell out of my house. You're free to observe, since you seem to enjoy that kind of thing."

Marv burst through the sunroom doors like he was conducting a raid. "Time to clear out, Mr. Wong." As Marv strode forward, Lisa Marie's hands flew to her throat. She ducked her head.

The two police detectives remained seated on the yellow sofa for a few beats while Marv stomped toward them.

Then one of the cops stood and calmly put up his hand in a halt gesture.

"It's *Detective* Wong, sir. And we can question your daughter here, or we can take her down to the station. Your call."

"Daddy..." whined Lisa Marie. She'd gotten dressed since I last saw her, but not by much. Merely a thin thigh-length tee-shirt dress and brown espadrilles. With her twig-thin body and stark bald head she looked like Yoda's granddaughter.

Marv backed out of the room at such a quick clip he nearly bowled me over. He slammed the French doors and stomped back down the hall.

"You ever hear of a country-western song called, *The Gambler*, Ms. Moon?"

"I'm not much of a country-western fan."

"Too bad; you can learn a lot from the lyrics. *The Gambler* talks about knowing when to hold 'em and when to fold 'em. The song's talking about a card game, but it's the same with everything. What I just did was let the cops think they won. I didn't order them off my property or demand to have my lawyer present, even though I know my rights. Nope, I let those bastards think it's just fine and dandy with me that they hassle my baby girl right under my nose in my own home."

I waited.

"But you know what, Ms. Moon? Marv Prescott didn't get to where he is by being a frickin' pussy. You're not offended by me saying 'pussy' are you, Ms. Moon? Where I come from, it's another word for 'loser'."

Again, I didn't respond.

He looked down the hall toward the sunroom. "You know, those cops in there should have done their homework. They should have asked around. I'm sure there are more than a few local theories about what happened to the sorry son-of-a-bitch who tried to stop me from building this house."

I couldn't help it: my eyes widened.

"Think about it, sweetheart. I got garbage scows leaving these islands every week of the year. Nobody knows what's on 'em and nobody much cares where it all ends up."

I told him I needed to get going and turned to leave. He stopped me with a hand on my shoulder. "One thing before you go, Ms. Moon. My sources tell me you're quite popular around here. I'd like you to do your friends a favor and give them a message: Nobody who plans to see their next birthday screws with Marv Prescott. Nobody."

20

I hopped in the Geo and bolted for the highway. It was almost three-thirty. The caterers were probably hard at work prepping for the seven o'clock rehearsal dinner.

Every day I'd sunk deeper in debt. Even after cashing the check from Todd Barker, which had come two days earlier, I still owed more than the entire five grand Tank Sherman would be paying me on Friday. Once my business and house were gone, all I'd have left would be my friends and colleagues. Marv had agreed to cancel the rehearsal, but without also calling off the wedding, the bills would keep mounting. I made a decision.

My first call was to Catering by Frank, also known as Paleke's Good Grinds.

"I'm afraid tonight's rehearsal dinner at Olu'olu has been called off," I said. "And the wedding dinner tomorrow, too. I'm really sorry to call on such short notice."

"No dinners?" Frank's calm response was a welcome departure from the freaking out I'd expected.

"No, *e kala mai*, Frank. I'm so, so sorry. Did you hear about that body washing up at Little Beach this morning? Well, that man was supposed to be the groom. The family's in mourning." I opted for the TV Guide version: short and sweet.

"Oh my, that's real *kaumaha* for that poor girl and her people. But they'll still need food, right? Gotta have something folks who come by the house. Do you want I should bring down some food for them?"

"*Mahalo*, but they're from the mainland: no family or friends here. And they're in total shock. I'm afraid your beautiful food would go to waste."

"No worries. I'll just invite our neighbors instead. My turn to have everybody to dinner. People up this way will go *pupule* when they see I'm laying out lobster and filet mignon."

"*Mahalo* for being so understanding. And do you mind sending me your bill? I'd pick it up but I have lots of people to get in touch with in the next few hours."

"Don't worry about no bill, Pali. You're a good customer. Me and my wife can handle the food costs. *Ho'omana'o* you call us to cater for you next time, okay?" He'd asked me to remember him next time. How could I forget his generosity?

I gushed my thanks and went down my list, cancelling everything and everyone associated with the rehearsal. Then I started pulling the plug on the fancy wedding. I scuttled everything except the guy I'd hired to take Farrah's place as the minister and the two bridesmaids, who'd also agreed to function as witnesses. No need to have flowers, photos and cake at a jilting. And if by some miracle Brad Sanders made an appearance, I was counting on Lisa Marie's I-told-you-so smugness to eclipse the simplicity of the event.

With each call, my suppliers offered to either forgo billing me altogether or they requested only a fraction of the agreed-upon cost. By the time I hit the bottom of the list, I was so choked up my voice had collapsed to a croaky whisper.

I locked up and drove home.

I found Farrah upstairs, sprawled across the open sleeper sofa with Lipton huddled tight alongside. The puppy box graced the foot of the bed. I had to step over two Snapple bottles and a crushed Doritos bag to get inside. The room smelled like corn chips and dog musk, a bad combination for even the calmest of stomachs, and pure hell on my stressed one.

"Do you want to talk?" I asked.

"I guess. I'm trying to pretend it's all a bad dream, but it isn't working."

"Yeah, I'm afraid it's real."

"On Monday night Kevin told me something."

"What'd he say?"

"He said Marv had threatened him and he couldn't wait to be done with DigiSystems so he wouldn't have to kowtow to Marv anymore."

"What was Marv's threat?"

"I didn't ask. I didn't want to seem snoopy, and besides, what did I care? You said yourself Marv's a total bull shitter. I figured he was just throwing around more *kukae*."

"Well, it looks like maybe this time it was more than *kukae*." I regretted it as soon as I'd said it.

"But it makes no sense for Marv to hurt Kevin. Especially before the wedding. They needed him." Farrah began to sob. "*I* needed him."

I sat down on the creaking sofa bed and took her hands in mine. A half-dozen trite expressions of sympathy came to mind, but thankfully I stifled the urge to utter any of them.

"I've been thinking about something else, too" she said. "It's been bothering me all day."

"What?"

"I'm worried it may be my fault Kevin got killed." Rough hiccups now punctuated the sobbing.

"That's ridiculous. Why would you say that?"

"Because I blabbed to Noni about Kevin buying the building." Farrah swiped tears from her cheeks. "She called to remind me about Tank coming in on Friday and I said 'don't bother.' I told her someone else was offering more money for the building and she could tell Tank to shove it."

"Did you tell her Kevin's name?"

"No, I just said it was some rich guy from Seattle."

We stared at each other in silence. Tank could've found out who'd put in another offer on the building by making three phone calls, tops.

"I don't know. Tank's a fat jerk, but he's no killer." I said.

"Seems maybe he is." She rubbed her eyes and dragged Lipton into her lap.

I wondered if I should call the police, but then thought better of it. Going to the police with anything on Marv or Tank would not only be a waste of time, but risky. Neither of those two would kill someone, they'd hire it done. And if the police contacted them, both Marv and Tank would quickly figure out who'd ratted them out. I needed more information before going all Citizen Tipster and throwing myself and my best friend under the bus.

"You know the worst part?" she continued. "I have a really bad feeling the police won't be able to figure it out. They'll just give up, like they did with Brad."

***

Steve didn't come home for dinner, but he called and invited Hatch to go bar-hopping with him later. He even offered to take him to a couple of straight bars after hitting his favorite haunts. With the two of them gone, it fell to me to keep an eye on Farrah and make sure she didn't start eyeing the kitchen knives. She'd holed up with Lipton and the pups upstairs, so my plan was to stay downstairs until sleep was my only option. Not only was it tight quarters up there, but the dog odor was suffocating. I fixed myself some popcorn and settled into Hatch's old spot on the sofa, a book propped in my lap. A few hours of peace and quiet seemed like a great idea, but within ten minutes I found myself pacing the carpet. I flipped through the channels, but there was nothing on TV. Never before had I been so bored on the night before a wedding: no bridal attendant gifts to wrap; no champagne glasses to inspect; no reception seating chart to fuss over. By ten o'clock the popcorn was down to the hulls, I'd read the last chapter of my book, and I'd put a serious dent in the battery life of the remote.

I called Steve. I rarely went out at night with him, since we both needed our personal space after living and working together day-in and day-out. But with Hatch added to the mix I was willing to give it a shot.

"You at the B and C?" I said. The Ball and Chain was mostly a gay bar, but since it was in Kihei—budget traveler central—it welcomed lots of straight singles and honey-mooning couples as well.

"Shh. Can't talk now. I'll call you back in a few minutes." The line went dead before I could ask what was going on.

I put the phone down feeling more than a little put out. It wasn't like I was going to horn in and wreck his evening. I'm considerate. I know when a trip to the ladies' room is in order. Besides, he had Hatch with him. Were they so determined to keep it a 'guys only' night that Steve thought it was okay to hang up on me?

By the time the phone rang, I'd worked myself into a royal snit.

"Hey," I said, not even waiting for his '*hello*.'"If I'm cramping your style, just say so. It's not like I couldn't find somebody else to hang out with."

"No, listen," he said." We're not at the B & C. Some of Hatch's buddies asked him to come by Cisco's." Cisco's is a celebrated Pa'ia watering hole made famous when a Maui tourist book mentioned Bruce Springsteen sometimes drops by when he's in town.

"Hatch's inside, but I saw Glen with a guy in the parking lot so I stayed out here to see what was going on."

"Are you talking about Glen Wong? The police detective?" I looked up the staircase, aware Farrah might have overheard me. The house was so quiet I could hear the trade wind rustling the palms in the yard.

"Yeah. He met up with some scrungy-looking dude. They got in Glen's car."

"Are they still there?"

"Yeah."

"You think it's official business or has he lowered his dating standards?"

"He's driving a plain vanilla so it's probably police business. I can't imagine him risking a cheap trick in a cop car." His voice brightened, "How's Farrah doing?"

"Not a peep."

"Why don't you come on down? I'll stick around until you get here. Everybody's talking about the murder. I'll bet someone would buy you a beer to hear you dish on Lisa Marie."

I felt a twinge of guilt for even considering such a proposition, but had to admit I wouldn't mind fifteen minutes of fame at Cisco's. And, after the day I'd had, I deserved a free beer.

Driving to the bar my adrenaline kicked in. It reminded me of my air marshal days when I'd snap my gun in the holster and wonder if this was going to be the flight where I'd get to use it. Never happened. My usual route was eleven and a half hours Honolulu to Taipei, then another three hours to Tokyo. The next morning I'd be back onboard headed for Honolulu. After ten months I never encountered anything more criminal than an airline meal. When I left the job I willingly gave up the gun and turned my focus to earning my black belt. I'd pit physical and mental skills over nickel-plated hardware any day.

I got to Cisco's by ten-thirty and couldn't find a place to park. It was a weekday night, but with the weather improving and the tourists returning, our little island was beginning to feel crowded again. I parked a block away.

I zigzagged through the back lot, slipping between tightly parked cars and dodging clusters of noisy party-hardies until I spotted a white four-door Ford: the kind the police refer to as "unmarked." Even with the armada of stripped-down rental cars cruising Maui, nothing shouts *cop* louder than a white bare bones Crown Vic with ugly black rims. I saw two men inside, but in the dark it was impossible to make out faces.

I punched the speed dial for Steve's cell number. It started to ring when I saw him trotting my way. I clicked off.

"Something's going down," he hissed as he came up beside me. He tipped his head in the direction of the cop car. He looked about as excited as a kid about to hop up on Santa's knee. "A guy I met inside said he thinks Glen's talking to a snitch."

"A *snitch*? Isn't that a Three Stooges word?"

He ignored my sarcasm. "The guy said it's a dude from Ma'alaea Harbor who called in on the crime hotline."

"How would a guy at Cisco's know who Wong was talking to?"

"How does anyone know stuff? People talk."

"You think this snitch knows something about what happened to Kevin?"

"Could be. I'm hoping Glen will fill me in later."

"Why would he do that, Steve? He's a cop. He's not some *brudda* who owes you a plate lunch."

"You forget, we are *bruddas*. And he knows I'm good with secrets."

Steve good with secrets? I was glad it was dark so he couldn't see the look on my face.

"Is Hatch still inside?" I said.

"Last I looked," he said. "A bunch of his fire station guys are here. They're fawning over him like he's the great American hero for getting run over."

"Yeah, what's with that? The guy's always got to be the center of attention."

"Well, I wouldn't go that far. He's making the most of a bad situation, that's all. And what's the deal with you two? I was hoping you might hit it off, but you take shots at him every chance you get."

"I'm not taking shots. I'm just not lining up to join the fan club."

"You might have to re-think that. He's in the fireman calendar for next year—August, I think. When that thing comes out, there'll be women making fake 9-1-1 calls just to get a look at him, up close and personal."

Two car doors slammed and we both looked over at the cop car. Wong was talking to a guy who'd climbed out of the passenger side. The guy was meth-addict skinny, with shaggy hair. When he moved off into the dark I detected a slight limp.

Wong started toward us. When he got within twenty feet, he stopped and motioned Steve over. For a second, I considered acting dumb and going with Steve, but I let it go. Wong didn't know me and, secret keeper or not, I knew I'd get the whole story from Steve later anyway.

I walked to the front door of Cisco's and flashed a smile at the bouncer collecting the cover charge.

"Hey, Pako, remember me? Pali Moon?" I'd met the guy at one of Sifu Doug's infamous blow-out luaus. I'd made a point of remembering Pako's name when I heard he worked the door at Cisco's. No use paying good money if you can play the *brudda* card.

"Oh, yeah," he yelled over the din of the over-amped band, rowdy crowd, and waitresses screaming drink orders at the bar. "You're that kick-ass lady from down at Doug's. You still doing the hook-up thing?"

Okay, it was good he remembered me; not so good that anyone overhearing him probably thought I was a madam at a dominatrix brothel.

"Yep, I'm still doing weddings." I leaned in close to make myself heard. "Say, I'm looking for someone. A fireman named Hatch Decker. He's on crutches—broken leg."

Pako nodded, his massive neck pumping like a piston. "Yeah, I know who you mean. Came in with some guys but he left about ten minutes ago with a fine-lookin' redhead." He paused for a beat. "Sorry."

"A red-haired *woman*?" I said.

"Well, duh. Weren't no Irish setter." In the hand-stamp black light his grin glowed white hot.

21

Valentine's Day dawned sunny with calm winds: perfect weather for a beach wedding. I'd slept on the downstairs sofa in lieu of joining the stinky huddle upstairs. My back was killing me, which seemed only right since this was the day I'd been dreading for more than a week.

I gimped into the kitchen to put on the coffee. The smell of hot water seeping through Kona coffee beans never failed to lure Steve out of bed, and as the pot filled, I heard his feet hit the floor upstairs. I was eager to hear what he'd learned from Glen Wong. Last night I'd scuttled home after hearing about Hatch taking off with the redhead. As much as I wanted a free beer, I'd lost the urge to gossip. When I got home, I stretched out in the living room and fell so dead asleep I didn't even wake up when the guys came in.

Steve came through the swinging door. The coffee maker hissed and burbled as I took four coffee cups from the cupboard.

"Thanks for putting on the joe," he said. "Oh, and Happy Valentine's Day."

"Yeah, you too. So, what'd you hear last night?"

"Glen's not giving out much," he said. "Fill me in on what you already know."

"Okay, I know Kevin died from a blow to the head, not from drowning. I know Wong and another cop went to

Olu'olu and questioned Lisa Marie. I know Kevin's the second guy from DigiSystems to meet an untimely end in Maui in the past couple of weeks. And, I know Farrah told Noni Konomanu that Kevin was buying the Gadda-da-Vida building out from under Tank Sherman—"

"Whoa," he said. "That's news to me." He poured me a cup of black coffee and then poured one for himself.

"She told me yesterday. I don't think the cops have made a connection between Tank and Kevin, but don't count on me to say anything. I figure if Tank's willing to whack someone over a failed real estate deal, there's no way I'm giving him a reason to point his fat finger at me."

"Well, don't worry about it. Seems the cops are pretty much focused on Lisa Marie anyway."

"Why is that? I can't for the life of me figure out why they think she killed him. Don't they know he was helping her pull off her fake wedding?"

"I said that, but Glen said the snitch works at the Ma'alaea Harbor Marina and he's pretty sure he saw Lisa Marie and Kevin having an argument out there the night of the murder."

"So?"

"Glen thinks maybe Kevin was trying to back out and Lisa Marie didn't take kindly to getting dumped twice."

"Brad didn't dump her. He *died*."

"Whatever. It still gives the cops a motive. They think she flipped out and killed him."

I held up my hand and listened for sounds of Farrah. I didn't want her to overhear Steve and me idly discussing her lover's murder.

I lowered my voice. "But Kevin was twice Lisa Marie's size."

"He was bashed in the head, remember? An oar, a fish hook, or even a good-sized rock could pretty much even the odds. And you said yourself that Lisa Marie can get pretty nasty when you cross her."

"Yeah, but she's a trash talker, not a killer. Now, Marv on the other hand..." I shuddered.

"Well, Glen didn't tell me much more than we already know, but he did say if what the Ma'alaea guy has is solid, it probably won't take them long to pull together a case against Lisa Marie. He said their goal is to solve a murder within forty-eight hours. After that, it gets tougher."

"Not much time," I said.

"Nope. So, by Saturday we should have a good idea what happened."

I'd heard enough murder talk. "Is Hatch still sleeping?"

"I guess. His buddies at Cisco's told me he found a ride home. I figured he left with you."

"No, I never even saw him." I didn't mention the redhead. I needed another cup of coffee before listening to Steve chide me about losing out to the competition.

"You want me to see if he's up?" he said.

"Yeah, if you don't mind."

He left and I heard him knock on Hatch's door. There was a pause, another knock, and then a squeaky hinge.

He came back into the kitchen. "Bed's made," he said, "and I highly doubt he's gone out for a run." His face wore an 'I told you so' smirk I found really annoying.

Time to take my lumps and bring up the redhead.

"The bouncer at Cisco's said he left with a woman right before I got there," I said.

"Oh." Steve seemed to mull over what to say next. "Maybe his leg was hurting him."

He got up and washed out his coffee cup. "I gotta go," he said. "That high school girl you promised I'd make look like Selma Hayek is coming in for her re-do's this morning."

"Oh, wow, I'd forgotten all about that." I cringed. Another load of work I'd foisted on a friend thanks to Lisa Marie's fake wedding. "Sorry."

"Don't sweat it. You owe me. I just hope she's not some 'bow wow' who hated her first pictures because she thinks 'Nikon' is Japanese for 'extreme makeover'."

"Her mom's nice looking," I said. Under different circumstances, I'd have taken him to task for the 'bow wow' remark. But, as he'd pointed out, I owed him—along with a half-dozen other people I was worried about paying.

"Well, let's hope nature trumps nurture and she's not into lip piercings or weird facial tattoos," he said. "I'll let you know how it goes."

The swinging door flapped once and then settled shut. For a house bursting at the seams, it sure was quiet.

I went upstairs to see if I could talk Farrah into getting up. When I opened the door, I found her already dressed in a red and yellow *mu'u mu'u*. She'd pushed the fold-out bed back into the sofa and was sitting at one end with a gossip magazine in her lap. The room smelled doggy, but either I was getting used to it or the breeze from the half-open window had toned it down a bit.

"Happy Valentine's Day," she whispered, as if offering condolences.

"Yeah, back at ya. You feel like going down to the store today?"

"I've got to. Last night Beatrice said she'd open the store for me, but then this morning when the flower delivery came she called all freaked out. Says there's no way she can handle all those orders by herself."

"You need some help?"

"That'd be great, especially around lunchtime. You mind driving me down there? I'll bet Bea's blood pressure's already in the red zone."

"No problem. Just let me take a shower. I'll help you for a while and then I need to start packing up my shop."

"Don't you think it'll be at least a month before Tank can actually buy the building and kick us out?" she said.

"Yeah. But in the meantime, I'm closing the shop. I'm not going to drum up new business for 'Let's Get Maui'd' and then shuffle off brides to Noni and Tank."

"I wish I could just close down, but the store's got to stay open. People depend on it."

"And working might help you take your mind off things. How are you doing?"

"I'm actually doing pretty good, considering," she said. "It's like when my folks died. At first I just wanted to die too, but I kept breathing in and out. You know: taking it one day at a time and all that. And now I've got Lipton and his pups. They're all counting on me."

I nodded, because I knew all about handling hurt by just breathing in and out. It sucks to lose your parents: especially when you're a kid. I've never met a child orphan who wasn't convinced somehow it was their fault.

"Well, if misery loves company, it looks like at least we'll both be spending Valentine's Day alone," I said.

"What about Hatch? I thought he'd come through for you."

"Hardly. He picked up some woman at Cisco's last night. In fact, he's still not home."

"The guy scored with his leg in a cast?" She smiled. "I'd love to be a fly on *that* wall."

"I wouldn't." I said.

"Sorry, I didn't mean it like that." She frowned and I felt bad I'd snatched away her smile.

I took a quick shower and was still dripping wet when the phone rang. It was Steve.

"Just got a call from Mitch, the bartender at the B and C," he said. "Apparently the snitch wasn't an eye witness after all."

No surprise there. The guy looked like a derelict sniffing around for some reward money.

"It's even better. The dude's got a surveillance tape of the marina, and on it, Lisa Marie's pitching a fit at Kevin."

"How does Mitch know this?"

"You kidding? Bartenders know everything."

"What was she saying? And did they go out in a boat or just walk around the dock?"

"Don't know. Mitch said the camera pans a one-eighty of the entire dock every couple of minutes. They're only on the tape for a really short time and there's no sound, just picture."

"Huh."

"Oh, but here's something else: Mitch said the snitch called Lisa Marie 'that little blond gal.' So, she had her hair when they were at Ma'alaea. The shave job must've come later."

I chewed on that for a few seconds.

"Gotta go," he said. "My high school do-over just pulled up. She's getting out...she's coming this way...and the verdict is..."

I didn't want to hear his verdict. In Steve's world, a perfect ten would be Victoria Beckham with a penis.

"She's pretty cute," he said. "This won't be that tough. Let's talk later."

I drove to Farrah's store and spent the morning doling out Valentine's Day flowers. By one o'clock the stream of sweethearts had dwindled to a final few procrastinators. We'd sold off Lisa Marie's wedding flowers and were completely out of roses, orchids, and even the prehistoric-looking protea flowers Farrah had special ordered for

Valentine's. Nothing short of a magic trick was going to make flowers appear for the eleventh-hour Romeos who'd be racing in on their way home from work.

At one-thirty I went next door to my shop.

As I'd expected, my message light was blinking. I wasn't up for another catastrophe, but I was curious, especially about Hatch's whereabouts.

You have three messages, said the disembodied voice.

The first was a reminder from my dentist about a cleaning appointment. The message ended with a request to call if I'd be unable to keep the appointment. I blew out a quick breath. I'd have no problem *keeping* the appointment, but *paying* for it was another story. I jotted down the dentist's number. I'd reschedule when I got a job with benefits.

Call received Wednesday, seven twelve p.m., said the voice. As the second message began, I recognized the distinctly brusque voice of Todd Barker, DigiSystems' Chief Financial Officer.

"What the hell's going on over there?" he snarled. "First Brad and now Kevin? Call me." He left various numbers, including office, cell, and home.

I called his cell, and when he didn't answer, I left a message saying I was returning his call. I wasn't about to track him down on the other numbers. I figured my obligation ended with one call.

The third message was from Sifu Doug, announcing Palace of Pain had been cleared by the health department and was open for business. It was good to hear at least someone's life had returned to normal. As I listened to his voice, I remembered that one of Doug's many brothers managed a big *luau* in Lahaina. I'd have a good shot at a job if I came armed with a reference.

The weather was gorgeous so I walked the half-mile down to PoP. Doug's car was parked out back. As much as I loathed groveling for a job that would pretty much involve non-stop groveling, I hated the idea of shopping with food stamps more.

"You're a trooper," Doug said. "I just called a half hour ago, and here you are, rarin' to go."

"Well, not exactly rarin'," I said. "I need to talk to you about something."

"Is it about that bald girl who knifed her boyfriend? Weren't you doing her wedding to another guy, that dude that got thrown overboard?"

Leave it to the island grapevine to scramble the facts.

"Where'd you hear all that?"

"Well, last night this girl's dad calls my brother, James. You know, the lawyer I told you about? Anyhow, he says his daughter was supposed to get married but her fiancé ended up shark bait. I remembered you told me how you were doing her wedding when we scrubbed down this place. He said now the police are all up in her face about killing the new boyfriend."

I nodded and he went on. "Now her dad wants my brother to be her lawyer. James told me she's bald-headed, and he's thinking it's 'cuz she's so stressed her hair is falling out. That happened to my brother when he went away to school on the mainland. He got all stressed, and his hair just fell out."

"Are you saying the police think she killed *both* guys? But the Coast Guard called the first guy's disappearance an accident."

"Yeah, well now the cops are thinking different. James said they're gonna arrest her any time now."

I let this new information roll around for a minute and find a place to settle. "How come you know all this, Sifu? Isn't lawyer-client stuff supposed to be confidential?"

"C'mon, Pali. He's my *brudda*. We talk."

In Doug's hard-core Hawaiian clan, lawyer-client privilege probably didn't hold much sway when it came to sharing a juicy tale with the family.

"So, Lisa Marie hasn't been arrested?"

"Not as far as I know. But I hear they're leaning tough on her. James told her like a million times to not say nothin' to nobody. He told her no matter what, keep her mouth shut."

Unlike some people.

"Well, *mahalo* for telling me, but I didn't come to talk about that," I said. "I need to ask about your other brother: the one who manages the No Ka Oi Luau."

"You mean my baby brother, Tommy."

"Yeah. You think he'll give me a job?"

"Why you think you need a job? You doing your wedding thing."

"Not anymore. Your brother James's new client was the only wedding I had this month. Thanks to the rain, I'm pretty much out of money. Tank Sherman's buying out my business, but he's not giving me much."

"Tank? Like anyone would want that weird dude fixing their wedding."

"He's buying the Gadda-da-Vida store, too."

"No lie? He's gonna run the store? Big dude like that'll eat up all the profits."

I figured my news about Tank had evened us up on the gossip score.

"So, can you help me get a job at Tommy's?"

"What you want to do there?"

"Serving. Waitress, hostess, whatever."

"You got a coconut bra and a grass skirt?"

I slumped my shoulders and nodded.

"Okay, no worries. I'll give him a call. You smart you'll wear somethin' sexy to the interview. Oh, and don't tell him about your black belt. He might think you wanna bounce."

Truth was, I'd rather work as a bouncer. But without tips, there'd be no way I could make ends meet.

"*Mahalo*, Sifu."

"No worries, Pali. Oh, and if I hear more from James about your girl, I'll let you know."

I looked longingly into the practice room. Working out was my go-to antidote to nervous tension, and every hour I'd been getting more concerned about Hatch's whereabouts.

First Brad, then Kevin, and now Hatch. Everybody knows bad luck always comes in threes.

22

My cell phone rang as I jogged up Baldwin. I'd promised Farrah we'd leave for home by two and it was already a quarter after. She'd probably had enough of faking a smile and delivering Happy Valentine's greetings while still reeling from the shock of Kevin's death.

"Aloha," I sang into my phone, trying to hide the huffing and puffing.

"Is this Pali Moon?" The caller's voice was a low growl interspersed with static.

"Yes, this is Pali." I slowed to a stop.

"Todd Barker here."

"Oh, yes. What can I do for you?"

"Well, for starters, you can get yourself out to the airport."

"Which airport?" I had an uneasy feeling I wasn't going to like the answer.

"I'm here in Maui. At the Katahoochie Airport, or whatever the hell it's called. I'd catch a cab, but these oily drivers look like they'll give me the scenic tour and then charge me a hundred bucks for the pleasure. I'll give you fifty if you'll take me to my hotel, pronto."

I was tempted to beg off and tell him to take his chances with a cab, but I had questions and he had answers. And besides, fifty bucks was more than I'd probably ever shake out of Marv. I told Barker I'd be there in fifteen minutes, then I called Farrah and asked if she could hold on for another hour.

I pulled into the white zone in front of baggage claim. I was fretting over how I'd identify a man I could only recognize by voice when I caught sight of a guy in a rumpled tucked-in white dress shirt, charcoal grey slacks, and black leather lace-up shoes. More than likely he'd taken off a necktie on the flight over. He'd slung his suit jacket over his shoulder and clutched an expensive-looking aluminum briefcase in one hand while wheeling a tiny black roller bag with the other. His medium brown hair was cut in the conservative style popular with politicians and news anchors. The guy wasn't bad looking, just absurdly out of place on a tropical island where all pants are khaki, and where tucking in your shirt is like setting your hair on fire: it really makes you stand out in a crowd.

I pulled to the curb and got out.

"Todd?" I said, coming up to him. He wore a forlorn expression and was nervously running a hand through his hair.

"Miss Moon?"

"Please, call me Pali. Is this your only luggage?"

"Yeah. With any luck I won't be sticking around long." He scowled at the milling throng of vacationers as if he'd been abducted by aliens.

We walked back to the Geo, which was garnering major stink eye from the rent-a-cop hired to keep people from doing what I'd done: parking in the loading zone. Being the considerate chauffeuress, I reached in front of Todd and wrestled the passenger door open. Then I leaned in and swiped the thin film of red dust from the seat. He got in and I put his suitcase on the back seat next to Lisa Marie's origami crane keepsake. The beautifully-framed picture of lotus flowers and koi fish made from the tiny golden cranes offered a sad testament to the events of the past couple of days.

I didn't have money to pay the framer and I'd asked if he wanted to keep the artwork until I could pay, but he'd declined. One more item on an already jam-packed list of mounting debts.

"Miss Moon?" Barker snapped.

I jerked my head up realizing I'd been lost in thought. The rent-a-cop was frantically blowing his whistle and waving his arms. Outrage and lack of oxygen had colored his face a brilliant fuchsia.

"Sorry." I hustled around to the driver door.

"Is today some kind of holiday over here?" Barker said as we pulled into traffic. "I didn't see a single man wearing a decent suit and tie. Hell, I didn't see anybody even wearing *socks.*"

Todd Barker didn't stop talking during the entire trip to his posh hotel in Wailea. He bounced from subject to subject: crying babies on the plane; Hawaii's ridiculous agricultural inspection form; the visitor's bureau asking for personal information; he even touched on the lack of decent toilet paper in the airplane restroom. As we left Kihei, heading south, he finally got around to his company losing its two key executives. Everything he knew about Kevin McGillvary's death had come second or third hand so he only had the basic facts.

"I heard Kevin was murdered. It wasn't from natural causes." He said it more like a question than a statement.

I knew better than to weigh in with my opinion. "It appears it wasn't an accident, but they haven't released the final autopsy report."

"Do you have any idea what this is doing to Digi-Systems? We're in a precarious position. For months we've been dealing with takeover rumors. And now we've lost both our founding members in less than two weeks. With Sanders and McGillvary gone, the share price is going to run off a damn cliff. Do you hear what I'm saying?"

Hearing him was no problem. When we stopped at Kilohana Drive—the intersection where you can make the turn into Maui Meadows—two local women in the car next to us looked over and stared. They most likely assumed they were witnessing a domestic dispute.

"And that asshole Marv Prescott. Acting all innocent. That guy's behind this, believe you me. He called me yesterday, barely able to keep from laughing. I tried to warn Brad against taking that sonofabitch's money, but would he listen? No-o-o."

"Marv told me he was just an angel investor during the start-up."

"Bullshit!" Barker shrieked. His voice was fast approaching a pitch only dogs can hear. "Marv Prescott's been called a lot of things, but 'angel' sure as hell isn't one of them. He's a manipulating self-serving bastard, and his fingerprints are all over this."

Todd blew out a sharp breath and dropped his tone a notch. "Don't you find it a bit too convenient that Digi-Systems' two key stakeholders died right under his nose three thousand miles from home? That's why I came over here."

"You think Marv killed Brad and Kevin?"

"I don't know what to think. What I *know*, as CFO for the company, is who stands to profit now that they're both dead."

A few beats went by before it dawned on me he was waiting for me to answer. "Would that be Marv Prescott?"

"Indirectly, yes. But he's too smart to be so obvious. He's handed his stake over to that dimwit daughter of his: Lisa Marie."

I was about to ask him to elaborate, but we'd arrived at the portico of the Royal Crown Kamehameha Resort and three valets had already dashed over to help. It appeared they were demonstrating first-rate customer service skills in moving so quickly, but I knew better. The faster they got my trashed green Geo out of their squeaky-clean tiled entryway, the better.

One valet opened Todd's door while a second lunged for the rear door to unload his meager luggage. I didn't get out. No sense creating confusion that we were a couple, and besides, my ears were nearly bleeding. I waited in blessed silence while Barker chatted briefly with the head bellman. He tipped the guy and then came around to my driver's window and leaned in.

"Thanks for your kind offer to pick me up," he said. I wasn't sure if he was being sarcastic or not, but when he extended a fan of three bills showing a twenty on top, I didn't care. I plucked the money from him and quickly tucked it in my bag.

"In Hawaiian, we say *mahalo* for thank you," I said. "You'll hear that a lot over here."

"Yeah, I'm sure." The snide had returned to his voice. "All these natives with their hand out, saying, 'Hollow.' Sounds like a pretty good description of what my wallet's gonna be in a few days. Pretty hollow." He stepped back from the car and gestured at me as if waving off an annoying panhandler.

The Pi'ilani Highway back to the Mokulele turnoff was wide open so I made good time getting back to Pa'ia.

"Girl, I was about to give up on you," said Farrah when I banged through the front door. The bell tinkled, and I got a catch in my throat as I realized that as of tomorrow even that damn bell would belong to Tank Sherman.

I peered into the glass-fronted refrigerator case. Not a single flower remained, just three rows of white plastic buckets. In one bucket a lone pink petal floated in green-tinged water.

"You hear anything from Hatch?" she asked.

"Not a word." I tried to keep the anxiety out of my voice since Farrah's anguish over Kevin was still raw.

"Maybe you should go next door and check for messages."

"Nah, I checked an hour ago."

"You never know. A lot can happen in an hour."

I put the key in my shop door and was surprised when it turned without resistance. Not locked. In my snit over Hatch I'd probably forgotten to lock up before going down to talk to Sifu Doug. But two steps in, the scent hit me like a tsunami.

Lavender.

A dozen lavender candles had been placed around the room, some burning, some still wrapped in cellophane. A lavender wreath the size of a spare tire hung on the divider wall; and two dainty white pillows embroidered with a lavender sprig hugged each of the arms of my tattered green sofa. An enormous basket festooned with a glossy violet bow was perched on my desk. In it was an assortment of fancy bath products.

Hatch hobbled out through the bead curtain and leaned on his crutch.

"You like it?"

"I don't know what to say. It's beautiful. Rather over-the-top, but beautiful."

"It doesn't upset you?"

"Not at all, it's lovely."

"Guess what?" He hopped over to the wreath and carefully lifted it from the nail in the wall. "Check it out. I made this all by myself. Up at the lavender farm in Kula."

"It looks good. You did a great job."

"So, will you be my Valentine?" he said.

"I guess."

He thumped toward me. Then he leaned on his crutch and reached out to lift my chin.

"What's the matter?" he said.

"Nothing."

He cocked his head, like a perplexed dog when the chew toy suddenly disappears into a pocket.

"C'mon. You may think I'm just a dumb smoke eater, but for seven years my life hinged on sizing people up. Something's wrong. What is it?"

"I didn't hear you come in last night," I was going for a nonchalant tone, but it came out kind of choked up.

"That's because I didn't come home. I stayed with a friend."

"Okay, fine. None of my business." I started blowing out candles.

"What's going on? Is there a house curfew you failed to mention? Steve told me he doesn't come home lots of times and it's no big deal."

"It isn't. You're a big boy. It's just that I need to get going. I promised Farrah I'd get her back up to the house more than an hour ago."

"You're not treating me like a big boy."

"I already told you: I'm late. I appreciate your Valentine's Day gifts, but I've got a lot on my mind."

He hopped over and hung the wreath back up on the wall. "Fair enough. Can I catch a ride back up the hill with you?"

"Of course."

The door squeaked open and Farrah poked her head in. "Well?" Her smile was back.

"Well, what?" Hatch and I shot back in unison.

The smile vanished.

"I thought I'd be interrupting a love-fest. But it looks more like a smack-down."

"We need to get going," I said, snatching up my keys.

"Yeah," said Hatch. "Don't get in her way. She's late and she's got a lot on her mind."

23

I arrived home with just enough time to change into tan capris and an earthtone aloha shirt. It's my go-to outfit when attending a beach wedding. I look semi-festive while still blending into the background.

Steve was out front packing his photography gear into the Jetta.

"I could make excuses if you want to skip this," I said.

"No way. If that long lost dude makes an appearance I'll have exclusive rights to the photos. Wouldn't miss it."

He offered to drive and I slid into the passenger seat. The ride down to Olu'olu was quiet, not only because Steve's car doesn't sound like there's a hive of angry bees under the hood, but also because we were both lost in thought.

When we pulled inside the gate the bridesmaid's black limo was already there. Marv's Mercedes was parked outside the garage, and Steve parked his black Jetta where I usually put the Geo. Seeing three shiny black cars in close proximity made me shiver. In the scheme of things, weddings and funerals aren't that dissimilar. Both are life-changing events; both usually involve flowers, ministers, and music; and both are expensive ways to pass a few hours with family and friends.

The funereal mood continued once we'd gone inside. Josie soundlessly led us to the sunroom to wait for the minister. I hadn't told Lisa Marie I'd switched out Farrah, but I wasn't worried. If Brad showed up, she'd be so excited she'd overlook it, and if he didn't, well, it wouldn't matter.

The two bridesmaids were perched on the far sofa, ankles crossed, hands primly clasped.

"Hi, girls," said Steve.

"*Aloha*, Mr. Rathbun."

Steve winced at the formal salutation and sat down in a cushioned wicker armchair. Through the window I saw Marv on the lanai, pacing, drink in hand.

I nodded to the bridesmaids and told Steve I'd be right back.

"Josie," I said coming up to her in the foyer. "Is Lisa Marie dressed?"

"Miss Moon, she lock her door. I don't know what she doing in there."

I went down the hallway to Lisa Marie's room. "Lisa Marie, it's me, Pali. Can I help with anything?"

"Go away."

"It's ten to five. We'll start no later than five-thirty, okay?"

"Is Brad here?"

"Not yet."

"Then how can we start? We have to wait for him."

At exactly five the minister arrived and joined us in the sunroom. We made quiet chit-chat for almost an hour and then a few minutes before six I went out to the lanai. It was nearly dark except for the light cast by a dozen tiki torches that had been lit as the sun hovered at the horizon. I told Marv we were all leaving now. He didn't turn around, but he gave a single nod to signal he'd heard.

In the two years I've been planning weddings I've had a few last minute changes of heart and even a couple of *can't wait* elopements, but I've never witnessed a jilted bride. I guess technically I still hadn't. Lisa Marie never made an appearance. As if we'd rehearsed it, we all quietly left the sunroom and slipped out to our cars with only our final *alohas* breaking the silence.

On Friday morning I awoke to a gentle rapping on the bedroom door. Lipton sprang into action, standing at stiff alert, a growl coming from deep in her throat. Farrah tugged the covers up to her chin and rolled over, taking the entire blanket with her. I had a deep dent in my spine from the crossbar under the thin mattress.

"Who is it?" I said.

"Pali? It's me, Steve. There's a guy named Todd Barker on the phone. He ordered me to wake you up. The guy sounds like Darth Vadar with a vicious case of hemorrhoids."

"Oh, joy." Barker probably wanted me to fetch him a latte.

I stumbled down the stairs, mistaking the second-to-the-last stair for the final one. I fell with a thud, striking my tailbone on the edge of the riser. I couldn't afford to break a bone so I pulled myself upright, rubbing my backside and shaking off the pain.

"Hey, Todd," I said picking up the receiver. "What time is it?"

"Forget that. You need to get down here right away," he said. "I've got something I want to run by you."

"I'll need a cup of coffee and a shower first," I said. "Then I've got to get some gas. You're a good twenty-five minutes from my house so the soonest I could be there is about an hour."

"I don't need a play-by-play of your hectic schedule, Miss Moon. Just get your ass in gear. I'll be in the coffee shop." He hung up.

I stopped at the gas station on Hana Highway and reluctantly parted with one of the twenties Barker had given me for the airport ride. The gas gauge ticked up to less than half a tank. My ancient Geo sipped gas like a guppy, but buying fuel for all the running back and forth from Olu'olu was tearing a serious hole in my already tattered balance sheet.

I parked on the street and walked onto the grounds of the Royal Crown Kamehameha. I'd never seen such well-behaved plants. Everything was in tidy rows, with no spent blooms and no wayward leaves littering the velvet lawn. I tiptoed across the manicured grass, glancing left and right for the ever-vigilant gardeners who would, no doubt, chase me off with a rake if they caught me leaving footprints.

As I crossed the lobby, Todd Barker waved from a table at the oceanside café.

"What'll you have?" he said.

The table was bare of food and drink. Either he wasn't having anything or his order hadn't arrived yet.

"Thanks, but I'm fine."

"I didn't inquire about your health," he snapped. "I asked what you wanted to drink."

The man really needed a vacation.

"Have you already ordered?" I said.

"Yeah, I'm having a BM."

I knew what BM meant in my morning routine, but I prayed that on the mainland it meant something different. I shrugged in confusion.

"A Bloody Mary," he said. "God willing, they'll have brains enough to serve it with a stalk of celery instead of throwing in one of those pineapple, cherry, tiny umbrella gee-gaws."

"I'd just like a glass of ice water," I said. I'd just spent twenty bucks on gas, and I still needed to get stamps, vitamins and toilet paper which would no doubt deplete the rest of fifty.

"I don't drink alone," he said. He gestured to an eager-looking waiter. "Bring her a BM along with some ice water."

"Right away, sir." The waiter smiled and bowed slightly before stepping away from the table. I felt uneasy with the guy's toady behavior, but it was probably because before long I'd be perfecting the fine points of toady-ism myself.

"I'll get right to the point." Todd held my gaze like a stare-down. "I'm here to proposition you."

Whoa, I thought. Becoming a toady waitress to pay the bills is one thing, moving into the sex trade was something else indeed. I felt a little thrill run down my spine. He wasn't that bad looking. His conduct could use a little polish, but at least he wasn't a fat slob like Tank Sherman. And, morals aside, hooker money would be a damn sight better than what I'd make trotting mai tais to pasty-faced tourists.

My reverie about a possible new career path was cut short when he continued.

"I need your help in nailing the Prescotts—or more precisely, Lisa Marie." He twisted his mouth into a sideways smile that looked like he'd just come from the dentist. "I've talked it over with my guys back in Seattle, and we're pretty sure she's up to her eyeballs in this, and her father's protecting her."

He fell silent while the waiter ceremoniously served us our drinks. The guy hovered for half a minute until Todd shooed him away with a dismissive wave.

"Why are you so sure it's her" I said.

"Oh, c'mon," he said. "She's not as dumb as she'd lead you to believe. DigiSystems finally starts grabbing some headlines and her two so-called fiancés bite it within a two-week period. She's left looking like a grieving widow: a very *wealthy* widow, I might add."

I wanted to ask how he imagined she actually killed the guys, but he started up again before I could get it out.

"Listen up. I took a cab down to their place late last night and that sumbitch, Marv, was almost gleeful. Oh, he made like the concerned father, but trust me, underneath all his BS he was laughing his ass off. And, Lisa Marie? She's psycho. She's probably counting on an insanity plea to get her off with a short stint in some high-class loony bin. And then when she gets out she'll just pick up her life where she left off."

"Todd, I'm not the police. I'm not even a private detective. I can't imagine how I could help you."

"Keep your ear to the ground, schmooze with the so-called grieving family and see what you can find out. Lisa Marie was all moony last night about what good friends you two are and how you've helped her get through this. Who knows, you might even get her to confess."

I wanted to laugh. Why would Lisa Marie tell him we're friends when she spits in my eye every chance she gets?

"Look," he went on. "I really need you to say 'yes' on this. And I'm not asking for charity. I got my board to approve a five-thousand dollar reward for information leading to an arrest of who killed our guys. Not for me, of course, but for whoever helps me. And, from what I can see, it isn't gonna be the cops who crack this. This morning I called and talked to some guy named Wong who's assigned to the case. He sounds like he means well, but he's clueless. Literally."

"Actually, I heard he may have some evidence." I regretted it as soon as it was out of my mouth.

"Yeah, what?"

"Oh, it's probably just gossip. But it seems the police have talked to a guy who called in on the tip line."

"Probably some beach bum who swears he saw a one-armed man fleeing the scene." He shook his head. "Look, I know Prescott's lawyered the girl up with some well-connected local. So even if she doesn't get off with the psycho act, it's not hard to see how this will go: the cops will screw up the investigation, then the girl's lawyer will bribe some on-the-take judge and in the end she'll get off with a slap on the wrist."

The more he talked, the more difficult it became for me to not throw my BM in his face and leave. But I wanted to hear him out. Eventually, he might say something of value. If nothing else, I owed it to Kevin, and Farrah, to gather whatever information I could. I'd promised Kevin I'd watch his back. And now his back was stretched out on an autopsy table.

Todd took a gulp of his vodka-laced tomato juice.

"I've got to hand it to her," he said. "She got both guys away from home so she'd get off scot free. Back in the States the police would have nailed her right away for Brad's murder; when he first disappeared. And Kevin would still be alive. But over here—"

I'd had enough. "First of all, Todd, Hawaii *is* a state. It's the fiftieth state. We vote for the president, and we even have our own state quarter. And Glen Wong is a first-rate homicide detective. He's bucking for promotion, so he has no reason whatsoever to allow this investigation to be compromised. And finally, our local judges have as much integrity, if not more, than any judge you'll find on the mainland. If Lisa Marie killed your guys, she'll be found guilty and she'll go to prison."

"Says you."

"Yeah. Says me."

"Then prove it."

24

In a martial arts competition, when an opponent makes an aggressive move it's crucial to respond immediately. Getting psyched out or waiting for the ideal set-up for a counter-attack is a formula for failure. I vowed to react quickly to Barker's challenge.

I turned left at the Honoapi'ilani Highway and headed down to Olu'olu. Although I had no doubt Glen Wong was a competent detective, I was baffled why Lisa Marie hadn't been taken into custody. After all, they had a videotape of her fighting with the murder victim the night he died. What were they waiting for?

The security guard opened the gate with little harassment. Maybe I was finally making an impression on the guy. This time I parked in a different spot: on the other side of the driveway, closer to the entrance than the exit. Although it's comfortable to stick with the familiar, I think a different perspective is essential to staying sharp. Even in wedding planning, what's hot one minute is often tossed aside the next. I've got six boxes of Chinese red parasols in my attic to prove my point. Last summer, every bridesmaid on Maui was twirling a flashy paper umbrella. Now, they're so passé only old ladies worried about skin cancer would be caught dead holding one.

Josie answered the door.

"Is Lisa Marie at home?" I said.

She led me to the lanai. Before opening the outside door she said, "Mr. Prescott is only one you can talk to. Miss Lisa Marie not talk to anyone."

But we're such good friends.

Marv sat at a table hiding behind a well-creased copy of the Wall Street Journal. He lowered the paper a few inches and peered over it when Josie announced me, then quickly put it back up.

I stood and waited, my blood pressure ticking up with each passing second. I wouldn't have made a good dog. If I'd had an owner like Marv, I'd have been more likely to bite his ankle than fetch his slippers.

"If you're here about getting paid, the answer's still *no* Ms. Moon." He kept the newspaper in place, as if looking at me was as burdensome as paying me. "No wedding, so no check."

"Our arrangement was Lisa Marie would pay for half the expenses and Brad Sanders' company would pay the other half. I've already received a check from DigiSystems even though Brad never got as much as a boutonnière. On Lisa Marie's instructions, my suppliers purchased paper and printing, cake ingredients, and expensive fabric. We flew in special flowers from South America, and I had little Girl Scouts working for days making origami cranes. Hours and hours of labor were spent getting ready for your daughter's wedding. It isn't their fault it didn't happen."

"Let's be clear, Ms. Moon. We received absolutely no value for the services you've described, so I don't feel any obligation to pay for them."

"I see. Well, my visit this morning is twofold. The first was to ask you once again to step up and pay your outstanding bill. The second is I need a few minutes with Lisa Marie."

"Why?"

"It's personal."

"There's nothing so personal it wouldn't affect me as well. If you want access to my daughter, you'll have to convince me it's in her best interest."

"As you're aware, there's speculation she's a person of interest in Kevin McGillvary's death—"

I didn't get a chance to finish before he launched out of his chair with such force I had to step back to avoid a collision.

Snapping the newspaper in my face like a bullwhip, he roared, "Lies! That poor girl spent what was supposed to be her wedding day locked in her room crying her eyes out. And then the cops show up again this morning to interrogate her. This has got to stop!"

His face crumpled.

"She doesn't need to be hassled, she needs help. Can't everyone see she's sick? She rambled on about Brad coming back, and then when Kevin died she just lost it. The cops are using her unstable mental state to extort a phony confession."

"Has she confessed?" He was right: Lisa Marie wouldn't be hard to break down. Even on her best days she struggled to separate fact from fiction.

"Not that I know of. But now her lawyer, Joseph Koko-something—"

"His name's James Kanekoa," I interrupted.

"Do you know *everyone* on this lousy rock? Anyway, even her lawyer's telling us she should consider a plea bargain."

"Maybe she should."

"No, no. I'm a thousand-percent certain she had nothing to do with any of this."

"Marv, I need to tell you to something that might affect Lisa Marie's decision about the plea bargain."

"What's that?"

"The executives at DigiSystems are offering a reward for information leading to an arrest for Brad and Kevin's deaths. And they're convinced Lisa Marie was somehow involved." I didn't bring up Todd Barker's name figuring if Barker ended up a floater, it'd be on my head.

"What? Those bastards. What are they thinking?"

"It seems they think it had something to do with gaining control of the company. Since you gave your shares to Lisa Marie, they're thinking she had a motive."

Marv's eyes dodged left and right, as if assessing whether anyone else was within earshot. I hoped he'd offer a plausible explanation, or maybe deny he'd ever transferred any stock to Lisa Marie. He leaned in closer.

"Do the cops know about this?"

"I'm not sure."

"Well, it's all bullshit. I gave Lisa Marie the stock as a small dowry. Brad seemed pretty pleased with the whole notion. But it was never a big deal to Lisa Marie. She's a pretty girl, but not the sharpest thorn on the bush, if you get my drift. Besides, she's already sole heir to my business, RRI: which is a damn site bigger than Brad's little sandbox. Money's the least of her worries."

Marv's mouth was still moving, but I'd stopped listening. I'd already taken in too much information for one morning.

"...we talking about?" His mouth clamped shut and his eyes locked on mine.

"I'm sorry, Marv. I drifted there for a moment."

"I said, those assholes at DigiSystems are nearly bankrupt as it is. What kind of reward are they talking about?"

"Five thousand dollars."

"Hell," he said, "I should be insulted. A cheap bunch of SOB's from the get-go. Tell you what, Ms. Moon: I find you annoying, but I respect your persistence. You help me get my daughter off the hook and I'll double it."

25

The ride back home was remarkably uneventful. Good thing, because I spent the better part of it locked in a mental fistfight with myself. I'd throw a punch for nailing Lisa Marie for being some kind of serial killer, and then I'd counterpunch she was simply an easy scapegoat and had undoubtedly been framed.

Todd Barker and Marv Prescott were both right about one thing: I knew a lot of local people. Even better, I could fly under the radar while I snooped around. But why was I even thinking of getting involved? Maybe it was to prove Todd Barker wrong about Hawaii being a corrupt backwater. Maybe it was simply to collect the reward money and pay my bills. Or maybe it was something else. Maybe it was a chance to quash the nagging feeling I'd had since they'd ID'd Kevin. Simply put, I'd failed him. Failure had been dogging me ever since I left the air marshal job. The government invested thousands of dollars training me and I up and quit after less than a year. How lame was that?

When I pulled in at the house, Hatch was sitting on the porch playing tug-of-war with Lipton. Hatch and I still hadn't cleared the air about the redhead sleepover and Valentine's Day debacle, but neither of us seemed eager to bring it up.

"Hey," I said.

"Hey, yourself," he said. "I've got some news." He dropped his end of the rope and Lipton started chewing it like a two-dollar steak.

"Not as juicy as my news," I said.

He looked annoyed.

"You go first," I offered.

"Guess who showed up here about a half hour ago?"

"No clue."

"That jerk you told me about: Toilet Tank or whatever."

"Tank Sherman?"

"I guess. He had some snarky-looking real estate guy with him. They snooped around the yard, but I wouldn't let them go inside. He said he'd see you later this afternoon."

"Yeah, he thinks he's buying me out today. But I've got a line on something that—if it works out—could pay me almost enough to save this house and keep "Let's Get Maui'd" out of his chubby clutches."

"You sign up a big wedding? Who is it: one of those Google guys?"

"Not a wedding. An investigation. There's a reward being offered to find out who killed Brad Sanders and Kevin McGillvary. I just need to dig up enough evidence for an arrest."

"Hate to break it to you, but somebody's already got that job."

"But the police are only focusing on Lisa Marie."

"For now." He patted his thigh and Lipton jumped in his lap. "These things take time."

"The police don't have time. While Wong's busy hassling loony-tunes Lisa Marie, the actual killer could be hot-footing it back to the mainland."

"*The actual killer*? You think Lisa Marie's innocent?"

"Who knows? I can think of at least three other suspects who ought to be brought in for questioning."

"Listen to you. You've been watching too much 'Law & Order.' No offense, but what makes you think you can out-cop the cops?"

"Because I grew up here. I know locals in every corner of this island, from the governor's office to the guy who scrubs toilets at the Maui Prince. I can ask questions and get answers without people clamming up. And even better, I sleep under the same roof as a guy who was a cop and still thinks like one."

I shot him a hopeful look.

His face turned to stone. "I don't do that anymore."

"Why not?" I said.

His face didn't soften. "Look, you're way out of your league here. Leave it to the professionals."

I went inside and made myself a sandwich. I scrounged a warped yellow pad from the kitchen junk drawer and while I ate, I jotted down what I knew so far.

"The homicide guys make murder books," Hatch said when he came in and saw what I was doing. He sat down at the table. "You know, investigations are complex. There are a million details you've got to keep organized."

"You're preaching to the choir, my friend. I put on weddings for women who swear a misplaced bow or the wrong shade of pink ranks right up there with a flesh-eating virus. Trust me, I'm all about the details."

"What's the deal with the reward money?"

I explained how Todd Barker had offered five thousand dollars and Marv had countered he'd double it if I'd prove Lisa Marie was innocent.

"That's what he said?"

I thought about it. "No, his words were he'd pay me double if I'd help 'get his daughter off the hook'."

"See? Details. World of difference between innocence and getting away with it." He looked at his watch. "I gotta go get ready for physical therapy. Like I said, stay out of this. This isn't a game."

After Hatch left I looked over my notes. I'd listed my possible suspects, starting with Lisa Marie. I included Marv, but I couldn't come up with a solid motive. Marv could most definitely be part of a cover-up, though. The third name was Tank Sherman because of the real estate deal. Finally, I'd written 'Takeover Company,' since Barker had mentioned that losing the two DigiSystems founders had hammered the stock price. Anyone looking to buy the company had good reason to do whatever it took to get a rock bottom price.

I looked up at the kitchen clock. It was noon: only four hours until Tank was supposed to show up. Before then, I wanted to talk to Todd Barker. I called and he agreed to see me at one-thirty.

***

As I trotted through the lush tropical lobby of the Royal Crown Kamehameha, I picked out Barker sitting at the same table he'd been at that morning. Was it a fluke or had he slipped the maitre d' a ten spot to let him camp out there for the day? Hard to know. The guy definitely had comfort zone issues.

"I hope you're bringing me a signed confession." He pointed to my beach bag purse.

"Hardly," I said. "I need to ask you a few questions about DigiSystems."

"I'm not at liberty to say much."

"Why?"

"I told you, there's a possible takeover in play. We're practically strip-searching our employees as they leave from work every day. Total confidentiality."

"Okay, well tell me what you can about Lisa Marie getting Marv's stock."

"That's no secret. Marv signed it over to her late last year. She got a pretty large chunk, but she didn't attend the stockholders' meeting last month. Probably trying to maintain a low profile while she plotted her massacre. "

"Can you tell me how much Marv's original investment was?"

"Can't divulge that."

"Do you think Brad and Kevin wanted to sell the company?"

"I don't know. But with the price climbing, it had to be tempting. But neither one of them ever talked to me about it."

"Can you give me the name of the possible takeover company?"

"No comment."

"How am I supposed to help you if you won't tell me anything?" I said.

He put two fingers on his neck as if taking his pulse on his carotid artery. "Look, Miss Moon, I'm not trying to stonewall you. I'm fighting for my livelihood here."

"So am I, Todd."

I check the time on my cell phone. Tank Sherman would be at my shop in less than two hours.

"I've got to go," I said. "If you think of anything you *can* tell me, please call me at home or on my cell. My business line's been disconnected."

26

Noni and Tank were due at four, but by four-thirty there was still no sign of them. My Auntie Mana used to say 'the servant waits on the *ali'i*, but never the other way around' so I refused to hang out any longer.

I was shoving the last battered cardboard box into my Geo when the black BMW pulled in across the street. Noni was driving, Tank riding shotgun. His head lolled against the passenger window as if his bulky neck was weary of holding up his fat face.

I turned my back and pretended not to see them. Then I slammed the trunk lid and race-walked to Farrah's.

Tank lumbered into the store before Farrah and I'd had a chance to rehearse how we were going to play it. I was still undecided whether I should pretend to go along with Tank's plan to buy 'Let's Get Maui'd' and then renege if I got the reward money; or take a chance and tell him I wasn't going to sell. If I didn't get the reward money I'd probably be sorry if I chose option two. Knowing Tank, if I refused him now, he'd punish me by refusing to pay me anything later.

"Well, well," Tank said as he waddled over to where we were standing. Noni was right behind him but I couldn't see her around his bulk. His porcine eyes took us in as if we'd been sculpted in chocolate. "My two favorite *wahines*. How's it hangin', girls?"

He'd gained even more weight since the last time I'd seen him. At only five foot eight the guy looked like he tipped the scales at three-fifty or better. He wore baggy cotton shorts that bunched up in his crotch. His gelatinous thighs slapped together with every step. I glanced down to see how he held up all the bulk. In his green rubber flip-flops, his feet looked like two Chinese pot-stickers with a green scallion garnish.

A cigar stub jutted from the side of his mouth.

"No smoking in here," said Farrah. She hauled out a sand-filled butt bucket from under the front counter. "Ditch it."

"No way," Tank shot back. "This here's a Cuban. Besides, it's not even lit."

"It still stinks, and this is a place of business. Use of tobacco products is against the law in here."

"Yeah, well don't sweat it, *ipo*, because I'm here to relieve you of your enforcement duties."

Farrah swallowed hard. I knew how she felt. It was one thing to verbally agree to sell your business to a slob like Tank, it was another thing altogether to actually hand over the keys.

"I'll need some time to move out," said Farrah. "After all, I live here. I need to look for a new place."

"Don't panic," he said. "Nobody's kicking you out today. Mostly I wanted to just drop by and make sure everybody's going to play nice before I set up a closing date."

"When will that be?" I said.

"Sometime around the end of the month."

"How's Farrah supposed to run the store and look for a new apartment at the same time?"

"Hey, you ladies knew I was buying this building. Not my problem you left it to the last minute to get your affairs in order."

"Yeah," Noni chimed in, "I came by and talked with you girls more than a week ago. You've had plenty of notice."

Tank scowled at her. She bobbed her head in submission and retreated a half-step.

Tank started walking down the first aisle, taking in the shelves. "Looks like you've been lax in restocking since I made my offer. I may have to factor that into my price."

"What are you talking about?" Farrah said. "We agreed on a price. Everything's the same. Ask my suppliers. I haven't changed my ordering in five years."

"Maybe. Maybe not. I'll need to take a look around."

He shuffled down the snacks and cookie aisle, grabbed a bag of Double Stuf Oreos and ripped into the package.

"That'll be four dollars and seventy cents," Farrah said in her proprietress voice.

"Oh, I think not," Tank mumbled back. Black cookie bits flew from his mouth as he chomped and talked at the same time.

Noni turned to me and said in a whisper, "I'd like to go next door and see where you keep everything."

We slipped out the back while Tank and Farrah argued the price of Oreos.

Once we got outside Noni said, "Mr. Sherman's asked me to operate the bridal business for a few months until he can move it to the new location."

"Why would he move it?"

"Because he's taking down this building. He's already got investors lined up to underwrite a three-story parking structure on this site. He'll be closing the store and the wedding shop by the end of summer." She shot me a saccharin smile. I couldn't keep my lower jaw from dropping open as I took in the news. I skidded to a stop.

"But this is a historic building. The store's been here for more than a hundred years."

"That's quaint and all, but we're not here to do a documentary for the History Channel. Mr. Sherman's bringing growth and prosperity to the island. And Pa'ia Town needs visitor parking way more than it needs this old store or your silly bridal shop. Now, let's go inside and see what you've got."

My shop looked beyond bare. I'd already rolled up the tattered throw rugs and I'd stripped the walls of the few items I'd hung there. I'd even disassembled the three way mirror and the changing stall. The pieces were haphazardly piled in a corner.

"What's all that over there?" she said pointing to the pile.

"Oh, those are your dressing room fixtures. They'll need to be put back together before you re-open."

"Why'd you take them down?"

"They need to be thoroughly cleaned. This is a very visual business, Noni, and prospective brides can get very turned off if they see any grime or smudges. Not to mention, I needed to spray for cockroaches and check out some fresh rat droppings."

She wrinkled her nose but said nothing.

"All the pieces are there." I crossed my fingers behind my back. Actually, all the *large* pieces were there, but the screws, bolts, and cotter pins had somehow ended up in the glove box of the Geo. They wouldn't be found for a while.

Of course all of Hatch's lavender gifts—the candles, wreath, basket, and pillows—had already been hauled up to my house. I'd asked a friend of a friend with a pickup truck to help me move my desk and chair later in the month. I planned to generously bequeath Tank with the sagging sofa and bead curtain. Both evoked memories of Kevin I hoped to leave behind.

Noni held out her hand, palm up. "Key?"

"Why should I give you a key? Tank hasn't bought the building yet."

"He's paying for the business and this place is a mess. I'll need to hire some people to fix it up so I can operate from here until I can find a nicer place. Face it, Pali, you're *pau*: finished."

I showed her where I'd hidden a key outside and then rushed back to Farrah's.

"Did he tell you he's going to demolish this building?" I asked.

"What? Why?"

"According to Noni he's going to put up a parking garage."

"Hell," she said, "I was feeling crappy enough, and now this." She used a box cutter to split open a cardboard box of paper towels. "Do you think he can actually do that? Don't you think the city fathers or mothers or whoever will stop him?"

"Well, he'll probably need to get a zoning variance. I think all of Baldwin Avenue is zoned for shops, restaurants and professional offices. I doubt if that includes parking garages. But way back when they did the zoning they'd probably never even heard of a parking garage. They'll probably hold a public meeting and see if anyone objects."

She shot me a look and we both barked a bitter laugh.

"As if local objections ever slowed down raging development on Maui," said Farrah.

"Yeah. I'm pretty sure a variance won't be tough for him to get. You know how hard it is for tourists to find parking around here. I wouldn't be surprised if they not only approve it but offer the county's bulldozers to help with the demolition."

"Total bummer."

"One glimmer of hope," I said. "This building could probably get historical landmark status. Didn't you tell me it was the original company store for the old sugar plantation?"

Farrah dropped her head and began paring her thumbnail with the box cutter.

"I didn't finish the paperwork." She said it so quietly I had to replay the comment in my mind to make sure I'd heard her correctly.

"What paperwork?"

"When my mom had the store, she got some paperwork from the historical society. I found it in her stuff later. She died before she got it filled out. I always meant to finish it, but every time I looked at it I just got too bummed out."

"So do it now."

"Can't. They only give you five years to apply after you record the deed." She shot me a defiant look. "It's harder than you think, Pali. The form's about thirty pages long, and they wanted all sorts of historical research stuff. It was impossible. I was just a teenager."

"Wow, it looks like Tank's going to be allowed to destroy a huge piece of Hawaiian history so he can rip off tourists coming to see historic Pa'ia Town. Kind of a weird oxymoron, don't you think?"

"I'm not sure what that means, but I'm sure I agree. Who'd of ever thought a high school loser like Tank would end up kicking our asses?"

We stood there, not saying anything, for a few moments.

"Oh, before I forget," she said, "he left us these. He called them a good-will gesture." She pulled two white business-size envelopes from a pocket in her *mu'u mu'u* and handed me one with my name on it. I ripped it open and saw a cashier's check drawn on a Honolulu bank for

MAUI WIDOW WALTZ **245**

five thousand dollars. He'd had the bank make it out to my legal name.

"Not much for all your hard work, is it?" Farrah said, leaning in to look at my check. "Oh wow, I'd forgotten all about your real name."

"It's a bitch." I said.

"What? Handing your business over to Tank Sherman, or your beastly name?"

"Both."

Farrah used the box cutter to zip open her envelope. She took out the check. Her hands trembled as she held it. Tears pooled in her eyes.

"That's a lot of money," I said.

"Dirty money," she replied. "I've let everyone down, starting with not honoring my mom and dad's memory. And then when Tank bulldozes this building a lot of Maui history will go with it. But most of all, I let Kevin down: in the worst possible way. I should never have told Noni anything."

Farrah waved the box cutter in front of her face. "If I find out Tank killed my darling Kevin over a damn parking garage I'll rip that fat bastard's beating heart right out of his chest."

So much for make love, not war.

27

At dinner Friday night, Farrah announced she'd be moving back to her apartment that in the morning.

"I'm crowding you guys, and I've got to find a new place to live before the end of the month. And since I don't have wheels, it'll be easier to look for a new pad if I'm down in town."

We all made the appropriate denials about her being in the way, but it was mostly nice noise. In the past couple of days, all three of us had privately voiced our dismay over the lack of bathroom time and privacy.

"You taking the dogs?" Hatch said.

"Of course."

He nodded, but a spark of anguish flashed across his face.

"Oh, and the little spotted pup's all yours if you want it," Farrah said. "It needs to stay with Lipton for a few more weeks though: until he's weaned."

"*Mahalo*, Farrah. I'd really like that." Hatch grinned as if he'd been chosen Employee of the Month and given his own parking space.

"What's with you two?" Steve said.

"Who two?" Hatch asked.

"You two." Steve wagged a finger at me and Hatch. "I practically need to grab a jacket when the two of you are in the same room. You guys have a fight or something?"

"Not that I know of," said Hatch.

"Me neither."

"It's me," said Farrah. "We're all getting on each other's last nerve. You guys were really nice to take me in but it's time for me to go. Things will get back to normal once I clear out."

Later that night I was sitting on the porch when Hatch thumped through the door.

"Sorry, didn't realize you were out here." He turned to go back inside.

"No, stay. I should be getting to bed anyway." I stood up.

He touched my arm. "Steve's right, you know. You've been acting pretty harsh toward me."

"Harsh? I don't think I've been acting any different than normal."

He leaned in and I could smell a slight hint of his after-shave.

"Are you mad because I won't muck around in this murder investigation with you?"

I thought about it for a few moments. "No. It would've been nice to have your help, but I understand why you might not want to do it."

"Why is that?"

"Because you're a fireman now and you don't want to be reminded of what you gave up."

He shot me a rueful smile. "Yeah, that pretty much sums it up."

We stood close together, neither one moving, for what seemed like a few beats too long.

"Something else is bothering you," he said. "What is it?"

"Let's sit down."

We each took a wicker chair and, once we got settled, Hatch pulled out a pencil and pushed it down inside his cast. "Man, this thing itches. I can't believe I've got to put up with this thing for another month."

"Speaking of itches: what's the story on you and that redhead you picked up at Cisco's on Wednesday?" It flew out of my mouth and just laid there like a rotting fish.

"Oh, so that's it. You jealous?"

"Jealous? No. I'm only asking because I was concerned about your welfare."

"Well, shoot." Hatch said. Even in the semi-darkness I could see the beginnings of a sly smile. "Sorry if I made you worry, but my welfare was in *very* capable hands."

I didn't say anything. No, truthfully, I *couldn't* say anything. I felt my throat constrict and my eyes burned as if I'd chopped a pound of onions. Thankfully the porch light was only twenty watts.

"You okay?" Hatch's smile faded.

I cleared my throat.

"Sorry," he said. "Bad attempt at humor." He reached over and touched my arm. "I was excited about going up to that lavender farm and getting you all that stuff for Valentine's Day. A guy on my shift lives up there, in Kula. His wife—the redhead you saw—offered to come down and get me so I could get an early start in the morning. I stayed up at their house with their two kids, three ornery Rottweilers and a pygmy goat. As I said, I was in *very* capable hands."

***

On Saturday morning I took Farrah and the dogs down to the store before it opened. As we pushed the door open, Lipton dashed inside and ran up and down the aisles, seemingly thrilled to be home among familiar smells. Farrah went back out to the car and carried the puppy box inside. She put it down near the front counter and Lipton immediately set to work hauling her offspring, one by one, out of the box and onto the wide plank floor.

"What if someone sees the dogs?" I said.

"Like I give a rip. I deposited Fatso's check in the bank right after he left. They put a hold on it, but if Tank tries to stop payment on it I'm sure they'll tell him it already cleared. None of the girls at the bank were very thrilled at the notion of this store being turned into a parking garage."

"Have you thought about what you'll do now?"

"The money's enough to keep me going for a while. I'll probably do some tarot readings and stuff like that to keep my skills up. And, if it's all right with you, I'll sign up to do weddings and flowers for some of the other wedding planners on the island."

"No problem. Unless I can pull off a miracle, it won't be long before I'm doling out watered-down mai tais at the No Ka Oi Luau."

"Oh gawd, don't say that. I feel so guilty. I should share my windfall."

"*Mahalo* for the thought, but there's no reason both of us should be poor."

"Well, at least I should go down there and work with you."

"No dis, girl, but you show up in a coconut bra and they'd cite you for indecent."

She looked down at her generous bosom. "Do they make a watermelon bra?"

I kissed her on the cheek and then got out of there before the laughing stopped and the crying got underway.

***

That night it was my turn to make dinner. I wasn't the cook Steve was, but I managed to pan-fry a piece of mahi mahi and serve it on a bed of fresh garlic-braised spinach. It turned out better than I'd expected.

"This is a really good, Pali," Steve said when we sat down to eat. "So good in fact, that even though you're being all hush-hush about poking into this murder investigation and you're completely shutting me out, I'll still share a tidbit you'd never find out on your own."

I gave him the *okay, spill* look. Hatch kept eating.

"Seems Wong's come up with a whole new scenario and a new motive."

I let my facial expression egg him on.

"Did you know there was some hinky stuff going on at Sander's and McGillvary's company? Word is a competitor was sniffing around, thinking of buying them out."

I didn't let on I already knew this.

"Glen Wong said he talked to your pal Barker this afternoon and Barker told him the stock tanked but now another company has stepped in and upped the bid."

"A different company?" I said.

"I guess. I don't understand all that Wall Street lingo but he said it's called an 'eleventh-hour rescue' or some such thing."

"Huh. Did Wong say how that might affect the murder investigation?"

"Not in so many words, but I'm guessing if he thinks maybe the first company had the two guys killed so they could buy DigiSystems on the cheap, then that expands the suspect pool to more than just Lisa Marie."

"Why's Wong telling you all this?" I said.

"Damned if I know. Maybe he's leaking information so witnesses will be more willing to come forward. You know, salting the mine."

"Or," I said, "maybe he's tossing around disinformation to make the killers think the cops are going down the wrong path. He's hoping they'll get cocky and blab."

"We got any more of that ice cream with the nuts in it?" said Hatch.

"I'll check," I said. I got up and checked. "Nope, all out."

"I've been thinking about that ice cream all day," he said. "How 'bout it Steve? You drive, I'll buy."

That night I mulled over Todd Barker's conversation with Glen Wong about a possible second offer on Digi-Systems. Barker hadn't said a word to me about any eleventh-hour rescue, and if he'd learned about it after our meeting, why hadn't he called? Weren't we both on the same side here?

That's when it hit me: maybe we weren't.

28

As if being a low value chip in Todd Barker's high stakes poker game wasn't bad enough, the Sunday edition of *The Maui News* upped the ante. When Brad disappeared, the paper reported Lisa Marie's plight with almost familial concern. Then Kevin showed up dead. After that, the reporter assigned to the story seemed to take a step back and re-evaluate. He no longer referred to Lisa Marie as 'the widow bride.' Now it was the '*maka wai* bride,' or 'tearful bride.' Although on its face the reference appeared sympathetic, I detected a touch of snide. *Maka wai* is also used by locals when referring to fake grief: what main-landers call 'crocodile tears.'

I was rummaging through the cupboards looking for something to fix for lunch when the kitchen phone rang. It was Marv.

"I lost out on golfing Pebble Beach yesterday," he said, hardly giving me time to say *hello*. "And I can live with that. But I've got to get back to work. I can't sit around while these local yokels screw around playing Hawaii Five-Oh."

I wondered if he'd dialed the wrong number.

"Anyway, Ms. Moon, I don't have time for chit-chat. I called to redefine our business relationship."

Was he going to try and weasel out on the reward money?

"Redefine it? How so, Marv?"

"Since they're calling Lisa Marie a 'person of interest,' she needs to stay here, but we don't. Tina wants to get the hell off this island tomorrow morning and so do I. Personally, I'd like to bring Lisa Marie back to the States with us and tell the cops to go to hell, but her lawyer thinks that could make matters worse."

"I hope you're not considering another proxy marriage."

"No, no. Nothing that stupid. What I'm proposing is for you to move in down here for a while. You know, to keep an eye on things. You could ferry Lisa Marie around when she needs to go to the lawyer's office or shopping or whatever. That way, Tina and I can leave and I won't be constantly worrying about my daughter."

"Well, I—"

"Look, I know Lisa Marie can be a handful. And now that she's doing this nut job routine, it's gotten pretty ugly. But I'm prepared to make you an offer you can't refuse." He chuckled at that. I didn't.

Before I could figure out how to gracefully decline, he continued.

"How about four C's a week to be her companion?"

"Four hundred dollars?"

"That's right. And if you manage to get her cut loose from this circus, you're still on for the ten grand. Think about it, Ms. Moon, this could prove to be the most profitable non-wedding you ever put on."

"Well, thanks for thinking of me, but I don't see how I could manage tracking down information to get Lisa Marie exonerated if I'm spending all my time down at Olu'olu."

"Okay, I'll make it seven C's: a hundred bucks a day."

I hadn't realized it was a price negotiation.

"Marv, I just don't see how I could do both things at the same time."

"Look, you put together weddings, right? And you don't think you can manage two tasks at the same time? Hell, you led me to believe that on any given day you're juggling twenty things or more."

Ah, my Achilles' heel: questioning my work ethic.

"Well, I—"

"I have faith in you, Ms. Moon. Only thing is, I can't have you bringing strangers down here to the house. I want you to personally account for her whereabouts every minute from seven at night until seven in the morning. But if during the day you need to leave for an hour or so to do this other business, I can live with that."

As much as I hated to admit it, Marv's offer *was* starting to look like an offer I couldn't—or shouldn't—refuse. How hard could it be to make sure she stayed put while she watched her soaps all day and then check in on her during the night? And the money was certainly tempting.

"What does Lisa Marie think about this arrangement?"

"Who gives a shit what she thinks? She's mental."

Seems I'd bumped up against the outer boundaries of Marv's fatherly concern.

"Oh, and just so we're clear," he went on, "this is the full meal deal. We'll keep the staff on until this thing blows over, so you're pretty much free to just paint your nails and chit chat with Lisa Marie all day. No work involved. She's been sleeping a lot, so that should leave you plenty of time to chip away at the cops' bogus case against her."

"Isn't that what her lawyer's supposed to be doing?"

"I suppose. But he's a grease ball. I don't think he's all that smart."

I probably should've stuck up for James Kanekoa, but I didn't want to debate James' intellect, or lack thereof, with a multimillionaire mob boss who probably hadn't even finished high school. And besides, I didn't know how dedicated James was to proving Lisa Marie's innocence. He might assume, as did nearly everyone else on Maui, that she was some kind of black widow killer. Maybe James' strategy wasn't focused on proving her innocence, but rather on getting her declared mentally unstable.

But I wasn't sold on her innocence either. I felt she was hiding something, and the whole whacko act might be just that: an act. If I found out she was involved in the killings, I'd be first in line pointing a finger. Screw Marv's ten grand reward.

"It's a generous offer, Marv, but I'll need one more thing before I say 'yes'."

"What's that?"

"A check for the wedding expenses: on your desk when I get there."

"Oh, for crying out loud. How much we talking about here?"

"I still owe my vendors almost four thousand dollars."

"Tell you what. I'll give you half that. You can use your Lisa Marie companion money to make up the rest."

"Make it three thousand and you've got a deal."

"I wish I'd met you under different circumstances, Ms. Moon. I'd have found a place for you in my organization."

"I'll take that as a compliment, Marv."

"You should. I need your ass down here tomorrow by eight a.m. sharp. We've filed a flight plan and need to leave by ten. Get here by eight so I won't have to leave the nut case alone by herself for too long."

"I'll be there, right on time."

"Good. And I'll have the check waiting for you in the guest room. I'd like you to consider my office off limits while you're here."

We said our good-byes and I went upstairs to get my laundry basket. I needed to wash a few things before packing for an extended stay at Olu'olu.

I came downstairs and found Steve and Hatch in the living room watching a golf tournament. Since neither of them had ever mentioned golf or, to my knowledge ever played a round of golf, I was pretty sure they wouldn't mind being interrupted.

"Guess what?" I did a 'tah-dah' thing with my hands to alert them I had something worthy of their attention.

"Tank Sherman's been found hanging by his ankles in Hana," said Steve.

"No."

"Your long lost father's turned out to be Donald Trump."

"No, and not funny."

"How about they've arrested Lisa Marie for Kevin's murder?"

"No, but you're getting warmer."

"How about you just spit it out because I'm getting tired of guessing?"

"Okay. Marv Prescott just called and hired me to move down to Olu'olu to keep an eye on Lisa Marie. He and the trophy wife don't want to stick around Maui and the police ordered Lisa Marie to not leave the island. Marv's paying me a hundred bucks a day to be her alibi."

Hatch's face darkened. "I don't like it. It could be dangerous."

"What? Watching Lisa Marie? I could be brain dead and do it. She's a tree sloth."

"No, I mean staying down there with those sleaze-balls." He looked over at Steve as if hoping to garner support.

Steve flicked his eyes back and forth between the two of us, apparently not ready to weigh in on which way he was leaning.

"Think about it," Hatch went on, "Lisa Marie's unstable and she may even be a murderer. Not to mention that 'Harry the Hacker' and 'Petey the Pervert' are probably regular guests at Prescott's mafia Camp David. I don't think it's safe, and I don't want you to go."

"I agree with Hatch," said Steve. "Tell him to hire some *schmuck* destined for the witness protection program to watch his crazy daughter."

"I've got three reasons I already said 'yes.' One, he's paying me a hundred a day, two, he's agreed to finally give me a check for his side of the wedding expenses, and three, I'll have a chance to really check out what's going on with Lisa Marie."

"What do you care?" said Steve. "Seems to me now that the wedding's a bust she's no longer your problem."

I hesitated. Steve didn't know about the reward money, or much else about my clandestine investigation. It was time to either come clean or dish up a pretty good fib.

Turns out, I wasn't in a truthful mood.

"Kevin was my client—I guess technically both Kevin and Brad were clients—and while I was working for them they both died. Not only that, because they died, I lost my business to the likes of Tank Sherman. In order to let it go and move on without regrets, I need to know what happened. I'm not feeling very positive about the police solving this case. It's been more than forty-eight hours, you know."

"Noble cause, Pali," Steve said. "But what'll you do if you stumble into something you can't handle? I say leave it to Wong and move on."

"I appreciate you guys' opinion, but this isn't up for a vote. I'll call every day to check in, but, as of tomorrow morning, my address will be Olu'olu."

"Can we visit?" said Steve.

"Afraid not. Marv's kind of skittish about having strangers in the house."

"Oh jeez, Pali. That's just great," said Hatch. "You're locked in and everybody else is locked out. Don't you see how insane this is?"

"Insane? Maybe you haven't noticed, but my whole life's gone nutso in the past couple of weeks. I'm trying to put a stop to it by earning enough money to pay my debts and hang on to my house and business."

Steve shook his head. "Isn't that the same speech you gave me a couple of weeks ago when you first signed up Lisa Marie?" He paused for a beat. "Oh yeah, and remind me again how that worked out?"

29

At seven o'clock Monday morning I zipped up my suitcase and quietly tip-toed down the stairs. Hatch got up from the sofa and hobbled over to block my exit.

"I really don't want you going down there."

"Did you sleep on the sofa?"

"Don't try and change the subject. I told you before, this could be dangerous."

"I know. But I'll be okay. You've never seen me fight, but trust me, they don't award black belts for congeniality. I can handle it."

"Can you catch a bullet in your teeth?"

I punched him lightly on his good shoulder.

"I didn't think so. Why are you doing this: for the money? 'Cuz if it's just about money, I'll loan you some, no problem."

"No, it's more than that. Please don't worry. I promise I'll call every day. What more can I say?"

"You could say you've wised up and you're not going to do it."

"Wised up? Are you calling me stupid?"

"You said it, not me."

I picked up my suitcase and dodged past him. When I left, I didn't bother closing the door.

I fired up the Geo and took a minute to savor one last look at my house and yard. There was no way I'd allow this place to go to foreclosure. Then I remembered Tank had threatened to buy it. I gunned the engine and headed out.

While driving to Olu'olu I did the math on my financial situation. Even without the reward money I was close to settling my debts. I had the two thousand dollars rent money from Hatch and I'd be getting seven hundred from Marv in the coming week. That was almost enough to catch up on my mortgage payments and pay at least the minimum on my past due bills. And with Marv's check for the wedding expenses I'd be able to reimburse nearly everyone except me for their out-of-pocket costs. Whatever craziness I'd be facing at Olu'olu was nothing compared to the relief of saving my home and my reputation.

Approaching Olu'olu I spotted a break in traffic and made a wild left from Honoapi'ilani Highway. I skidded toward the gate. Luckily it was open. Maybe Marv and Tina had just left for the airport or maybe the security guy was expecting me. I parked in my favorite spot, as close to the exit as possible. I popped the trunk and took out my scruffy black roller suitcase with the gimpy wheel.

"I'll take that." It was the big Fijian guy who'd harassed me when he'd caught me sneaking around the house.

"Thanks." I didn't know if Fijians used the word *mahalo*, and I didn't want to draw attention to our differences. For all I knew, the guy could have been third generation Hawaiian-born and raised, but from the looks of him, I doubted it.

Josie met me at the door with a big smile and a glass of guava juice on ice.

"Lisa Marie is in the sunroom," she said, leading me to the now familiar room. "I think it's nice of you to come and keep her company."

I didn't know if it was the language barrier or if my role had been misconstrued, but I decided against setting her straight. After all, I was rather fond of guava juice.

"Miss Pali is here," Josie announced as we stepped through the French doors.

Lisa Marie, in a two-piece French terry lounging outfit, was propped up on one of the brilliant yellow sofas. Her face was buried in a Hollywood gossip magazine. She peeked over the top, then raised it again and continued reading. I couldn't miss the eerie resemblance to Marv's behavior with his Wall Street Journal.

"Bah wahp," she said, her voice muffled by the magazine.

"Pardon me?" I said. It was more reflex than any real curiosity about what she'd said.

"I said, *big whoop*." She lowered the glossy magazine and stared at me as if hoping to make me vanish through sheer will. "Like I'm supposed to be glad Daddy's hired a gopher to spy on me."

I told her I was there to make sure she had an alibi witness since the police were still investigating.

"Like I'm going to go and, like, kill a bunch of *other* people?"

Her cold snarl made me want to shake all over like a wet dog, but I kept it in check.

"I don't think your dad thinks you're planning to do anything. He just wants to make sure you don't get accused of something."

"Like anybody's going to believe you." She stretched out on the sofa and draped the magazine over her face.

I took the hint.

Josie showed me to my room. It was the one I'd seen earlier, the first bedroom on the left with the mahogany bed swathed in mosquito netting and the enormous ceiling fan slowly churning the humid air. The Fijian security guy—

who Josie told me was named Kamisese, but went by George—had placed my suitcase on a luggage stand at the end of the bed. The zipper was open a couple of inches and I wondered if he'd taken the opportunity to sneak a peek. Didn't matter; I'd left the family jewels at home.

As promised, Marv's check for the wedding expenses was on the nightstand. He'd made it out to Polly Moone. Maybe he was being ornery or maybe he didn't know how to spell my name, but it didn't matter. I was on a first-name basis at the bank so I'd have no problem cashing it.

I peered out the large shuttered window. It opened onto a tiny courtyard tightly packed with dense tropical foliage: a banana tree, birds of paradise, and philodendrons with dinner-plate sized leaves. When I flipped the shutters aside and pulled the window open, ocean-fresh air flooded the room.

I plopped down on the bed to see if the obscenely rich had the same notion of comfort as the rest of us. I'm not much for rock-hard mattresses. No matter what so-called back experts say, I don't sleep well on anything approaching 'firm.' The nights I'd spent on the sofa bed squished next to Farrah and Sir Lipton had left me tired and achy. I longed for Baby Bear plush, or at least Mama Bear middle-of-the-road.

My prayers were answered. The mattress was a vast expanse of memory foam that brought to mind snuggling up to Auntie Mana's cushiony bosom. I considered taking a short nap while Lisa Marie snoozed under her gossip mag, but figured I should first give Hatch and Steve a call to let them know I'd survived the settling in.

"Hey, it's me."

"I was just going to call you," said Steve. "The second you left the phone started ringing. You in a place you can talk?"

"Yep, fire away."

"Well, first of all, your buddy Septic Tank called. He's demanding you call him back. He wanted your cell number, but I wouldn't give it to him. He sounded pretty steamed about something."

"I couldn't care less. Now that I got this babysitting gig I'm ripping up his check so whatever he's bitching about isn't my problem."

"From the way he was going off, you still might want to give him a call.

"I'll think about it, but I was kind of looking forward to telling him to 'pack sand' in person."

"He's heading back to Honolulu this morning, but he'll be on his cell later on."

"Did he leave a number? I don't exactly have him on speed dial." I was hoping he'd say *'no'* and I'd be free to ignore Tank for the rest of the day.

"Hang on, the guy's got more numbers than a deck of cards." He rattled off Tank's cell, pager, answering service, and home.

"Moving on," he continued, "Doug at your kung fu place called. He said to tell you, and this is right outta his mouth: 'My brother James is *the man.*' He said to stop by the gym and he'd explain."

"Huh. That sounds good."

"And finally, I don't want to burn through your cell minutes, but I thought you'd want to know that Mitch—you know, my bartender friend—told me he heard there's something hinky with the surveillance video from Ma'alaea Harbor. You know, the one with Lisa Marie and Kevin arguing."

"What's hinky about it?"

"Not sure."

"Where'd Mitch hear this?"

"Beats me. But you know what they say, only three people you can trust: your momma, your barber and your bartender."

I thanked him for the messages and asked him to put Hatch on.

"Sure, just a second." There was a rattling sound as he put down the phone. When it was picked up again it was still Steve. "Sorry, Pali, but he's in the john or something. Says he can't talk now. But before I sign off, I want you to promise me you'll stay safe down there. Call every day. If I don't hear from you, I'm marshalling a posse from the Ball and Chain and we'll come looking. You know, my friends love a party; even a search party."

"Now there's an image." In my mind's eye I saw the rainbow coalition storming the gate at Olu'olu: all bare chests, coifed do's and well-oiled pecs.

"Anyhow, you watch your back, sweetie, okay?"

I agreed and signed off. Then I went searching for Josie. I found her vacuuming an immense round rug in the foyer. It was a work of art: a pieced wool tapestry of palms, hibiscus flowers, and red ginger. The roar of the vacuum drowned out the sound of my approach, so I positioned myself in front of her and waved. She shut off the machine and the motor wound down with a whine.

"Sorry for interrupting your work, but I need to leave for a while. Would you mind keeping an eye on Lisa Marie?"

She puckered up her face as if not pleased to be thrust in that role, but after a couple of seconds she gave me a one-shoulder shrug signaling she'd do it.

"Is she still in the sunroom?" I said. "Maybe I should tell her I'm leaving."

"She taking a shower."

"Okay. I'll be back by…" I looked over at the immense grandfather clock. "No later than ten o'clock."

I zipped up to the Palace of Pain. The back parking area was nearly full, which meant there was a class in session. I quietly opened the back door trying to not interrupt. As I slowly pulled the door shut behind me, the hinge shrieked, and Sifu Doug glanced up and waved. He was leading a tots class for kids who looked about three or four years old. A group of moms sat in a circle of folding chairs in one corner of the room. They were chatting and laughing; each one clutching a coffee mug. It appeared they were enjoying pre-school martial arts a heck of a lot more than their offspring.

The kids wore black uniforms with thick white sashes wound around their waists. Some of them were so skinny their sashes were double-wrapped around their body yet they still hung down past their knees.

"I'll come back later." I stage whispered.

"No, no," said Sifu Doug. "Hang on a minute." He instructed the students to practice the form they were working on and told them he'd be back in a few minutes to check their progress. A couple of the moms lifted their heads and nodded as if to assure Doug they'd keep an eye out for shenanigans.

At his office door Sifu Doug kept an ice-filled picnic cooler stocked with water bottles. He motioned for me to help myself and I grabbed two waters, offering one to him before taking one for myself. In all things martial arts there's a protocol; a hierarchy of respect.

He pulled the top off his bottle and took a long pull. Then he made his way into the cluttered space of his tiny office. Pushing aside a tangle of padded headgear, an unopened cardboard box embellished with FedEx stickers, and a broom with a broken handle, he sat down in his creaky desk chair. He pointed to a white plastic chair behind the door.

"Pull that over and have a seat. I told you I'd call if I heard anything more about your killer bride."

I politely reminded him that everyone's presumed innocent until proven guilty. The look on his face told me I'd failed to make even a small dent in his opinion.

"It don't really matter if she's innocent or guilty, 'cuz James is pretty sure she won't even get arrested." He scooted his chair in and lowered his voice. "The video the cops have is messed up. Time code's all off."

I bit my lip. This must be what Steve's bartender meant about the tape being 'hinky.'

"What's that mean: time code?" I said.

"The time code on a surveillance tape is a bunch of numbers in the lower corner that shows what time the tape got recorded. On the video it shows a time code of 20:32, that's eight-thirty at night. But the sun sets before seven and on this tape it's bright daylight, so something's messed up. And without that tape, they got nothing linking your girl to either of the guys on the night they died. James says he's thinks she musta hired a pro to do the hit."

I considered correcting him once again about the presumption of innocence but I let it slide. I still hadn't been successful in getting Farrah to call Lipton a *she*—and the dog had the goods to prove it—so how could I expect to change anyone's mind about Lisa Marie's guilt?

"The cops have only been working the case a few days," I said. "Something else might come up."

"Might, but James is real stoked. He says they got nothin' and they're not gonna get nothin'."

We chugged from our water bottles.

I asked if he'd had much fallout from the MRSA scare. He said two students dropped out, but they weren't hardcore, so he thought they probably just used it as an excuse to get their money back.

A couple of minutes later, I got up to leave. I thanked Doug for calling me about the tape and gave him a short bow.

As I walked out to my car, I felt something shift. Finding out who killed Brad and Kevin was no longer just about collecting some reward money or even making good on my pact with Kevin. I flashed back to my air marshal days, when I imagined myself grabbing a couple of scumbag terrorists by the hair and pitching them out of a plane at thirty-five thousand feet. In my world it's crucial the good guys win. No, to be truthful, it's more arrogant than that: in my world I need to make sure the bad guys lose.

30

I got into my car lost in thought about the faulty surveillance video. The information had been passed down two or three times, so I wasn't ready to take it as fact. And even if the video was thrown out, maybe Lisa Marie's lawyer was being premature in his smug belief that the cops had no additional evidence against his client. Maybe they had eye witnesses and fingerprints and a pile of other stuff they were planning to throw at her in court. Then it dawned on me. They didn't. If they did, she'd already be cooling her Jimmy Choos in the Wailuku jail.

Even Daddy Prescott's considerable means would be of little use to her if she was arrested and charged with premeditated murder. Forget bail. She was a flight risk, literally, and wealthy enough to shrug off walking away from even the most outrageous bail bond. With no ties to the community, and a lifestyle that wouldn't vary whether she lived in St. Tropez or St. Louis, the judge would realize chances were slim to none she'd bother returning to Maui for trial.

So now what? With no evidence against Lisa Marie, and the cops unwilling to consider other motives, the official investigation would soon sputter to a halt. A sad scenario played out in my mind: Wong placing the puny amount of evidence they had—Kevin's autopsy report, the inadmissible videotape, and a few pages of interview notes—

into a white cardboard box labeled 'cold case.' In time, the box would get shipped off to Honolulu where it would join hundreds of other forgotten white boxes in a dimly-lit warehouse off Beretania Street. Todd Barker's snide opinion of Hawaii's police work and judicial system was beginning to look regrettably accurate. Two deaths in two weeks. Both questionable, both unsolved.

To be fair, unlike the other forty-nine states, the seven major inhabited islands of Hawaii present unique challenges for law enforcement. To start with, we're completely surrounded by water: three thousand miles of ocean in all directions. If a body is recovered from the ocean, normal forensic work is nearly impossible. Salt water erases the killer's fingerprints, washes away blood spatter and DNA, and even messes with toxicology reports. Tox reports generally are deemed "inconclusive" if the victim gulped copious amounts of seawater before dying.

What's more, if a killer dumps a victim's body into the ocean, chances are high it will never be recovered. The ocean has its own 'circle of life.' A hunk of dead flesh—human or otherwise—is like a Publisher's Clearinghouse Prize for sea creatures up and down the food chain.

I started my car and drove slowly down the alley. As I waited to make the turn onto the Hana Highway I had to yield to a yellow Maui County Fire engine as it screamed past me and took a left on Baldwin. I pulled out and stayed back a few car lengths. I remembered something on the driver's license exam about giving emergency vehicles at least fifteen feet, or was it fifty?

It didn't take fifty feet for me to figure out where they were headed. Smoke billowed from under the eaves of the Gadda-da-Vida and from a big hole in the roof over my shop. The police had blocked off Baldwin at Akoni Place so I pulled over and jumped out to follow on foot.

I was in an flat-out sprint when a firefighter in full gear—SCBA tank on his back and plastic face shield down—extended a gloved hand to halt my progress.

"Day bat," he said behind the mask.

I squinted in confusion.

"Stay back," he said, exaggerating the words so I could read his lips.

"That's my shop." I pointed to the roiling smoke.

"Sorry." He took my elbow and steered me toward a cordoned off area where a knot of bystanders had gathered.

"No, you don't understand—"

With his big gloved hand he gave my shoulder a slight push toward the yellow tape. I moved toward the onlookers, all the while watching the oily black smoke engulfing the building. As I bent to duck under the 'caution' tape, I heard the *click whir, click whir* of a film camera with an automatic advance.

"Hey," it was Steve. He was crouched on the ground, a few feet behind the tape. "You okay?" *Click whir, click whir*.

"Have you seen Farrah?" I peered at the front window of my shop. The glass was intact, but it looked as if it'd been painted black.

"No, but Beatrice is out here somewhere. She's the one who called 9-1-1. You run into Hatch yet?"

"He's here?"

"Yeah. We caught the call on his scanner. Got here about the same time the first engine pulled up." *Click whir, click whir*.

I scanned the crowd. No sign of Hatch or Farrah.

Steve lowered his camera. "You might try sneaking around back. Last I saw he was talking to a guy headed that way."

The access to the alley was blocked by fire apparatus, but I glimpsed a three foot opening between the fire engine and the alley fence. There was a guy working the pump panel on the near side of the truck, but the rest of the firefighters had congregated along the hose line laid out in front of my shop. The front door had been forced open and the nozzle man was poised to enter. A guy in a white helmet yelled into his walkie-talkie and the hose team marched through the door, lugging a fat snake of khaki hose inside.

After four or five minutes the crowd control guy turned his back and I took the opportunity to slip away. I wedged myself in the space between the fire engine and the sagging chain link fence and crab-walked alongside the vibrating truck until I was behind the building. I checked up and down the alleyway for a guy on a crutch. Or a *mu'u mu'u* clad woman with a wide halo of frizz. Nothing.

I looked up. Farrah's apartment door stood open. No firefighters in sight. I bounded up the stairway, smelling the bitter stench of burning wood and calculating how many bones I'd break when the stairs gave way.

The smoky haze inside the living room made it look like a black and white photograph. My eyes stung and quickly filled with tears; my nose refused to suck in even a shallow breath of the acrid air. An aluminum crutch was propped on one end of the sofa.

"Hatch? Farrah?" I don't think I actually said it out loud; it was probably just my brain screaming.

Hatch was on hands and one knee behind the coffee table on the living room floor. His broken leg with the stiff white cast was stretched out behind him. As I made my way over to him, he reached out his hand and swept under the table as if trying to locate something.

I bent down so he could see me. By now my lungs were beginning to feel starved for air, but I grabbed the back of his shirt and nodded toward the bedroom. I probably should have stuck around to help him get up, but I didn't. I figured he wouldn't leave until he'd found what he'd come up there for, and I felt the same.

I scanned the bedroom and looked under the bed. One good thing about a tiny apartment: it doesn't take long to search.

The box was in the bedroom closet, right where it'd been when I'd first seen the pups. Lipton had positioned herself over her puppies, so I couldn't do a headcount. Her eyes looked defiant, but she didn't make a sound as I grabbed the box and roughly jostled it into carrying position.

Hatch and I got to the door at the same time. He gave me a little 'after you' wag of his crutch and I dashed down the stairs, trying my best to avoid dumping mother and brood onto the pavement below. Hatch thumped hard at my heels.

"Hey! What the hell are you two doing?" It was the white helmet guy yelling from the end of the alley. He sprinted toward us.

If I'd had any air in my lungs, I might have answered. Instead, I sucked in huge gulps of oxygen and just held up my hand in a *give me a minute* gesture. I tried to talk but only managed to cough up sticky phlegm.

Meanwhile, Hatch busied himself taking stock of the pups. He pulled them out one-by-one and checked their eyes and then ran a finger inside their mouths. Lipton was still in the box. When he got around to lifting her out, she drooped like a half-filled sack of rice. Her eyes were glassy, her mouth slack.

Hatch laid her gently on the pavement and bent over her. He gripped her head and put her nose and mouth into his mouth, and blew in three quick breaths. Her torso expanded. He released his mouth and pressed his palm against her chest, one-two-three.

Hatch kept up the doggie CPR, even though it appeared futile to me. Lipton's chest rose and fell with Hatch's breaths, but other than that I saw no change. By then, three firefighters had entered the alley through the back door of my shop. They'd flipped their face shields up and I saw them shoot each other amused glances, but they said nothing.

Steve showed up just as Lipton's legs began to twitch. *Click whir, click whir*. Lipton lifted her head and bicycled her legs as she tried to stand.

A firefighter came forward and clapped Hatch on the shoulder. "Good job, man." The guy had caught him on his bad side, but Hatch didn't flinch.

"No sense letting things die," Hatch said. It looked like he might have had tears in his eyes, but smoke does that.

Farrah arrived at the entrance to the alley only minutes after Lipton's return from the Great Beyond. I ran to her.

"What happened?" she said. "I went out to look at rentals and the next thing I knew there were sirens every-where."

I hugged her and we both took in the scene. The back doors to both her store and my shop stood open. Dark gray water trickled over the threshold of my shop, but the store was dry; just a veil of smoke wafted outside.

Before I could say anything the white helmet guy came forward. "You the occupant of these premises?"

"That's my shop," I managed to rasp.

"Yeah, and that's my store. And my home." Farrah pointed to the stairway.

"Well, turns out we didn't need to send any crews over there. Got it knocked down before it could spread." He turned to me. "Any idea how this got started?"

I didn't say anything. Wasn't figuring that out his job?

As if he read my mind, he went on, "So far, we're not ruling out arson. First-in team noticed a slight accelerant smell and what appeared to be an intentional fuel load in the back: a pile of lumber. But it doesn't take much; one spark and these old buildings go up like kindling. I'm calling in the fire investigator."

"What should we do now?" Farrah said.

"Well, you might want to consider a fire sale." He grinned at his own lame joke, then looked around and saw nobody else sharing the humor. "Seriously, you have some pretty extensive smoke damage in there. I think you should call your insurance company. But you came out better than your neighbor here. I'm estimating that side of the building at a near total loss."

He glared at me as if hoping I'd clap my hands and say, '*Goody*', so he could be the star witness at my arson trial.

"I've run a successful business here for over two years," I said.

"Well, the investigator's on his way from O'ahu, so I'm not going to speculate. And, like I said, old wiring and ancient wood's a bad combination. We get calls on these plantation-era buildings all the time."

"Can I go in and look around?" said Farrah.

"I'd rather you wait until the investigator's had a chance to get here, but if you need to go upstairs to pick up a few personal effects, I can have a firefighter go with you."

I lobbied to go into my shop as well. Since I'd pretty much cleared out everything on Friday, I wouldn't have lost much, but I wanted to grab my address book and my box of vendor files.

"Wait 'til we can escort you."

When Farrah was finished upstairs, the firefighter asked me what I needed from my shop.

"I'd like to go in and get some things from my desk."

"Still too hot in there. Tell me what you need and I'll get it."

"Okay. I need the cardboard box from the bottom right-hand drawer of the desk. And if my address book is still on the desk, I'd appreciate it if you'd grab that too."

He put his plastic face mask back on and went in. When he came out, he handed me my address book, soot-covered and wet, but intact. He flipped up his mask.

"Thanks, I said. "But what I really need is that file box."

"There's no box in the desk."

"The right bottom drawer," I said. "It's the big one: a file drawer."

"Nothin' in there."

We stood there, staring each other down, until he blew out a breath and flipped his mask back into place. Then he went inside. When he did, I peeked in behind him.

The odor knocked me back on my heels. I'd expected it to smell like a luau pit or maybe a bonfire, but it didn't. The wet charred wood smelled dank and sulfurous. The air swirled with particles and with the windows smoked over it was dark as night. There were plate-sized holes punched in the walls.

The firefighter came out lugging two file-size drawers, one in each hand. He dropped them at my feet. They were both empty.

He flipped up his mask. "Anything else?" His tone said he was done playing fetch for me.

"That's all," I said. "And I really appreciate you looking."

Farrah came over and put an arm around me. "You get what you needed?"

"No, and it doesn't make sense. The drawers were both in pretty good shape. How could everything inside them just burn up?"

"Maybe the investigator guy can tell you." We walked over the small pile of clothes and personal belongings she'd piled up near Lipton's box. "Steve says Hatch rescued Lipton. Is that true?"

"Yep. Pulled her and the pups out of your closet and then gave Lipton mouth to mouth once they got outside."

"You jealous?"

"Of Hatch sucking face with your dog? Trust me, it's a good thing it was Lipton. If I'd been the one trapped in a burning building, he'd have let me croak."

"What's with you two?"

I shrugged.

"What do you think Tank's gonna say when hears about this?" she said, gesturing toward the still-smoking building.

"Who cares? He's tearing it down, remember?"

By now, a small crowd of neighbors had come into the alley. They swarmed Farrah offering condolences and help in getting the store back in business. I walked out to Baldwin where my car was parked and checked my cell phone. Tank's cell number came up as a missed call. I set my crap detector to 'maximum' and dialed.

He answered on the first ring. "Don't even *think* of trying to cash that check, Pali. I knew you girls weren't happy to sell out but I never thought you'd do arson on me."

Ha! I wanted to tell him if I'd figured I could have gotten away with 'doing arson on him' I'd have picked up a can of gas and a Bic lighter three days ago.

"I didn't do it, Tank. And neither did Farrah. The fire almost killed her dog." The conversation was absurd, since he was planning on taking down the building anyway. What did *he* care if the walls were punched in and the floor warped by water damage?

"Hey, no skin off my nose. You girls did me a favor. When the city condemns the building I'll get it for half of what I was willing to pay. But Noni tells me you swiped those business files I paid for. She says when she went by this morning they were gone. So forget the five grand. In fact I already stopped payment on it. Oh yeah, and have a nice day."

He clicked off.

There were a few ways to look at this: Noni stole the files and lied to Tank; Tank has the files but doesn't want to pay me for them; or someone else took them. But who besides Noni and Tank would care about a box of 'Let's Get Maui'd' files?

My money was on the fat man. He'd already proven himself to be a cheat. Now I could add 'liar' to his list of regrettable qualities.

I checked the time on my phone: almost noon. I'd been gone from Olu'olu for over three and a half hours which made me more than two hours overdue. I called Josie and told her I'd had an emergency come up but I was on my way back. She said Marv had called from his plane and he'd sounded upset that I'd left so soon after arriving. When I inquired about Lisa Marie, Josie told me she was napping.

"I'll be there in fifteen minutes," I fibbed, knowing full well the drive to Olu'olu would take at least twice that long.

"Maybe you call Marv now," she said. "He not know where you are when you call on the cell phone, right?" The woman was a lifesaver. She gave me Marv's cell number and I memorized it. I knew I might need it again in the near future, so it seemed like a good investment to spend a few brain cells making it permanent.

"Prescott," he said, answering the call. He had to know it was me. There was no way a guy like Marv doesn't check caller ID before picking up.

"Hello, Marv. Josie tells me you called." I willed my voice to sound upbeat, as if I'd just lathered up with sunscreen and was pulling up a chaise next to Lisa Marie.

"Where are you?"

"At your place. It's a gorgeous day here."

"Josie said you left hours ago."

"I had a quick meeting regarding Lisa Marie's situation. I can't promise too much yet, but it's looking better and better."

"You're supposed to be watching her, not traipsing around the countryside. If you need to talk to someone, that's what phones are for, Ms. Moon." He let a beat go by so I could offer an apology, but I didn't. He went on, "What'd you find out?"

"It appears the only evidence they have against Lisa Marie is tainted." I gave myself a mental pat on the back for coming up with such an official-sounding word: *tainted*. Seemed like the kind of word a real private investigator might use.

"What the hell does that mean: *tainted*?" Ah, pearls before swine, for sure.

"It means it's messed up and the prosecutor won't be able to use it. I can't really give you the particulars, because the information's not been released yet. I promise I'll call as soon as I hear more." I passed two dawdling cars I'd been following for the past couple of miles. Soon the road would start curving and the center line would change from dashes to double solid.

"Put Josie on."

Busted.

"Ah, she's not out here right now."

"Where is she?"

"She's around the house somewhere, but not where I am."

"Go get her. I'll wait."

I took the sharp curve just before the little tunnel on Honoapi'ilani Highway. In about five seconds, the rock walls would suck up any transmission microwaves, effectively putting an end to the call.

"I'm not sure where she is. It may take me a minute to track her down." I said. I'd entered the dark passage. Water dripped from the slate gray walls.

"You're breaking up. Where are you? You better not be lying to me, Ms. Moo—?"

And then he was gone.

31

I gunned it past Papalaua and Punahoa Beach and passed four cars in a row in the straightaway near Ka'ili'uli. When I arrived at Olu'olu I roared up to the gate, my bald tires grappling for purchase as I slammed on the brakes. I didn't even have time to start the 'mother may I?' routine with George on the speaker box when I saw the gate slowly grinding its way open. I waved my thanks in the direction of the gate house and scratched to a stop just beyond the front door. I felt like every second I gained was a little chit in my favor. As if Marv would consider my lying less egregious if I called him back in eight minutes instead of ten.

It was Lisa Marie who answered my quick rap at the door.

"Oh good, you're up," I said. She stepped in front of me, blocking my way.

"Yes, I'm up. And I've been up for hours. Why do you smell like that?" She leaned in and sniffed me like a dog.

"Well, I've had—"

She held up her hand. "No one cares, okay? Anyway, it's good you're finally back because I need to go out." She cupped my elbow in her palm and steered me back outside.

"Wait. Your dad gave me a message for Josie." I pulled my arm free. I don't like being physically restrained, and I found her bossiness offensive. As of this morning, I now worked for Marv, not her.

"Hang on," I said. "I'll be back in a minute."

I sprinted down the hall. Through the tiny window in the kitchen door I saw Josie sitting on a stool at the counter. She popped up quickly when I entered.

"Hi Josie, sorry to burst in like this, but Marv Prescott wants you to call him on his cell phone." My voice sounded out of breath, but I wasn't. My lack of oxygen probably stemmed more from recalling the way Marv and I had left it: him accusing me of lying and being correct.

Josie's narrowed her eyes in a confused look. "I just talk with Mr. Prescott a few minutes ago. He ask if you are here. I told him your car is outside but I not sure where you are. I said I would find you and he say 'Forget it. No big deal.'" She said *deal* like *dill*, but I got the drift.

"*Mahalo*." I put out my arms to give her a hug, but she stepped back, ducking her head as if uncomfortable with public displays of affection by deceitful co-workers.

"No worries," she said. "Everybody who work for Mr. Prescott take care of each other." She glanced over at the cook, who shot me a pinched smile and a one bob nod of the head.

"I'll remember that."

I walked quickly back outside. Lisa Marie was leaning against the driver door to the Geo, her arms crossed.

"Not nice to keep me waiting."

"Where're we going?" I said.

"I'm sick of people staring at me," she said. "I want you to take me to buy a wig."

Wig? I'd lived on Maui almost my entire life, but I'd never run across a wig store. I rubbed my forehead in contemplation.

"I have no idea where to buy a wig. You may need to order one from Honolulu."

"Get in, I know where." She slid into the driver's seat. When I didn't move, she leaned over and cranked down the passenger side window. "C'mon. I looked it up on the Internet. It's over on the other side, near the hospital."

I reluctantly got in. "Do you know how to drive a stick?"

"A stick? You mean a shifter car?" She rammed the gear shift up and down a few times without putting in the clutch. I winced.

"Doesn't seem too hard."

It took four tries to get out of the gate. Lisa Marie would kill the engine, scream a cesspool of expletives, and then try again. After the first kill, I tried to coach her, but she slapped my hand off the gear shift knob. I resigned myself to mutely riding shotgun.

Once we'd made it onto the highway and were cruising along in third gear, she turned to me.

"See? I'm a fast learner. My dad says there's nothing I can't do, and he's right. And besides, if I mess up, big whoop. Money can fix ninety-nine percent of all screw-ups. Did you ever think of that?"

"Not in so many words, but you're probably right. Money's the next best thing to having friends."

"What's that supposed to mean? Are you saying I don't have friends?"

"Lisa Marie, since you're in a philosophical mood, consider this: everything's not always about you."

"Well, consider this Pali: it's *never* about losers like you."

Deep breath, deep breath.

When we approached the stop light at Ma'alaea, Lisa Marie failed to push in the clutch as she braked. The engine shuddered, then shut down.

"What's *wrong* with this piece of crap?" she shrieked.

"It's going to be harder for you to drive the stick in traffic with all the stopping and starting. Do you want me to take over?"

"No! Back off, bitch. I can do this if you'd just shut your yap." She was at full volume now. Cars behind us had started to honk. She threw a middle-finger salute out the window with her left hand while trying to shove the gearshift into first with her right. The steering wheel was on its own.

I stared out the side window, trying to imagine myself sitting on my porch at sunset; Steve sitting companionably alongside.

The final four miles to Wailuku were a series of stalls, blue language, and grinding gears. The starter was sounding like it was contemplating a strike. As painful as it was, I managed to stay silent.

The shop near the hospital was called "Rx for Beauty." The window display included a dozen white head-only manikins with placid features and an array of wigs in different colors and hairstyles: black ringlets, a chestnut-red pageboy, and a mahogany brown bob. Three of the manikins wore jaunty small-brimmed caps, and two modeled silky gypsy-style headscarves. I wondered what it would be like to work in a shop where everyone who came in—except, of course, cue-ball-by-choice Lisa Marie—had been to the gates of hell and back.

"That one's cute," Lisa Marie said as we gazed at the window display. She pointed to a platinum pixie cut, which I thought would look good on her.

"Let's go in and you can try it on," I said.

"No, it's cute, but I'm going for a more natural look. I want something that just hangs there. Like yours."

My reflection in the store window showed my shoulder length hair in deep distress. Frizzy, split ends cried out for a trim. My bangs hung down past my eyebrows, making it look like I lacked a forehead. This was the look she was going for?

"Are you sure? There are some pretty cute short styles here."

"I know exactly what I want."

We went inside and a plus-size local woman with russet-colored skin came out from the back of the store. She was wearing a red and black *mu'u mu'u* and knee-high nylons she'd rolled down to her ankles. On her feet she wore a pair of blue mule-style bedroom slippers. Even though her dress was billowy, it was obvious her chest was washboard flat. I figured she'd chosen to forgo the breast prosthetics to show her customers she was walking the walk.

"Oh my dear," she cooed, fixing on Lisa Marie's bald pate. "And so young."

"I've been through a lot." Lisa Marie put two fingertips to her lips and triple-blinked a couple of times, as if holding back tears.

"You just let it go, honey. We're all survivors here; we honor your journey."

"Thank you. You're so kind. Unlike some people who've been making fun of me." She nodded in my direction, and the store clerk gasped and shot me a nasty look.

I sidestepped Lisa Marie's con game. "You're looking for a mid-length wig, right?"

She turned to the clerk. "Even though my older sister here has been calling me stuff like 'slickie sickie' and 'baldy-locks,' we're still family. No matter how mean she gets, I love her anyway. You know, when we were little girls our mother dressed us in matching clothes and we always had the same haircut. When I was in chemo I'd keep myself from barfing by thinking back to those happy times with my big sister. Do you have a wig that looks like that?" She pointed to my hair.

The clerk shot me a second contemptuous look. No doubt she believed the wrong sister had been stricken with cancer. I silently repeated to myself, 'a hundred bucks a day, a hundred bucks a day'.

The clerk waddled to the back of the store and brought out a shoulder-length wig of light brown hair. She gestured for Lisa Marie to take a seat in a fussy little boudoir chair facing a gilt-edged mirror. Using a wig comb, the clerk smoothed and tucked the hair until it was a tidy long bob that just grazed her shoulders. As I stood behind her, my reflection in the mirror brought to mind a "before" picture for a hair conditioner capable of miraculous results.

"How's that, honey? It looks *ten* times better than your sister's, but it's nearly the same color and style." She made no effort to pull the punch, shooting me yet a third look of disapproval.

"It's fine. I'm kind of worried though," murmured Lisa Marie. "It's so nice, I don't know if I can afford it. Can you tell me the price?"

"This one's a classic, so it's very reasonable." The clerk went to the cashier desk and consulted a battered three-ring binder. "Let's see. Yes, the Patti Pageboy is only fifty-nine ninety-nine. It's not real hair, you know."

"Oh, that much?" Lisa Marie started up the blinky-eye thing again. "I only have forty dollars to spend."

The clerk bit the side of her lip.

Lisa Marie reached up and pulled the wig from her head. She laid it down on the tiny dressing table and let out a theatrical sigh.

"Okay," said the clerk. "I won't make any money on this, but you're such a sweet girl. And besides, no cancer survivor should have to put up with *kukae*—that's our word for crap—from her own sister." Once again, I was treated to the death-ray glare.

"Thank you. *Mahalo*, so much!" Lisa Marie jumped up from the chair and jogged over to the cashier stand. She stepped behind the counter and leaned into the clerk's non-existent bosom like a child seeking a hug.

"You're so kind. I will never forget you."

Until we walk out the door.

The clerk carefully wrapped the wig in pink tissue and placed it in a round yellow hat box decorated with brightly-colored butterflies. Lisa Marie mused she was worried the wig would lose its shape if she kept it stored in the box and the clerk threw in a free Styrofoam wig-stand. When we finally made our way out to the car, I pointedly marched to the driver's side door. She owed me, big-time, and I wasn't about to put up with car torture all the way back to Olu'olu.

"What was that little charade all about?" I said once she'd slammed the passenger door.

"Oh, nothing. I just get a kick out of messing with people."

"You enjoy telling lies and cheating a nice lady who has had *cancer*?"

"Don't get all high and mighty with me, Pali. You'd do it if you could. But you're not smart enough, rich enough, or cute enough to get away with it. But me?" She shot me what my brother would call a *shit-eating grin*. "Messing with people is my number one talent."

No argument there.

32

As soon as we left the parking lot, Lisa Marie tore into the exquisitely wrapped hat box and plopped her new wig on her head. She pulled down her windshield visor, probably expecting a mirror, but my Geo lacked the 'convenience package.'

"You sure have a crappy car." She grabbed the edges of the wig above her ears and tugged, adjusting it side to side. "How do I look?"

I gave her a quick once over. A red Jeep in front of me had its left-turn signal blinking, and I was keeping an eye out for brake lights.

"I think it may be a little too high on this side." I reached over to fine-tune it, but she jerked her head out of reach.

She yanked the left side down just as I braked hard to avoid hitting the Jeep which had come to a complete stop. The wig ended up forty-five degrees off-kilter.

"You bitch! You did that on purpose!" Her shriek nearly made me kill the engine. I downshifted and dodged around the inert car. A glance in my rearview mirror confirmed my suspicion: the driver was holding up a newspaper-sized map. Traffic behind him bobbed and weaved to avoid a collision. I figured it was just a matter of time...then I heard a *bam*! Normally, I would've stuck around to give a witness report but I couldn't trust what might come out of Lisa Marie's mouth.

She spent the next few minutes of the ride rummaging through her Prada bag. She pulled out a gold clamshell compact encrusted with semi-precious colored stones. Okay, if it had been *my* compact they would have been semi-precious stones. The green and red stones on *her* compact were probably real emeralds and rubies. She clicked it open and used the three-inch mirror inside to admire her new hairdo. She also freshened her lipstick, spit-smoothed her eyebrows and investigated her chin for stray hairs. I marveled at her ability to preen with such concentration, seemingly oblivious to the stunning ocean views passing by on the highway.

We pulled into Olu'olu twenty minutes later. As soon as the gate parted, I saw the detective's car parked in the driveway. Lisa Marie snapped her compact shut.

"Oh, hell," she said. "What now?"

I figured they'd come to officially release her from being a suspect. I wasn't clear on how the police worked, but it seemed to me if they'd ordered you to stay put, they were obliged to formally advise you when you were free to go.

Lisa Marie snatched the wig from her head and shoved it into the hat box before getting out of the car. "No use giving away my beauty secrets," she said when she caught my confused look.

Josie met us at the door and told us in a whisper the police were waiting for Lisa Marie in the sunroom.

"I tell them you go to doctor's." She gave Lisa Marie an expectant smile, but instead of a *thank you* for covering for her, Lisa Marie snapped, "You shouldn't lie, Josie. Your nose'll grow."

Josie looked bewildered. Maybe Pinocchio wasn't a popular kid's story in the Philippines. She recovered quickly, though, and looked down at Lisa Marie's hat box.

"You buy something nice?"

Lisa Marie nodded and handed her the box. "Put this in my room. But first, bring me a drink. I'm going to need it."

"Ice tea? Coke?"

"No, I said a *drink*. A screwdriver, with two shots and no ice."

Josie turned and went down the hallway.

"Do you want me to go in there with you?" I said to Lisa Marie. "They may tell me to leave, but at least they'll see someone's here at the house with you. I'm pretty sure they know your dad's gone back to the mainland."

"Suit yourself."

I took that as tacit approval and followed her into the sunroom. The two detectives were perched on the bright yellow sofa, spines ramrod straight, feet flat on the floor. Each wore taupe-colored pants and a muted beige print aloha shirt. They looked like two spots of drab in a sea of luminous color. Two tall crystal glasses of ice water sat untouched on the coffee table in front of them.

Josie came in and handed a matching glass to Lisa Marie. It appeared to be an enormous serving of orange juice. No doubt the cops figured Lisa Marie must be some kind of health nut.

"Ah, Ms. Prescott," said Wong. He'd stood when Lisa Marie entered the room, and he remained standing. "Nice of you to join us. Did we or did we not have an appointment this afternoon at one?"

"As my maid already told you, I had something personal I had to do."

I looked at the clock on the wall. It was one thirty. Lisa Marie wore an expensive Rado watch, but I'd never seen her even glance at it. In fact, time seemed of little significance to her.

"And who might this be?" Wong nodded my way.

"She's my personal assistant. I've asked her to be present to make sure you don't pistol whip me or plant drugs in my pocket or something." Lisa Marie shot him a coquettish smile. His face remained impassive but I noticed his right hand clench into a fist.

"Does your assistant have a name?"

I weighed my options of stepping forward and introducing myself versus letting Lisa Marie handle it. I chose the latter. It wasn't my fight, and if the cops were there to release her, I'd probably be following them out the door anyway.

"She's nobody. Do you want her to leave?"

"Yes. If you're unwilling to provide us with her name and her connection to this case, then I'm afraid she'll have to step outside while we talk."

I felt strangely stung by the dismissal, but figured it was probably for the best. I went down to my room to call Steve and Hatch and make sure everyone had gotten home safely after the fire. I figured I'd keep it short and use the extension in my room. No use burning up my cell minutes.

Steve answered.

"Hey," I said.

"Hey, yourself! You okay? I lost track of you. Are you still at the fire? I didn't recognize the caller ID."

"No, I'm back at Olu'olu. Wong's here and I'm using the guest room phone."

"I never got to tell you about that hinky videotape. Guess what they found out?"

I didn't have the heart to pop his balloon. "What?"

"It's got a bum time code. Seems it was recorded at a different time and even on a different *day*."

Okay, so maybe discretion *is* the better part of valor. A different day? Sifu Doug hadn't mentioned that.

"How'd they figure that?"

He explained about time code, which I already knew, and then he continued. "The cops reviewed the dock worker's schedules for the past couple of weeks and matched the names against the images of the people on the video. The tape with Lisa Marie and Kevin arguing was from Sunday afternoon, three days *before* Kevin's body showed up on the beach."

"Huh. So that would explain why Lisa Marie still had hair."

"And that's why the tape is worthless. At least a dozen people saw Kevin after that."

"Yeah, including me."

"Guess what else has happened? *The Maui News* bought three of my shots of the fire. They especially liked the one of Hatch doing CPR on the dog."

"Speaking of the Canine Crusader," I said, "How's he doing? He sucked in a bunch of smoke up in Farrah's apartment."

"He's taking a nap. I had to practically carry him into the house he was so worn out."

"I'll bet. Dragging that cast up and down Farrah's back stairs had to take a toll. But if he hadn't shown up and brought Lipton back to life, I don't know if Farrah could've handled it."

"Yeah. So are you coming back home? I mean, without that video, what've they got on Lisa Marie?"

"Wong's here now. I'll wait and see what he says. If he says she's free to go, I'm sure Marv'll have her going back to the mainland on the next thing smokin'. Why don't I give you a call in another hour or so? Say, three o'clock?"

"Sounds good. I'm stickin' around," he said. "I've had enough excitement for one day."

We hung up. The call had gone on longer than I'd intended. I wouldn't put it past Marv to deduct for time I'd spent on his phone, so I looked around for my purse to call Farrah from my cell. My bag wasn't in my room. I must have left it behind in the sunroom when I'd been hastily booted out by Glen Wong.

The French doors to the sunroom were standing open. I looked in. No one was there. I scanned the entry table just inside the doors. I was certain that's where I'd put my purse and keys when I'd come in, but now the top was just a clear expanse of highly-polished hardwood.

I left to go search for Josie. She was in the far hallway, running a dry mop across the tile.

"Did you happen to pick up my purse and keys from the entry table in the sunroom?"

She looked puzzled. "How did you drive your car away without your keys?" she said.

Okay, we were having one of those conversations where Part A is not, by any stretch of the imagination, fitting into Part B.

"I haven't driven anywhere. I was in the guest room on the telephone."

"Oh no." She ran to the front door and pulled it open.

The police car no longer blocked the driveway. Trouble was, my green Geo was long gone as well.

33

I sprinted to the gate house and startled George, who had his head down gawking at a magazine. I averted my eyes as he slapped it shut and shoved it under a shelf below the open window.

"Hey man, it's not dirty," he said when he saw me looking away. He pulled the magazine back out and showed me the cover: *Surfing*. I felt myself start to smile, visualizing a guy his size struggling to get upright on a long board.

"Did Lisa Marie just leave in my car?"

"No," he said. "You did. A couple minutes ago."

That took me a few seconds to process. But it didn't appear he was burning up any brain cells processing it along with me.

"No, George. I'm here. I'm not in my car. Lisa Marie's in my car."

"It looked like you." He came out of the gate house and stared out toward the highway, as if hoping to spot the Geo parked on the other side of the gate.

"Did you see which way she went?"

"Not sure, but I think she turned right. Like I said, I thought it was you. I figured you were headed back up to Pa'ia."

I glanced around for a means of pursuit, and settled on the four-car garage at the far end of the property.

"What's in there?" I pointed to the garage doors.

"Mr. Prescott's cars."

"Good. I need to use one of them."

"Can't." He shrugged and shook his head, giving me a forlorn look.

"Oh, I think I *can*. You see, Lisa Marie's father hired me to keep an eye on her since the cops are watching her every move. Now she's stolen my car and taken off. I need to find her, and fast. Otherwise, *somebody's* going to have to explain to Mr. Prescott why he opened the gate and allowed Lisa Marie to drive out of here all by herself."

Now he looked like he was burning up some brain cells.

"Mr. Prescott took the Benz to the airport this morning and it's still over there," he said. "The Bentley's got something wrong with the fuel injectors so it stalls. The only other car is Mrs. Prescott's little Porsche." He pronounced it *porch*, but I knew what he meant. "She don't let nobody drive it; not even *Mr*. Prescott." He chuckled, as if anyone daredevil enough to say 'no' to Marv Prescott deserved his admiration.

"Please get me the keys, *now*."

"I can't. She'll kill me."

He crossed his arms in front of his massive chest and smiled a Buddha smile. I reached out and gripped his right wrist in my right hand, while stepping to his side. Then I twisted the wrist up behind him while sweeping my foot around his well-muscled calf. I had him locked in a lopsided leg wrap. His face froze into an astonished look as he teetered on the edge of a fall.

"You can give me those keys standing up or from the ground nursing a bad sprain. Up to you." I pulled his arm up higher.

"They're on the wall in the shack." He nodded toward the gatehouse.

I released him and went to the gatehouse door. At the back of the tiny space was a pegboard with metal hooks. Four sets of keys hung there, but only one set sported the red, yellow and black Porsche logo. I unhooked the key chain and trotted back to George. He was rubbing his wrist and shooting me major stink eye.

"Open the garage door," I ordered.

"You press the button on the keys."

I looked at the key chain in my hand. In addition to ignition and valet keys it had a tan plastic fob with a green button in the center. I pressed the button and the furthest garage door slid up. The overhead light spotlighted a dazzling red Porsche Boxster convertible with a gray top.

"That's it?"

"Yes, ma'am. But you can't drive it outta here unless I open the gate."

"So? Open the gate."

He shook his head. "I do that and the Missus finds out, I'm a dead man."

"Then don't open it. Problem is, when Marv calls, I'll let you explain how you let Lisa Marie leave on her own when the cops said she couldn't. Think about it, George. Who'd you rather piss off? Mrs. Prescott or Mr.?"

"Okay, get out of here. But bring Miss Lisa Marie back real fast. And don't do *nothing* bad to that car."

***

I could barely see over the steering wheel of the low-slung convertible. My Geo was not an especially high-sitting ride, but this felt like I was fanny-buffing the pavement. If I came into a big inheritance this particular model probably wouldn't make my shopping list. But whew! talk about acceleration.

I careened through the turns on the Honoapi'ilani Highway sneaking up on slow-pokes and blowing around them like they were in neutral. I mostly waited for the center line to turn from solid to dashes, but sometimes I risked it. I knew every inch of the highway, and Tina's car could outrun and outmaneuver not only the wimpy rental cars but probably cop cars as well. In a fit of bravado I considered trying to tune the radio to KPOA-FM, but I had too much going on with keeping an eye on the road ahead, downshifting when necessary, and scanning side roads and turnouts for my green Geo.

I sped straight up the highway toward Kahului. I knew Lisa Marie didn't have much of a head start, but with only George's tentative confirmation of which way she'd gone I was pretty much going on gut feeling. Since this was the road we'd traveled to the wig store, it made sense if she was just out for a joyride she'd stick to the tried and true rather than risk getting lost.

At the Kuihelani Road turnoff, I caught a glimpse of a scabby green car making a dog-track right turn. I tried to convince myself it wasn't my car. In fact, I was mortified to see how pathetic the car looked, even from this distance, but it was the right size, shape and color. It took the Boxster only seconds to get close enough to confirm the disgrace.

Kuihelani becomes Dairy Road and then heads straight on out to the Maui airport. Maybe Lisa Marie was planning to head for home now that she'd been sprung. But why steal my car? Why not summon a limo, with cut glass liquor bottles and mirrored windows?

My theory about her making a dash to the airport was nixed when the Geo took a screeching two-wheel right turn, without stopping at a red light, at Hana Highway only a few blocks short of the airport entrance. Oncoming traffic dodged and horns bleated, but Lisa Marie barreled ahead. She was now on the road to Pa'ia. Was she headed to my shop? Maybe she'd learned of the fire and wanted to see the damage for herself.

At the intersection of Highway 37—Haleakala Highway —she fooled me again. She slipped into the right lane and, again without signaling, took another right turn. Okay, now I was totally confused. Highway 37 leads to the Upcountry area: a place with no major shopping or entertainment and certainly no exodus off the island. It offers peaceful farms and cooler temps. Nothing up that way, short of an invitation to Oprah's lavish estate, would hold much appeal for Lisa Marie. I made the turn.

Haleakala Highway is steep. In fact, we learned in driver's ed that it's one of the steepest paved highways in all of the United States. If you take it all the way to the top, you'll climb to ten-thousand feet above sea level in only thirty-eight miles. After a couple of miles, it was obvious the Geo was struggling. Smoke belched from the tailpipe. I imagined Lisa Marie, foot smashed to the floorboard, screeching obscenities as the little green machine wearily clawed its way up the incline.

I eased up on the gas pedal. The Boxster was raring to go, but if I'd downshifted and let it have its way I'd have overtaken Lisa Marie in less than a minute. By this point, apprehension wasn't my goal. My curiosity peaked, I wanted to see where she was headed. I promised myself I'd intervene if her joyride threw her into the category of 'harmful to self or others,' but until then, I was willing to go along with her game.

I had to move in closer than I'd liked as the highway approached Highway 377, the turn-off for Crater Road. Straight ahead on 377 is the farming town of Kula; a left turn feeds into the twisting, turning ascent to the national park, ending at the cliff rim of Haleakala Crater. Lisa Marie turned left. I checked the gas gauge on the Porsche. It was still nearly full, but by now the Geo would be hovering near the "E." Even if it made it up the steep road to the summit, there was no way it'd make it back down again.

I hadn't been to the crater since I'd moved back to Maui after college, and I'd forgotten how much cooler and windier it was up there. I hung back so she wouldn't see me, but I was fooling myself. Most likely by now, Lisa Marie had noticed she was being followed by a red car identical to her stepmom's.

I gripped the wheel while keeping an eye out for stragglers from the bicycle tour groups that coast down the mountainside every day. The number of injuries and even deaths from these alleged 'easy rides' from the top was a grim statistic rarely shared with tourists, but you sure as hell never see locals paying good money to risk life and limb on the narrow twisting roadway.

At this point there were no more intersections or turnouts, so I kept back a quarter-mile to avoid being a constant presence in her rearview mirror. Every time I'd encounter a switchback I'd see a flash of green as the Geo relentlessly chugged uphill, a white plume of exhaust spewing from its tailpipe. Within seconds the exhaust mingled with the patchwork of low-lying clouds we encountered as we climbed higher.

From the looks of things, Lisa Marie was heading straight to the top.

34

About ten miles up Crater Road a big brown sign alerts drivers they're nearing the entrance to Haleakala National Park. By the time I passed the sign the ground-level clouds had thickened and visibility was down to less than fifty feet. It dawned on me I'd probably have to pay a park entrance fee and I didn't have my purse. Who was I kidding? Even if I'd had my purse I wouldn't have been able to come up with the fee.

I pulled off the road, throwing up a cloud of red dust that tinted the surrounding fog the palest of pinks. Rummaging through the minuscule glove box I found a wrinkled one-dollar bill and a diamond stud earring. The earring looked to be a carat, maybe more. In anyone else's car I'd have figured it for a fake, but I was in Tina's Boxster. No doubt the DeBeers diamond brokers could probably provide a pedigree tracing the sparkling gem from that glove box all the way back to where it was pulled out of the earth in Botswana.

I pulled up at the park entrance kiosk and lowered my window. Along the road leading up to the entrance at least three signs had warned drivers to be ready to fork over ten bucks to enter the park. I couldn't pretend I didn't know about the fee so I figured I'd play "Let's Make a Deal" with the park ranger. Maybe he'd see the upside of waiving the fee in return for surprising his wife with a big ol' diamond on their anniversary.

"Welcome to Haleakala National Park," said a shivering female ranger in a short-sleeved dark khaki shirt and Smokey-the-Bear hat. She said Haleakala in the Hawaiian way, stressing the final 'la' with all she could muster. She was short, with a squat build and freckled skin. She looked like the kind of woman who'd been offered a long-sleeved shirt and maybe even a jacket, but refused, preferring to prove her mettle with bare arms in the chilly temps.

"The park entrance fee is ten dollars," she said, handing me a vanilla-colored brochure printed in brown ink. She leaned her head into the car window, ostensibly poised to take the fee. I figured the lean-in was also an effort to snatch up a little warmth while waiting for me to dig out the money.

"I'm sorry, I only have a dollar. But I'm not staying. I'll just be driving up and out again." I'd given up on the notion of trying to dazzle her with the diamond. She didn't look like a gal who was into bling.

Her eyes surveyed the Porsche. "It's *ten* dollars."

"I know. But I'm a local, and I just need to go up and turn around. I won't use the bathrooms and I won't toss out any garbage. If you'll just let me pass, I'll be in and out without causing any problems."

"You're already causing a problem," she said.

An older guy in a ranger uniform opened the door to the ranger shack. I noticed he was packing a sidearm on his utility belt. "Need some help out here?"

"No, thanks," said the female ranger. "I've got it."

He nodded and disappeared back into the shack.

"Okay," I said, "here's the truth. My purse was taken and the person who took it was the young woman who just went through here. She's got shoulder-length brown hair, like mine. I'm following her to get my stolen purse back."

"There's been no woman with shoulder-length hair through here since I came on duty, and I collect all the entrance fees."

For a second, I was stumped.

"How about a skinny bald guy in a trashy green car with smoke pouring out the tailpipe?" I asked.

"Well, yeah. A guy like that came through a few minutes ago."

"That's who I'm talking about."

She stared at me. I stared at her. I thought about rethinking the diamond ploy, but knew trotting out Plan B would just cost me precious time in pursuing Lisa Marie. I was also pretty sure bartering the admission price was against ranger policy, and by the looks of things I was dealing with a hard-liner for Uncle Sam.

Then I did something that reminded me why I'd never quite fit into the squeaky clean team at the U.S. Federal Air Marshal Service. I threw the car into first gear, popped the clutch, and fishtailed away from the ranger shack, tires smoking. Luckily there wasn't a gate across the entrance. If there had been, it probably would have done some pricey front-end damage to Tina's baby.

But Tina's baby was in second position to Marv's baby. I already regretted not apprehending Lisa Marie when I'd had the chance. I'd abandoned any curiosity over what she was up to and just wanted to nab her and get her safely back to Olu'olu before Marv got wind of her leaving. Our little foray to the wig store and then her stealing my car had me concurring with Marv that her mental state was iffy. And he'd have every reason to hold me liable if she took a swan-dive off the crater rim.

I drove as if the ranger was in hot pursuit and didn't slow down until I glimpsed the Geo passing the Halemau'u Trailhead. The elevation marker showed we were at eight thousand feet. I stayed back, hoping to avoid pressuring her into a Thelma and Louise, but I never let the little green car out of my sight for more than half a minute.

The road climbed and climbed. I'd forgotten how far it was to the top. At mile sixteen I approached a hairpin turn. The Geo was just above me, taking the sharp curve. I'm sure if Lisa Marie had glanced down, the shiny red Boxster would have stuck out like the proverbial sore thumb. Still, she kept up her speed. I wouldn't have thought it possible for my little beater car to keep going at that pace. The engine must have been running on fumes and Lisa Marie's sheer force of will.

Just after the Leleiwi Overlook turnout, I lost sight of the Geo. I hadn't noticed Lisa Marie pull into the parking area, but it's kind of a tricky curve and I could have missed it. As I climbed out of another hairpin turn, I checked my mirrors. Nothing but open road behind me and ahead. She must have turned off. I hesitated, then whipped the car into a tight three-point U-turn and headed back to Leleiwi.

Nearing the tiny parking strip for overlook visitors I saw the Geo. She'd pulled it into a spot at the very end, tight alongside a Jeep Wrangler. It had been impossible to see since a nondescript beige van blocked it from view on the uphill side of the road. I parked the Porsche in the first available space, near the road, so I could make it out of there in a hurry if she decided to resume her travels. Across the street from the parking area was a sign marking the entrance to a rocky half-mile trail that led to the overlook shelter.

I got out of the car and in a half-crouch made my way down to the Geo. I crept up to the back side window and looked in. The contents of my purse was strewn across the back seat. How embarrassing. All sorts of personal items were on display: an overdue notice from the Kahului Library, a creditor's demand letter with the words *Urgent Attention Required!* in bright red letters on the envelope, and a tattered Tampax that had poked through its paper wrapping. My wedding emergency kit: a shoe box with safety pins, aspirin, super glue, and so on, was on the floor behind the driver's seat. I looked through the driver's window. My cell phone was flipped open on the passenger seat. I tried the door. It was unlocked. I leaned in and grabbed my phone, snapped it shut, and slipped it into my pocket.

Right next to the Geo was a new black Jeep Wrangler with a soft top. The windows were down so I checked inside. There was a large wad of dirty clothes balled-up on the passenger side floor and a portable GPS on the seat. The keys were in the ignition.

I looked in the back and saw a jumble of stuff. I pulled the door open to get a better view. Under a filthy tarp was a red and yellow metal can with an aluminum cap. I turned it over and the word *Gasoline* was written in a diagonal line across the can. Under yet more grubby clothes was a cardboard box: a banker's box. Right away I recognized the white, pink and lilac-colored file folders I used to color-code clients, vendors, and service providers for "Let's Get Maui'd."

I left the door hanging open and bolted for the trailhead.

35

I picked my way down the trail to the overlook, moving as fast as I dared without twisting an ankle on the rock-strewn trail. How Lisa Marie had managed it in kitten heels, lugging her ever-present oversized designer handbag was a mystery. At about the halfway point, a guy Farrah and I would have dubbed a 'tree hugger' came into sight coming the other way. He nodded hello, I smiled in return, and we kept moving.

As soon as the metal roof of the overlook came into view I scrambled up the rocks and advanced from above the trail. From that vantage I could see most of what was going on below, but whoever was on the overlook wouldn't notice my approach.

When I was a few yards from the end of the trail I ducked behind a large boulder and cautiously peered into the covered shelter. Lisa Marie was against the Plexiglas viewing window and a guy stood in front of her with his back to me. I couldn't see Lisa Marie's face very well because the guy was in the way, but on her arm she still carried the same black Dolce & Gabbana purse she'd had at the wig shop. The guy wore a blue golf shirt that looked too tight under the armpits and baggy khaki cargo shorts. The lookout offered a stunning vista of cloud-shrouded Haleakala Crater shimmering in the late afternoon sun.

Lisa Marie and the guy were talking in low tones. Anyone coming upon them would assume they were just two nature-lovers taking in the spectacular view. From my observation point I couldn't hear what they were saying, but I had a decent enough view of what was happening. Lisa Marie came in and out of sight as the man shifted his position. She kept her arms crossed and she nodded a few times, but it appeared she wasn't doing much of the talking. Since Lisa Marie rarely listened to anyone for very long without disagreeing or interrupting, it was fascinating to watch.

I turned and surveyed my surroundings. The tree hugger guy was probably the driver of the beige van, and by now he'd left. That left only Lisa Marie, the guy, and me out here at the overlook. When I focused back on what was happening on the platform below, the man had moved in closer to Lisa Marie. He pulled a folded paper from his pocket, opened it up, and held it out to her. She didn't take it.

The sound of her mocking laughter carried to where I was crouching. He responded by yelling a word that would have been bleeped out on TV. Then he roughly refolded the paper and put it back in his pocket. Lisa Marie used the opportunity to duck around him. I finally got a good look at her. Her cheeks were red and her eyes fixed on the path out of there.

The guy grabbed Lisa Marie by the upper arm and pulled her back. By now their voice levels had risen to a point where I could make out almost everything they were saying.

"I thought you were screwing around on me," he yelled. "Then I realize *I'm* the one getting screwed!"

"No, no, you've got it all wrong," said Lisa Marie. "Kevin said you were just being stubborn. He said you'd thank me later."

"I'd *thank* you? Well, here's my thanks."

He grabbed at her purse. She tried to hold on but he was a lot stronger and within a couple of seconds he'd wrestled it off her arm.

"Give it back," screamed Lisa Marie. "Purse snatcher. Thief, thief!" She turned and looked toward the pathway, her eyes bulging in indignation.

He dumped out the contents of the bag.

"You're so predictable," he said, picking through the stuff at his feet.

I caught a quick flash of sunshine glinting off chrome. I'd been trained by the TSA to identify handguns in an instant. We'd had timed tests where they'd flash photos of an armed perp and we'd have to write down the make and model of the weapon and then provide the basic stats: how many rounds it carried, what caliber, and so on. No one complained about the tedious training. It'd be a critical skill if we ever found ourselves facing an armed assailant thirty-five thousand feet up.

The guy was holding a Beretta 92 S. Not a big gun, but certainly big enough at a point-blank range. He waved the gun in Lisa Marie's direction and my mind downshifted. I didn't need to see her face to guess her reaction. I slowed my breathing and ceased all movement as my body ceded control to my brain. I could hear Sifu Doug's patient voice, 'Matches are lost when we fall back on human instinct or emotion; especially if your opponent presents a superior weapon.'

"Look," the guy said. "I didn't want to do it but he wouldn't listen. If you're smart, you will."

My thighs were burning in protest over maintaining the low crouch, but I couldn't just jump up and startle a guy waving a gun around until I had a plan.

He again pulled the folded paper from his pocket. "Sign it," he said.

Lisa Marie snatched the folded paper and tossed it over the overlook wall. I watched as the white square disappeared into the abyss below.

"You crazy bitch!" He stiff-armed the gun and screwed up his face as if readying himself for what came next.

I'd seen and heard enough. I stood up and picked my way around the boulder, trying to avoid alerting him to the sound of my approach. When I was six feet behind the guy, Lisa Marie ducked left and we made eye contact. Her eyes darted from him to me and he whirled around.

I bent my knees to give me more power and leverage. I delivered a roundhouse kick to his ribcage that sent him staggering backward onto the floor of the lookout. The gun flew from his hand and came to rest near the far edge of the rock wall.

As he pushed himself back up to a standing position, I raised my elbow and jabbed him hard in the solar plexus. I heard his breath stall in his chest, and he made an *uh* sound as his knees gave way. His head took a heavy hit as it slammed into the concrete floor. I cringed. Without a mat to soften the blow, a fall like that could be fatal. I calmed down a little when he started moaning.

He curled into a fetal position and didn't attempt to get up. I stood over him, studying his face. He'd lost some weight and his bad haircut was shaggy and uneven. The goofy goatee was gone and he wasn't wearing wire-rim glasses, but there was no mistaking it: I'd just kicked the crap out of missing tech mogul Brad Sanders.

"You okay?" I said to Lisa Marie.

"Yeah. But Brad killed Kevin."

I looked at the crumpled man at my feet. His moans had become a kind of guttural breathing, but his eyes remained closed and he still wasn't making an attempt to get up.

"Lisa Marie, I need you to go over there and get that gun," I said.

She stepped over Brad and picked up the gun.

"Hang on to it for a minute while I make a call." I wondered why Lisa Marie had been packing a handgun, but I figured it'd all come out when the cops arrived.

I pulled out my phone and called nine-one-one and reported an armed man at the Leleiwi overlook in Haleakala National Park. The dispatcher said she'd send a police cruiser, but it'd take a while since they'd be coming from Kahului. She told me she'd also alert park security.

"You sure you're okay?" I said to Lisa Marie after hanging up. She nodded. "Well, hang in there. Cops are on their way. It'll be a while, though, so give me the gun. I'll keep an eye on him."

"It's my gun. Why should I give it to you?"

"Suit yourself. But the police just released you as a suspect, and they're probably not too happy about it. You want to be pointing a handgun at him when they get here? The State of Hawaii's rather picky about who gets to pack heat."

She bit her lower lip and handed it over.

"Now I need you to go up to my car and get some duct tape. There's a roll in a shoe box behind the front seat."

"Duck tape? Like for taping a duck?"

"No, like for keeping Brad still until the cops get here. It's silver-colored, on a roll about this big." I made a circle with my thumbs and forefingers to show her the size.

As she trotted up the trail, I slipped the gun into my back waistband. I'd need both hands if Brad suddenly decided he didn't want to stick around for the cops.

A few seconds later, my cell phone rang.

"Pali? You at the overlook?" It was Steve.

"Yeah, I'm here. Where are you?"

"I've got Hatch with me and we're a few minutes away. Are you okay?"

"I'm fine. Everything's good."

"Well, hang in there, because the lady ranger at the gate's real concerned about you. She took off in an official pickup as soon as we told her we thought you were in trouble. She had the siren going, driving like a bat outta hell. Keep an eye out, she should be pulling up any minute now."

Great. Ranger Hard-Ass already had it in for me for stiffing her for the park fee, and there I was, squatting next to a guy I'd cold-cocked halfway to heaven. Oh yeah, and don't forget the unpermitted gun I had stuffed down the back of my pants.

36

Amazingly, Lisa Marie did as I'd asked and brought me the duct tape. I quickly trussed Brad's hands and feet and tossed what remained of the roll across the overlook floor. Five minutes later I heard the sound of boots on gravel. I didn't look up from watching Brad, but I clearly heard only one set of footfalls coming down the path.

As the sound of the steps changed from gravel to concrete, I stood up, held my arms above my head in surrender and flashed the ranger a smile. She smiled back, but it was a *gotcha* grin. I glanced over at Lisa Marie and saw her gearing up for a performance.

"Thank God you're here! This woman tried to kill my fiancé."

Ranger Hard-Ass turned to me, her smile so wide I thought it might dislocate her jaw. "I made a mistake in not pursuing you when you trespassed on federal property. For that, I guess I owe this gentleman an apology."

She gazed at Brad's prone body, trussed up like a prize pig. He was dazed, but his eyes were open. He didn't look at her. He didn't struggle against his restraints, but instead blew out an irritated breath like a guy stuck in heavy traffic.

The ranger turned back to me. "As an agent sworn to defend federal property and uphold the laws of the United States of America, I hereby arrest you for aggravated assault, improper restraint and kidnapping. You will remain in my custody until proper law enforcement authorities can arrive to transport you to jail."

I was pretty sure she was hoping the police would take their time. No doubt this was as close to an orgasm as Ranger Hard-Ass had had in months.

Might as well mess with her a little. "Aren't you supposed to read me my rights?"

"Uh, I don't have my card with me."

"You were never issued a Miranda card, were you, Ranger..." I glanced at the difficult-to-read bronze name plate over her shirt pocket. "...Masterson. In fact, you're not a sworn federal agent at all. You're a gatekeeper, a ticket taker. You have no authority to arrest me, here or anywhere else."

Lisa Marie was observing us closely, her face showing she wasn't enjoying watching me not only play, but triumph, at her favorite game. She piped up, "I don't care whether you're a cop or an outhouse janitor. I need you to cut that tape off my fiancé's hands and feet. He's got a plane to catch."

Ranger Masterson whipped out a Leatherman tool from her back pocket. I wasn't surprised. I'd bet she had some chew and a church-key bottle opener back there as well.

"Don't be so quick to free him," I said. "He's a confessed murderer. And this woman," I pointed to Lisa Marie, "stole a car."

Lisa Marie snorted. "Oh yeah, some car. I don't think it's against the law to take a pile of crap to the dump." She turned to the ranger. "It didn't have hardly any gas in it."

Masterson glared at me, her eyes like two steel ball bearings. "Why should I believe you?"

"Better safe than sorry, right? You said yourself you wish you'd pursued me when I blew through your toll booth. Now you have another chance to take precautions. Can't hurt to leave this guy tied up until the police arrive."

She twisted her mouth to one side, not pleased to be forced to agree with me.

"Maui Sheriff's deputies have been called and they're en route," she said. "I'll secure the crime scene and maintain physical custody until they arrive."

Touché, Ranger Hard-Ass. Good save.

At this point, Steve appeared. "What the hell happened here?"

"Long story," I said. "Hatch didn't come with you?"

"He's on his way. But it's a slow go with crutches. Why's this guy tied up?"

"This gentleman is the formerly deceased Brad Sanders. It seems he asked Lisa Marie to meet him up here. He had some paperwork for her to sign, but she wouldn't do it."

"Liar," said Lisa Marie. "Brad called me to come up here because he wanted to talk about getting married. He felt bad about missing Valentine's Day."

"Ditching a wedding isn't grounds for a thrashing,'" said Steve. "Why's he tied up?"

"You'll have to ask her," I said.

All eyes turned to Lisa Marie. She shrugged.

"Why don't you start by telling us why Brad pulled a gun on you?" I said.

"Because—." She halted. I could imagine the little liar cells in her brain scrambling around, all talking at the same time and bumping into each other.

"Yes? We're waiting," I said. I'd seen Lisa Marie in action enough to know she wouldn't stay stumped for long.

"Because Brad loves me so much he wanted to get married right away by a justice of the peace and I really, really want a fairytale wedding. When he got out the gun he was desperate to change my mind. It was...uh, a crime of passion."

Not one of her better snow jobs.

I shook my head. "I give that one about a C minus. You want to tell what really happened, or do you want me to do it?"

"I hate you! I wish I'd never met you. You ruined everything! That ugly dress, the stupid crane picture, and then you hired that whore for the wedding ceremony. You screwed it up so bad Brad pretended to disappear and then he had to kill Kevin. If it hadn't been for you, it could've worked out. That company would've bought DigiSystems, and Kevin would be rich, and Brad and me would be on our honeymoon instead of him working twenty-five hours every day. It's all your fault!"

Somewhere in that messy haystack was the needle of truth I'd been seeking.

37

Hatch made it down the trail about ten minutes later. He looked pissed he'd been dragged into this, but he didn't say anything. Then another ten minutes after that, none other than Glen Wong and his sidekick showed up. Their beefy Crown Vic must have really screamed up Crater Road to make it that fast. Wong was unable to hide his confusion as he took in the scene: a hog-tied man, tear-stained Lisa Marie, and me, the so-called 'nobody assistant' he'd ordered out of the Olu'olu sunroom only a few hours earlier.

"Well, I guess we meet again," he said, turning to me. "This time I need to insist on seeing some identification."

"My ID's in my purse and my purse is in my car. Or at least I hope it's still there. This woman," I nodded at Lisa Marie, "stole my car and my purse and drove up here. I followed her and when I arrived I witnessed a man threatening her at gunpoint." Just in case there might be some confusion over what man I was talking about, I pointed down at Brad.

"Quite an interesting story. But until you're able to recover your ID, why don't you just tell me your name."

"Certainly. I'm Pali Moon. I live up in Hali'imaile, and I have a wedding planning business in Pa'ia." I probably should have said a bankrupt business in a burned-out building, but I wanted to appear to be a respectable tax-paying citizen.

"That your full legal name?"

"That's the name on my driver's license, yes." I'd be damned if I was going to amuse this sorry lot with the name on my birth certificate. If it showed up in a police data file, I'd deal with it then.

"And if this person allegedly stole your car, how did you manage to get all the way up here? Did these gentlemen bring you?" He nodded toward Hatch and Steve.

Leave it to a detective to want to cross all the T's.

"No, Detective. I borrowed a car. They arrived later in their own car."

"And who did you 'borrow' a car from?"

"From her stepmother." I nodded toward Lisa Marie.

"The stepmother gave you permission to use her vehicle?" Oh great. I could see where this was headed, so I decided to play it straight.

"Not exactly. She's on the mainland. But her husband hired me to keep an eye on Lisa Marie at all times, so I was following his orders."

"I see. Well, we'll deal with that later."

"And as for you young lady," he looked at Lisa Marie, who was sitting on a boulder wearing the sulky look of a teenager caught with a joint in her pocket. "I didn't take you for a nature lover, Miss Prescott. Fascinating to find you up here admiring the view."

He finally went over to Brad and crouched down beside him. "And you. Let me guess. You bear a striking resemblance to a guy whose picture we were showing around a couple of weeks ago. That guy disappeared off a boat and was never found. Any chance you might know something about that? His name's Bradley James Sanders."

Brad grunted and turned his face away.

"And the gun used in the alleged assault. Where is it now?"

I reached back and pulled the Glock from my waistband.

"You got a permit to carry?" Wong asked.

"I was an air marshal with the TSA."

"Good for you, but we're not on an airplane. Most people new to Hawaii don't know we're pretty strict about folks carrying unpermitted firearms."

Here we go again. "Detective, I've lived in Hawaii all my life. I was raised here on Maui, and I took criminology courses at UH Manoa."

He smiled and turned to his partner. "Whew. Seems we've got a local girl who used to work for the feds. And, she took cops and robbers classes in college. Does it get any better than that?" The partner grinned and shook his head.

They cut the tape off of Sanders feet and hands and replaced it with handcuffs. We were then all marched single file up the trail to the parking lot. Hatch huddled with Wong for a few minutes while we waited for the Maui Fire EMT's to arrive in their fancy panel truck fitted out for medical assistance. Wong told me he wouldn't cite me for carrying Lisa Marie's gun, and he even allowed me to gather my belongings from my Geo and return down the mountain in Steve's car. I was ordered to appear at the police station before going home, though.

Lisa Marie wasn't so lucky. When they told her she'd be riding in the police car, she howled "unfair"—adding a few choice expletives regarding Wong's mother—and demanded to drive her stepmom's car instead. Wong explained that once they'd gotten her statement she'd be free to retrieve the Porsche at the impound lot. What he didn't tell her was that toting around a loaded handgun is a class A felony and he'd be citing her for it once they got down to the station.

Brad Sanders didn't get to join Lisa Marie in the cop car for the scenic ride down the mountain. The EMT's strapped him to a backboard and fitted him with a neck collar. They radioed the hospital to report they were bringing in a possible concussion. They whispered the last few sentences; probably alerting the Emergency Department this was a criminal transport so prepare for a phalanx of cops as well.

"How'd you find me?" I asked Steve.

"Hatch figured it out. When you didn't call or come home by three, we got worried. I called your cell and right away I recognized Lisa Marie's voice. She was blabbing nonsense so I asked her to put you on and she screamed a bunch of swear words and hung up. She wasn't smart enough to turn off the phone, though. Hatch got the cops to trace your location through the embedded GPS in the phone."

It was ironic I'd used part of Lisa Marie's initial deposit to pay my overdue cell bill.

I arrived at the Wailuku Police Station assuming I'd be out of there in an hour or so, but after three hours I'd answered the same barrage of questions, or variations thereof, at least a dozen times. I'd also downed about five Diet Pepsis. Finally, despite the caffeine, I was nodding off and they told me I'd be named as a witness but I was free to go. I got a little speech about Hawaii firearms laws, which was actually a repeat of a lecture I'd attended in college, and they warned me not to leave the island without permission because I'd be summoned to testify at trial.

The next morning I called Todd Barker and gave him an abbreviated version of Monday's events. He was quiet when I reported Brad had been alive all along, but when I said Brad had killed Kevin and was now facing a felony murder charge, he gasped.

"Why'd he do it?" he said.

"From what I've pieced together, Brad disappeared to halt the sale of DigiSystems. Remember you told me there were rumors of a takeover? Well, I guess Kevin was backing the takeover and he'd secretly convinced Lisa Marie to vote for it too. But when Brad went missing the sale went into limbo. Then Kevin stepped in with the idea of a proxy marriage. Marv said he'd have no trouble getting a judge to sign off on it, and that would allow Lisa Marie to not only vote her shares, but Brad's as well, as his widow."

Barker sighed. "I always held out hope Brad might be still alive. He took DigiSystems from a spark of an idea to a corporation worth more than three hundred million in five years. The guy's a freaking genius."

"Maybe so, but don't you think a genius could've come up with a better way to hold on to his company than bashing his partner's brains out?" I winced. I hadn't meant it to come out like that.

"I don't know. He was just so passionate about it. And Kevin was, well, I don't mean to speak ill of the dead. But his priorities were never in synch with Brad's. For Kevin it was all about the money." I heard him suck in a deep breath and then let it out with a *whoosh*. "I suppose you're going to be testifying against Brad."

"I have no choice. I witnessed him confessing to Lisa Marie about the murder. And then I saw him pull a gun on her."

"I hear Marv Prescott offered a reward for clearing Lisa Marie. You gonna get it?"

"Fat chance. I had to resort to extortion just to get him to pay me his half of the wedding costs. But I'll survive. I've got friends."

"Tell you what. I'll tell the board we need to shake a little reward money your way. After all, with the sale of the company, any cash on our balance sheet will just go to the new guys anyway. Give me your bank's wiring instructions and I'll send you the five grand. A goodwill gesture, Miss Moon. Marv mentioned you're having some cash flow problems."

Bells went off in my head. Barker had been talking with Marv Prescott about *me*? And now they're on a chummy first-name basis?

"When did you talk to Marv Prescott?"

"This morning. With Brad in the slammer and Kevin gone, Lisa Marie's our majority stockholder now. Well, more specifically, she's the only stockholder who can vote. Marv offered to spearhead the sale of the company for us. The next time you call here, pretty much anybody you talk to will be a millionaire. Brad gave stock options to everybody; even the secretaries and the cleaning crew. All those little pieces of paper are worth a lot of coin."

There was an awkward pause as neither of us seemed prepared to sign off for the final time.

"Miss Moon, I know this may sound a bit out of line, but I feel obliged to let you know I've recently gotten engaged to be married."

"Well, congratulations." I managed to put a smile in my voice. It's simply proper etiquette to congratulate the groom. But that didn't keep me from conjuring up an image of a tall, busty blond purring in his ear that she'd be *honored* to be his wife, not to mention co-custodian of his newfound millions.

"Anyway," he said, "for some crazy reason, my fiancée's adamant about getting married in Hawaii. Maui, to be precise."

"Smart lady." Okay, so maybe Todd Barker wasn't so bad after all. The *nouveau riche* deserve a fabulous wedding as much as anyone else.

"How much advance notice do we need to give you?" he said. "You know, to have you help us put on this thing."

"I'm usually booked a couple of months in advance, but let me know when you set the date and I'll make sure your wedding gets top priority. But first, a bit of advice, Todd. Aim for late spring or summer. Winter around here can get a bit rainy.

EPILOGUE

Brad Sanders was convicted of first-degree murder in the death of his friend and business partner, Kevin McGillvary. He'd struck him in the head, then did a lousy job of burial at sea. At trial, Lisa Marie testified Brad called and asked her to meet him at Haleakala Crater and she was so excited to hear his voice she mistook my car for one of her father's many vehicles. She went on to say Brad confessed to killing Kevin, but it was justified because he was so in love with her he was heartbroken when Kevin stepped in to take his place. She burbled on, reverting to her original fantasy about Brad falling from his boat and washing up on a 'desert island' with amnesia. She said once his memory returned he asked Kevin to step aside, but Kevin refused.

My testimony pretty much blew that story out of the water, and it was corroborated by Todd Barker, various members of the DigiSystems board of directors, and even Kevin's executive assistant who'd been privy to his campaign to convince Lisa Marie to vote for selling the company. By the trial date, DigiSystems had been sold to a competitor and many of the former employees were busy putting up mini-mansions on Lake Washington, east of Seattle. To them, Kevin McGillvary was a martyr: a guy who'd sacrificed his life for the greater good.

No one sided with Brad Sanders, even though without Brad's original vision and relentless passion they'd all still be writing code and eating Top Ramen.

Since Hawaii doesn't have the death penalty for any crime—even capital murder—Brad was sentenced to life in a maximum security prison. I like to think he keeps himself busy conducting Computer 101 classes for guys with shaved heads and biceps bristling with tattoos, but that's because I always prefer the Disney ending. More than likely though, prison life for him is a never-ending gauntlet. He probably considers it a good day if he makes it from sun-up to sun-down without requiring medical attention.

At trial, Brad pleaded the fifth on a lot of things but he did cop to breaking into my shop and taking my file box. He said he did it to retrieve the wedding license he'd taken out with Lisa Marie. He stopped short of admitting to arson, and the fire investigator ruled it 'inconclusive' so who knows?

Farrah and I managed to prevent Tank's efforts to turn our building into a parking garage. We were stunned when a throng of local folks showed up to protest the condemnation order. It was the first time rampant development on Maui had ever been dealt a serious blow. Maybe at long last people here aren't buying the sweet talk about how economic growth always trumps culture and history. Maybe they're finally sick and tired of seeing everything our forefathers and foremothers held dear getting scraped away by bulldozers.

And Hatch? Well, that's another story in itself. Come to find out he didn't just up and quit the police force because he wanted to be a firefighter hero. Seems heartbreak and guilt played a big role in his decision. Once we both cast aside our need to BS each other, he told me the truth. And knowing the truth was a huge step in giving our relationship a chance.

From where I'm sitting now, it looks to me like a very *good* chance.

ACKNOWLEDGEMENTS

There are always a bunch of people who help get a book out. Some aren't even aware of how much they helped. But, even at the risk of forgetting someone, I'm going to take a shot at naming a few names. Thanks to Deputy Chief (he's probably chief by now) Mike Ciraulo for teaching me a thing or two about firefighting; and to Amy Roth for clearing up a question about the TSA and private aircraft. Also thanks to Marianne Gaertner for taking me up to the Kula lavender farm, and to Chef Bev Gannon of the Hali'imaile General Store for chatting with me about the area and for giving me a great reason to drive completely across the island just to have lunch. Closer to home, I'd like to thank local friends such as Bev Wait, Diana Paul, and Deb Migdalski who kept pestering me to "finish the book," and not-so-close to home, but close in other ways, my friends Sue Cook and Wendy Lester with whom I share an interesting past. Also a big *mahalo* to my friend and fellow writer, Jackie Edwards aka Nora Barker, who did the final copyedit and usually offered to drive because she had the hybrid. Finally, a lifetime of thanks to my DH, Tom, who read draft after draft and never complained.

And, my warmest *aloha* to you, my readers. Without you, these hours at the computer would just be me whistling in the dark.

Titles in the "Islands of Aloha Mystery Series"
—in series order

Maui Widow Waltz
Livin' Lahaina Loca
Lana'i of the Tiger
Kaua'i Me a River
O'ahu Lonesome Tonight?
I'm Kona Love You Forever
and coming soon...
Moloka'i Lullaby
Hilo, Good-bye

Other books by JoAnn Bassett:

Mai Tai Butterfly
and coming soon...
Lucky Beach

Look for updates on new titles on Facebook at
"JoAnn Bassett's Author Page"

And check out her website:
http://www.joannbassett.com

CPSIA information can be obtained
at www.ICGtesting.com
Printed in the USA
FSHW020450191218
54525FS

9 781463 606657